LIES SHE DIDN'T TELL

Angela C Nurse

F & J
Publishing

F&J Publishing
Fandjpublishing.co.
uk@gmail.com

First e-book edition May 2023
First paperback edition May 2023

Covers designed by GetCovers

ISBN 978-1-914597-09-1 (paperback)
ISBN 978-1-914597-10-7 (ebook)

www.angelacnurse.com

A NOTE FROM THE AUTHOR

Please note this book is written by a British author and is set in Scotland. All spellings are the British versions.

A couple of helpful notes;

Bovril is a salty meat extract paste similar to marmite that can be mixed with hot water for a savoury drink.

When the new A92 was built in the 1980s the old one was renamed the A921 and there is reference to both in this book.

Scottie dogs Jock and Wallace star in this book as a tribute to the real life dogs of a very good friend.

Also by Angela C Nurse

**THE ROWAN MCFARLANE DETECTIVE
MYSTERIES**

Discarded (Novella)
Jack In A Box
Sally In The Woods
What She Didn't See
Bloody Snow (Novella)

LIES SHE DIDN'T TELL

A ROWAN MCFARLANE DETECTIVE MYSTERY

Chapter One

My brother has been missing since 1983

Normally the 'contact me' forms I received through my website were much more along the lines of 'I think my partner is cheating' etc, so this one caught my eye immediately. I clicked to read the rest of the enquiry.

> My younger brother Iain went missing in June of 1983, his car was found in a ditch at the side of what is now the A921 between Burntisland and Kinghorn. The police did investigate at the time, albeit briefly, and could find no trace of him. I understand that this was a long time ago, but having researched you a good deal, it would seem you have rather a talent for old cases. I will be 72 this year and have reached the point in my life where I need to know what happened.
> Many thanks, Elspeth Thorogood (nee Blair)

As well as being by far the politest request for my services that I have ever had, the abandoned car piqued my interest. I did a quick Google search and it returned very little. In 2003, twenty years after his disappearance, there was an article about Iain and a handful of other, still missing people who were last seen between 1983 and 1993. The police had given their assurances that their cases were still open, and if any new evidence came to light, they would investigate.

I replied to Elspeth saying I was keen to meet with her to find out more, asking when she would be available. It would likely be a while before I heard back from her so I turned on the radio so I could listen to the local news. I'd missed the start and they were already in the middle of a report.

> The victim, Pamela Blackstock, who is in her late sixties is in a critical condition at the Victoria Hospital in Kirkcaldy. The attack took place early on Sunday morning whilst she was walking her dogs on Silver Sands beach. We now have a statement from Detective Chief Inspector Johnston.

George's voice filled my office.

> We understand that Ms Blackstock was a regular on the beach and was well known by other dog walkers in the area. We are appealing for witnesses to come forward. The attack took place at approximately 7.30am on Sunday morning. If you have any information that might help us track down the assailant, then please contact us immediately. In the meantime, we are asking people to be vigilant, especially if they are out alone.

Back on the radio station they gave out all the details for contacting the police. I listened to the remainder of the news before turning it off. I checked my emails and there was no reply from Elspeth.

The house felt empty. I'd taken Alana to Dundee last week to settle into her university accommodation. It was a journey we should've taken last year when she went into first year, but the pandemic had meant there was precious little point in living in Dundee when all her courses and lectures were going to be done online anyway. I'd had an extra year of her living at home, and I'd been grateful.

She'd been excited and nervous, all the things you're supposed to be when you set off on a new journey in your life. She made me promise not to make a scene when I said goodbye and I had just about held it together. Sitting in my car afterwards though had been another matter. I had let myself feel a little bit sad and that had led to me sitting there for nearly twenty minutes moping. I knew we were both going to be fine, the last few years had been intense, and we were closer now than we had ever been.

Now, sitting in my office, everything felt too still. It would take some time to get used to it. I was getting ready to wallow in another bout of loneliness when the doorbell rang. I pulled myself up from the slumped position in my chair and opened the door.

'Hello love,' Maureen said as she walked in through the door past me towards the kitchen.

I looked down the drive to see Eddie following, a carrier bag in each hand. 'Morning Eddie, is everything okay?'

'All good with us petal,' he said smiling.

I closed the door and followed them both through to the kitchen. Maureen had the fridge door open and was peering inside.

She stood up, 'well I was right Eddie, barely a scrap of food in here.'

'I just haven't had the chance to go shopping, that's all.'

'I said that you wouldn't be taking proper care of yourself with Alana away, didn't I Eddie?'

'You did.' He agreed.

'And here we are and all you have in your fridge is some scabby cheese and some celery that is definitely past its best.' She held the pathetic looking vegetable up in her hand, the stalks hanging limply to one side.

'Maureen thought you could do with a little bit of help on the meals front,' Eddie said. 'You know how she worries.'

'This is so kind of you, I promise I was going to go to the shops.'

Maureen gave me a look, 'I've done a bit of batch cooking for you so it's going to be no effort at all for you to eat properly. I'll pop some in the fridge for the next couple of days and the rest can go in the freezer. They'll be better re-heated in a pan but I'm sure you'll end up using the microwave.'

I gave up protesting, in truth I'd been telling myself I needed to go to the shops now for the last three days and a diet of tinned tomato soup and bread was starting to wear thin – even for me.

'Also, I baked, so there's some chocolate cake, a wee batch of scones and a fresh loaf for you.'

I hugged her, 'thank you. This is amazing, just what I needed, you're staying for a cup of tea I hope.' I could see Eddie eyeing up the chocolate cake, for all the baking Maureen did it seemed like it was always for someone else.

She sat down at the table next to Eddie, 'that would be lovely, do you need any help?'

'No, it's fine,' I said quickly before she had a chance to get up out of her seat. 'Let me do something for you for a change.' I put two cups of tea and two plates of chocolate cake in front of them, Eddie stuck a fork in his and took a mouthful before Maureen could tell him off and say that she'd made it for me.

'How have you been with Alana away?' Eddie asked.

It felt selfish to tell them that I'd felt more than a little lost when I knew that they hadn't seen their own children for so many years, but I knew that they wouldn't mind. 'It's odd without her.' I replied.

'That's understandable,' Maureen reached across the table and put her hand on top of mine, it was warm from holding the mug of tea. 'It'll be better when you're busy, you need a new case to get your teeth into.'

'Actually, I think something has come up that could be quite intriguing. Do either of you remember a man going missing in 1983, his car was left abandoned at the side of the road.'

'You're going back a fair while there,' Eddie said sitting back in the chair but still not letting go of the plate of cake. 'Not off the top of my head, you got any more for me to go on than that?'

'Does the name Iain Blair ring any bells?'

Eddie was deep in thought. 'It's not that much of an unusual name mind you, but I'm sure he worked on the roads same time as me.'

'The A92?'

'That was the year Gordon finally got the all clear for the cancer, so it sticks in your mind a bit.'

'You got that big promotion that year as well,' Maureen said then she turned to me, 'the extra money was a god send.'

'I got made foreman, not sure it was that big a promotion, but it helped. I'm still friends with a couple of the folk from those days, of course some of them are dead now, but I'll ask around and see what I can find out for you.'

'I appreciate it, you'll be discreet though?'

'Of course, you can trust me,' he said.

Chatting with Maureen and Eddie had been a pleasant way to spend the morning. When they finally left, I had promised to make sure I ate properly and to let them know if I needed anything at all. It had been four years since I discovered they were my maternal grandparents and having a new extended family had been easier to get used to than I would've previously expected. I was tempted to have another slice of chocolate cake for lunch but with my aforementioned promises in mind I had a bowl of homemade lentil and ham soup.

I checked my email, relieved to see that Elspeth had replied.

Thank you for replying so promptly. I am free all day today. I have put my phone number at the bottom of this message, please call me so that we can arrange a time and location. Regards Elspeth

Chapter Two

Elspeth had been hesitant about meeting me in the Sunshine Café, until I explained that I was friends with the owners. Originally, she had suggested that I come and visit her at home, but for many reasons, my security included, I never went to a client's house for the first meeting. I'd learnt the hard way last year that being in someone else's house could have serious consequences for me.

Star, despite being six months pregnant, was still working as hard as she ever had. It had been a lovely surprise when Star and Billy announced the pregnancy.

'Shouldn't you be taking it easy.' I said as she waddled over to my table with a mug of camomile tea and a slice of her raw carrot cake.

She sat in the seat opposite me, 'you sound like Billy,' she laughed, slipping off her mask for a moment.

'I hope he's taking good care of you.'

'He's driving me round the twist, especially after the doctor called me a geriatric mum.' She looked mildly outraged. 'I'm 36 for goodness sake.'

I laughed, 'I'm pretty sure it's just a medical term. You look well though.'

'Truth be told I'm starting to think I need to slow down a bit, but with the place being shut a lot of last year we really need all the custom we can get.'

Billy had told me how worried he'd been when Covid struck and all of a sudden their regular income had stopped, but Star had adapted well and had an online pick up or delivery service of afternoon or morning teas and a website up for the bookshop part of their business within weeks.

'I know but you need to look after yourself.'

'Honestly, I can't tell you how glad I am that Chantelle and Mohammed decided to move back to Scotland, Chantelle is such a help. I know she's going to be such a doting Aunty. I do feel a bit bad though, I know how much she'd like to be in my position.'

Billy's sister and her boyfriend, now husband, Mohammed had fled the country after her career criminal cousin had attacked Chantelle causing her to lose their baby and needing to have an emergency hysterectomy. With him dead they'd been able to return home.

'I think she'll be so pleased to be part of this little one's life,' I said.

'And Mohammed, he's been shadowing me in the kitchen almost every day to make sure he can run this place whilst I'm on maternity. I'm actually starting to think he's better than me.'

'I doubt that, but I am glad you'll be able to take some time off without thinking about what's going on here.'

'Anyway, is this a social visit or are you waiting on someone?'

'New client.' I replied.

'Hmm, thought so, you've got that new case look about you. I know I don't need to remind you, but be careful, we want to keep you in one piece. Right better get on.' She covered her nose and mouth with the patterned cloth mask and levered herself out of the chair, her pregnant bump accidentally knocking into the shoulder of a customer.

A few moments later I heard Elspeth ask for me at the counter, one of the waitresses showed her over to me and took her order.

'I've never been in here,' she said taking her coat off and draping it over the back of the spare chair next to her. 'It's nicer inside than I expected.'

'It's a little alternative,' I agreed. 'But Star and Billy really do make the best food, and they're lovely.'

'Well, you certainly have interesting friends, not that it's any of my business.'

Elspeth was a very neatly put together woman. She was wearing pale blue jeans with a crease ironed down the front and a yellow shirt with only the collar visible underneath a navy-blue jumper. She looked good for her age, her white hair was cropped short, not much make-up – a bit of eyeliner and bright pink lipstick which was revealed when she removed her mask.

'Tell me about your brother,' I asked hoping to get the conversation going. 'Were you close?'

'The three of us were close, I was the eldest, then there was Rodger, and then Iain the youngest. I always thought he was spoiled being the youngest and so much responsibility was put on me, being the oldest and a girl. Our parents were good people, but old fashioned. I wanted to go to university, I had dreams of being an archaeologist but Dad said that it was a ridiculous thing for a woman to do and that I'd be better spending my time learning secretarial studies.'

'What did you do?'

'I learnt typing and that sort of thing, but I also studied hard and got lucky with a female head teacher keen on getting girls involved in science, not that the male teachers were particularly for it. But that didn't bother me. My dad got me a job as an office junior at the offices where he worked not long after I turned sixteen, but Miss Green persuaded him to let me stay on at school for the next two years. I got a place at Edinburgh University and took on a part time weekend job using my secretarial skills to help fund my living costs.'

'How did your dad feel about that?'

'Proud as punch as it turned out. You'll think I'm rambling, but I have a point, I promise. I've spent my career travelling the world, going to digs and on a couple of occasions helping with the excavation of war graves, so you see I understand what a difference it can make uncovering a loved ones remains and providing closure. I want to find Iain before I die, do you understand?'

I nodded.

'I didn't have any children of my own and Rodger passed away from a heart attack in his forties. I'm still in touch with his partner Stewart, but they had no children either, it wasn't the done thing then to let gay men adopt. Which means it's up to me to find out what happened.'

'What was Iain doing before he went missing?'

'Being a pain in our father's backside. Iain was by far the cleverest of us all, he did his degree in mathematics and was working for some insurance company afterwards, then he decided to do his PhD. He would have been less than a term away from completion when he jacked it all in and took a temporary construction job working on the new A92.'

'Any idea why?'

'None, I was in Singapore at the time. My parents contacted me asking me to come home and help knock some sense into him, but I couldn't just up and leave. Rodger tried his best but according to him Iain had had enough, and he wanted to do something physical and not remotely academic. There were promises he'd finish the PhD, but of course he disappeared before any of that was possible.'

'Elspeth, I'd like to take your case, but first I think it's important that I set your expectations. It's been a long time since Iain disappeared and many of the people who were around at that time will be difficult to locate or may even be dead, so this may take some time and it's possible that I won't be able to give you the complete closure you're hoping for.'

She took a sip of tea, placed the mug back on the table and stared into it for a few moments, before lifting her head to look at me. 'I completely understand, this is a tall order. As I mentioned earlier, I did a lot of research before I reached out to you, and I wouldn't have bothered if you didn't strike me as the sort of young woman who'll exhaust every avenue before giving up. All I'm asking is that you do what you can to find out what happened to my brother.

Chapter Three

An afternoon of wading through old newspaper articles hadn't turned up much more than I already knew. The car had been reported by another motorist, fearful that there had been an accident and the driver and any passengers might have been hurt. Police attended but found no sign of the occupant. There were several appeals made for witnesses but from all accounts they were thin on the ground.

The abandoned car had later been connected with the missing person's report for Iain Blair. Either Iain drove his car off the road himself and disappeared into the nearby woodland, ending up who knows where, or his car was stolen and crashed at the same time as he went missing. The latter sounded too convoluted to be likely.

I could make an official request for details of the police investigation through the Freedom of Information Act, but it would take ages. Instead I would, as always, chance my arm and ask George.

I rang his mobile and got his answer machine. Reluctant to leave a message and wait I called the police station. Sergeant Olsson on the front desk recognised my name and put me through to the team without any further questions.

'Are you looking for me?' George's voice said on the other end. 'I saw your missed call on my mobile, is everything okay?'

I felt momentarily guilty for my impatience. 'You know me, can't wait for anything.'

He harrumphed.

'I've just taken a case and I could do with seeing an old police file.'

'You know there are procedures in place specifically for this kind of request that don't involve calling a DCI?' I could hear the sarcasm in his tone.

'If I don't have the patience to wait for you to return my call, what makes you think I have any for going through the proper procedures,' I laughed.

'How old?'

'1983, it's a missing persons case.'

'Well at least this one can't have anything to do with me. Text me the details and I'll get copies arranged for you.'

'Thanks George, how's your case, is the woman going to be okay?'

There was a small pause before he spoke, 'It's a tricky one, no witnesses, except for Jock and Wallace and they're not much help.'

'The news said she was alone...'

George laughed, 'they're her dogs, a pair of Scotty's, Mel and I are currently dog sitting.

We don't know if she's going to pull through and given the nature of the attack it's hard to accept that this was random or unprovoked, but we can't find anything to suggest otherwise.'

'Very strange, was she known to the police?'

'Nope, she was just an old lady that moved into a house on the outskirts of Aberdour a year or so ago, she lived alone. Her neighbours said that she was pleasant and always happy to chat about gardening and that kind of thing and she was an active member of the bowling club.'

'Hope you find something soon,' I replied.

'That makes two of us, I'll email you over the file later today.'

'Thanks.' I hung-up

With Alana away at uni, the evenings were the worst. Even though she would most likely have been in her bedroom studying, I would have known she was there and at some point she would have appeared in the doorway to my office suggesting ice-cream or hot chocolate, depending on the time of year. I would get used to it I told myself over and over again. For someone who would have adamantly stated that they were a natural loner I hadn't expected to feel so bereft.

I put a portion of Maureen's casserole in the microwave with a slight pang of guilt, knowing that she'd told me to heat it on the stove. I was sure she was right that it would have tasted better, but five minutes later I was sitting down to a lovely plate of food that was significantly nicer than anything I would have made for myself.

George emailed the police file on Iain Blair at just after half past six. I read through the statements. His parents said that Iain hadn't been himself for some time and that dropping out of his PhD course so close to completion was particularly out of character. His workmates on the road project had described him as standoffish and said that he didn't fit in with the other lads.

'POSSIBLY QUEER?' was scribbled in the margins of one interview, there had been nothing in what the other workmen had said that would've led me to that thought, but the 80s were a different time, not fitting in with the lads may have been enough to make Iain's sexuality something worth mentioning.

Those that knew him said that his behaviour had been odd for a while and those that had only just met him thought he was odd full stop. The only statement that was of any interest was that of a woman called Deborah Marchmont. She lived near to the woods and close enough to the path that she would have been able to see anyone passing by from her window. She said that she had seen a couple walk up the path towards the woods at approximately the time it had been estimated that Iain's car came off the road. She had said that they seemed to be arguing or distressed. 'NUTTER' was written in very faint writing next to her name, with no further explanation.

I read through the interview notes, Deborah had been interviewed by PC Dave Hampton.

> Witness: Deborah Marchmont age 21, address: Inver Cottage, Fife
> On the evening of Friday 10th June 1983 Deborah saw a man and a woman run up the path past her house into the woods. She states that they came from the direction of the main road. The man was white with dark hair, looked to be in his late twenties to early thirties and was wearing light blue jeans and jean jacket.
> The woman; white, late twenties to early thirties, blonde hair and was wearing light blue jeans and a black jacket with a long fringe on the arms. Deborah says that she wrote down the time they passed her house in a "note book" she keeps and says it was 1800 hours exactly when they came into sight and it took approximately 1 minute for them to move far enough along the path to no longer be seen from her bedroom window.

There had been no follow up interview and no indication that there had been any search of the woods. Scrolling through the rest of the file on Iain Blair, there was nothing to suggest that he had been with anyone else at the time of his disappearance and so I suspected the sighting had been written off as unrelated.

A thorough search of Iain's car had turned up nothing of any interest. There had been an AA roadmap of the UK, something that was in practically every car before sat nav and smart phones. There were several years' worth on a shelf in my office, most of them had been inherited from Jack, but I'd kept up the collection after realising how helpful it was to be able to see how far places were from each other and to track the way the roads had changed over time.

I wondered if Deborah still lived locally. She was twenty-one when she had given her statement so she would be fifty-nine now. She could be anywhere in the world and could've changed her name a number of times over. The telephone number on the report was so old that the dialling code was the old style, before everything was '01'. It was worth a try, but when I dialled it, the number was dead.

Tomorrow morning I would take a drive out towards her house. Perhaps she'd changed number, or like lots of people these days, didn't have a landline anymore. The fact that the original investigation had ruled her out as a credible witness so quickly made me intrigued by her.

Chapter Four

The next morning, before I had a chance to get ready and head out to Deborah's house, Eddie had phoned to tell me that he'd managed to round up some of the old crew that worked on the roads at the time.

'They'll be at the club this evening at 6pm,' Eddie said.

'The club?'

'The working men's club, here on the estate.'

'Oh, okay.' The only time I ever went to the Robert the Bruce estate was to visit Eddie and Maureen.

'Listen Rowan, I know you're not going to like me saying this, but…well love it's just that I think it might be an idea if I came with you.'

'I'm pretty sure I can handle it Eddie, don't worry,'

'I'm sure you can love, I'm not doubting your abilities at all, god knows you've proved yourself time and time again. It's just that this lot, well some of them aren't as enlightened as me and I wondered if I could go a long with you just to smooth the road.'

On one hand, having Eddie there might get them talking easier, but on the other they might see me as weak, someone who needs a man beside her to make sure she's okay and that was not the impression I wanted to give off.

'How about we go together. You can make the introductions, then perhaps sit somewhere else whilst I chat to them?' I desperately didn't want to offend Eddie.

'That sounds like an ideal compromise,' he replied. 'Would you like to come for dinner after?'

It was no good saying no, Maureen would've insisted and besides having some company for a couple of hours sounded good. 'Okay I'll come to you for quarter to and we can walk round together, will that give us enough time.'

'Sounds good to me.' Eddie replied.

I sent Alana a quick text telling her that I had taken a new case and was going to Maureen and Eddie's this evening in case she was trying to get hold of me and couldn't. She replied with a brief 'have fun xx'

I swithered about still going to visit Deborah Marchmont's old house in the hopes of finding her, but Eddie had set up this evening's meeting and I didn't want to go anywhere that might jeopardise that. It might only have been 10.30am, but experience had taught me that it was very easy for a day to get away from me. Instead, I decided to see what I could find out about PC Dave Hampton, his name had appeared on the majority of the interviews. His notes in the margins gave me a clear indication of his opinions of people. Along with 'POSSIBLY QUEER' he had written 'DOESN'T BELONG HERE' alongside his interviews of Iain's work colleagues.

I phoned George.

'What now?' He asked.

'Do you know a Dave Hampton?'

'Do you mean Inspector Hampton, as was?'

'I don't know, he was a PC in 1983, he worked on this missing person case I'm investigating.'

'That would probably make sense.'

'Do you know where I can find him?'

'I think there's a plaque at the crem, he had a heart attack about 10 years ago, died on the golf course.'

'Bugger.'

'I'm sure his family will be sorry to know his premature death inconvenienced you.'

'You know that's not what I meant,' I replied, although I was aware that George was mostly mocking me. 'What was he like?'

'He was alright, well respected but you didn't want to get on the wrong side of him because his punishments were harsh, he was old school, I think is how you'd term it.'

'Any chance he was homophobic?'

'Why, what's Dave's sexuality got to do with your investigation?'

'Nothing and I wasn't asking about his personal sexuality, just his attitude to homosexuality, that's all, why so defensive.'

'Sorry, force of habit. He definitely wasn't homophobic.'

'How can you be so sure?'

'Everyone thought Dave was a confirmed bachelor because he liked to go out with the lads, play golf and the job hadn't left him enough time to find a wife but later in his career it became known that he wasn't a bachelor, he was gay. He'd had to keep his private life hidden, when he joined the police it was still illegal to be gay. Even then when it became common knowledge he faced some backlash, comments were made behind his back, that kind of thing.'

'Such a lovely organisation you work for.'

'It's getting better.'

'Why would he have made reference to the missing man's sexuality in his notes do you think?'

'It's possible that he was just reflecting the general opinion he was getting from the people he interviewed. Or perhaps he wanted it recorded somewhere just in case he turned up dead, especially if he'd been murdered. There had not long been that serial killer Nilsen arrested for killing gay men in London, could've been that Dave made a habit of recording suspected sexuality on the notes of missing men at that time, just in case.'

'Okay, thanks.'

'No problem, see if you can make it a whole 24 hours before you call me next time,' George teased before he hung up.

Chapter Five

The working men's club reminded me of a variety of pubs I'd been in. The only women in the place were behind the bar, and they were the sort that didn't put up with any nonsense. I bought Eddie a pint and I had a coke on tap, which is the sort of drink that doesn't taste like any of the big brands that bear its name, but instead reminded me of the cola cubes I used to enjoy when I was little.

I followed Eddie as he moved through the tables towards a group of six men varying in ages from late fifties upwards.

'Alright Eddie,' one of the older men said nodding his head in our direction.

'Nice to see you Wullie,' Eddie replied. He turned to make sure I was next to him. 'This is the detective I told you about, the one who's looking into that lad Iain Blair's disappearance. I told her you'd tell her all that you can.'

'When you said detective this wasnae what I had in mind.' Wullie said and a ripple of agreeing grunts followed.

'I'm not sure I follow,' Eddie said taking a sip of his drink.

'No offense hen, but you don't exactly look like a private detective do you!' One of the others said.

Before I had the chance to reply Eddie said, 'and what does a private detective look like John?'

'You know what I mean,' he replied.

'Now you listen to me, you'll not find a better private detective in the whole of Fife and if you don't believe me perhaps her name will help some of you see sense.' Eddie looked to me to introduce myself.

'Hi, I'm Rowan McFarlane,' I said.

I noticed as they glanced between themselves, quietly muttering. 'The lass that killed Jimmy Murray?' Wullie asked.

'Aye, the same, so how about you hear her out?' Eddie replied. Wullie nodded, 'aye alright.'

I sat down on the only free seat, Eddie patted my shoulder, 'right I'll be over at the bar with my mate Bert.'

I took another sip of my drink before putting it down on the already crowded small round table, sticky from previous spills.

'I appreciate your time,' I said.

'Aye well this estate has been through a lot and it's coming out the other side and if Eddie says we've got you to thank for that then we're happy to help, right lads,' Wullie said.

'I know 1983 is a long time ago and you might not remember, but from the information I got from the police file and Iain's sister, it seems like he was working on the roads when he went missing and I was wondering what you remembered about him.' I sat back and hoped they would start to reminisce.

'John you started at the same time as Iain, did you not?'

John nodded, 'he was odd like. I'm sure he'd been doing something quite intellectual before and I couldn't understand why he was doing this now.'

'Didn't he ever give you any reason?'

'Needed the money, that's what he said to me.' A small man in his late fifties, early sixties spoke.

'Did he say what he needed it for?'

The man paused for a minute, 'nope, but and I know this lot will take the piss when I say this, but I wasn't surprised when he disappeared. He seemed weighed down by something.'

'Any idea by what?'

'I wondered if he might have a gambling problem at first, he had a keen mind for working out all the odds on the horses, but then I found out he was a mathematician and that explained it.'

'Was he having any trouble at home that you know of?'

'With his wife? I don't think so, they seemed happy enough.'

'Wife? There's nothing in his file about him being married.'

The man shrugged, 'I can only tell you what I remember, he showed me a photo from their wedding day, didn't look like it was a fancy affair, he said they eloped.'

'I didn't know that Seb,' Wullie interrupted.

'We used to take our lunch at the same time, he liked to talk about things, I thought he was alright.' Seb said.

'I thought he was gay,' said John.

'Did you mention that to the police?' I asked.

'No, I wouldn't have done that, if they'd thought he was gay, well the likelihood of them looking for him properly was going to be slim. The 80s weren't kind to homosexuals, despite what you'll read in history books.'

'Was there anyone on the crew who really didn't like Iain?'

Wullie cleared his throat and rubbed the palm of his hand round the back of his neck. 'It'll all come out in the end so I might as well tell you myself, I had one or two run ins with him. Me and Eddie we were foremen, we'd been doing the job for a long time, knew what we were doing and then along comes this lad, who doesn't look like he's done a hard day's work in his life by the way, and he's telling me that we've got some of the measurements wrong and it's going to lead to issues when we start…I didn't like his tone and I told him so.'

'He was right though, wasn't he,' Seb said quietly as he finished his pint.

'Aye he was right,' Wullie admitted.

'Wasn't him that got the glory when you pointed it out to the higher ups though was it,' Seb continued.

'That was wrong of me, I shouldn't have made out that I spotted the error, but I was pissed off at the lad and I thought it would teach him a lesson, that doesn't mean that I wanted any harm to come to him though.'

'Didn't say you did,' Seb replied before standing up and heading towards the bar for another drink.

'Don't mind that pair,' John said, 'I'm sure it sounds like there's no love lost, but they're family.'

There was no further explanation of who they were to one another. 'Did Iain rub anyone else up the wrong way?' I asked.

'He fell out with a few folk, it was to be expected, but it wasn't anything serious,' John said.

'Why was it to be expected?' I asked.

'It's just the way it is, he wasn't like the rest of us, we'd all been doing hard labouring since we left the school and for most of us that was at fifteen. It wasn't his fault he was different, he just was. He might've been smart, but he wasn't good at talking to people, struggled to fit in, we didn't have anything in common with him nor he with us and in those days it was hard to trust outsiders in case they were plants by the higher up bosses to tell tales on us,' Wullie said.

Seb had returned to the table to hear the last part of what had just been said. 'It's not like many folk actually gave him a chance though is it.' He turned to me, 'from my point of view Iain was a nice guy, something was going on with him and I'm sure that's why he had the sudden career change, though I promise you I don't know what it was. He tried to get on with the other guys, but he was actively shut out by most of them.'

'But you gave him a chance.'

'I know what it's like to be on the outside. I'm Polish, I had to learn to change everything about myself to be accepted and it was doubly hard back then. Wullie looked out for me when I started, and I was just doing the same for Iain.'

'That was cos you had the cheek to marry his sister,' someone said.

Seb smiled, 'this is true.'

'Other than yourself was there anyone else that Iain was friendly with?'

'Michael Swanage,' he replied after a few moments. 'They seemed to get on well and I think they might even have socialised together.'

'Where's Michael now?' I asked, assuming that he wasn't amongst the men here, otherwise surely he would've said something by now.

'He moved away, Inverness I think,' Seb replied.

'Does anyone still keep in touch with him?' It was a tall order imagining that someone who'd left the area in the 80s was still on the Christmas card list.

There was a collective murmur of 'no'. I guessed that this was as much as I was going to be able to glean from this meeting and glanced across to Eddie. He put down his glass and walked across to join us.

'Thanks for your time,' I said. 'And if you remember anything else here's my card, just give me a call.' I handed them each a card, hoping that if any of the less vocal participants in this evening's discussion had something to say they would feel able to speak to me in the absence of their friends.

Chapter Six

By the time we got back to the house I was starving and very grateful for Maureen's home cooked dinner.

'How did you get on petal? I hope they minded their manners.' The second part of the sentence was directed towards Eddie, who Maureen clearly thought had gone along as my guardian.

'They were fine, it was really useful, thank you for setting it up.'

'I'm glad it was helpful,' Eddie said. 'Do you think you'll be able to find out what happened to him then?'

'Of course she will,' Maureen replied on my behalf. 'She's a genius at this stuff, just like her dad.'

I smiled, they had only known Jack as a young man, but it was always nice to hear people talk about him with such affection.

'I hope so, it is a very long time ago though. Today was a good start, especially with Seb saying Iain was married, that's not documented anywhere. One of my first jobs will be to try and find out all I can about his wife.'

We ate in silence for a few moments, 'How's Carol?' I asked, Whilst it had been easy to make the mental shift that Jack was my dad and not my uncle, thinking of Carol as my mum had been much harder, and I wasn't sure I'd ever think of her as anything other than Carol.

Maureen and Eddie shot each other a look, 'she's doing fine.'

A small lump formed in the pit of my stomach. When we'd first met, Carol had been sick, desperately in need of a kidney transplant. Eddie had made that possible and now I worried that she'd had some sort of relapse.

'Is it her kidneys?' I asked.

'No, nothing like that,' Eddie said to me and then to Maureen, 'we should tell her.'

'Tell me what?' I asked.

'It would be better coming from Carol,' Maureen protested.

'What would?'

'I know but we're worrying Rowan now, so I think it's best that we just tell her,' Eddie said.

'What's going on?' I asked.

'Carol's got a fella, they've been stepping out for a couple of weeks now. We've not met him yet, but she says she's happy.'

'Is that all,' I sighed in relief.

'You don't mind?' Maureen asked.

'No, why would I mind, I'm glad she's found someone.' And it was true, I was glad, even if Jack was alive I couldn't imagine them together as a couple after all these years apart.

'I thought it might've upset you,' Maureen said quietly.

'Not at all, I'm honestly happy for her.'

They spent the rest of the meal enquiring after Alana, and when she'd next be home. It had been a lovely evening, I'd been grateful for the good company and the amazing food and now that I was back home, I was thankful for the quiet. I took off my boots and left them near the front door.

I sent Alana a text telling her I was back home and went to bed.

The clattering of my letterbox woke me the next morning, I could see the pile of post on the mat from the top of the stairs. I flipped through the envelopes on my way to the kitchen; a company offering me a house insurance quote, another reminding me to get my eyes tested, a sailing catalogue addressed to someone who had never lived here and a plain white handwritten envelope.

I put the other correspondence to one side and opened the letter:

Dear Rowan

It's been brought to my attention that you have been asking questions about Iain Blair. Please stop. I will tell you this much, the man you seek is dead and that should be closure enough for those that still think of him.

After all, what's a life anyway? We're born, we live a little while, we die.

If you choose not to heed this warning then know you are setting off on a path that can bring no peace to anyone, least of all to those that need it most.

Please do not put yourself in danger once again for someone as undeserving as Iain Blair, save yourself and your talents for answering the call of those who deserve it.

Much love
A friend

I didn't recognise the handwriting, as warnings went it was one of the nicest I'd ever received. The question was had it come from someone trying to protect themselves and their own deeds from being uncovered or from someone who knew too much about what had happened to Iain and was genuinely trying to protect me. Experience led me to believe it was the former.

The envelope was postmarked Dunfermline, other than that there was very little to tell from it. I placed both items into evidence bags and made myself a coffee. I'd been investigating Iain's disappearance for a couple of days and the only people who knew about it were George, Eddie and Maureen and the old road crew I'd met the previous evening. It was possible that one of the road crew knew more than they had let on, but even so this didn't feel like it had been written by one of them, the others I trusted with my life.

I read the letter over again, I'd received warnings and threats before, it was inevitable, something I'd just got used to, but this one intrigued me. There was no point pondering over who my new pen friend was just now, instead I wanted to find out more about the possibility of Iain being married.

I phoned Elspeth. 'Hi, something has come up in my enquiries and I wanted to run it by you,' I said.

'That was quick, I'll help any way I can.'

'I spoke to some of Iain's co-workers on the A92 project, one of them recalled Iain showing him a picture taken on his wedding day,' I paused.

'I think he must've been getting Iain mixed up with someone else.'

'You have no recollection of Iain being in a serious relationship?'

There was a sigh on the other end, 'honestly I don't think I would have known if he was, I was on the other side of the world and you have to remember in those days it wasn't as simple as phoning or Facetiming someone, you had to write letters and I doubt him being in a relationship would've been considered stamp worthy but getting married, that's another thing altogether.'

'Any chance he could've eloped and done it without telling anyone?'

'Anything is possible I suppose, I just really don't think he would've done that to our parents, mum especially. She'd have been devastated by something like that.'

'What happened to Iain's possessions after he went missing?'

'As far as I know Rodger and Stewart dealt with all of that.'

'Would they have kept his things?'

'I don't know. I'll speak to Stewart later today and see what he remembers.'

'When your parents died did you find any of his things in amongst theirs?'

More silence, 'You'll be getting the impression that I've not been a very good daughter and maybe I wasn't, but my job kept me busy, right up to retirement. When dad died I was lecturing at a university in Munich, I came home for the funeral of course, but to my shame I let Stewart deal with everything, he got rid of most of the furniture, but the rest was put into storage. I always intended on dealing with it, but I've never felt like it, I'm not a great keeper of things. Ironic really that if an archaeologist was trying to find a trace of me, they would be hard pushed to know I'd even existed.'

'Would you mind if I took a look through the things that Stewart kept?'

'I think you're barking up the wrong tree but I have no objections.'

'I can come to you to collect the keys if you would like me to?'

'I'll be in for the next couple of hours if that suits?'

I told Elspeth I would be there in an hour or so and hung up. I understood that family dynamics could be difficult but leaving everything to your brother-in-law to arrange made me think there was something else going on between Elspeth and her parents. I absent-mindedly took a mouthful of the slice of chocolate cake I'd cut myself for breakfast. According to what Elspeth had told me, her parents, particularly her father, had been proud of her achievements and surely wouldn't, therefore, have begrudged her a fulfilling career afterwards.

I made a mental note to get Stewart's details and see if he remembered the situation differently. In the meantime, I swallowed down the rest of my coffee, feeling only a tiny bit guilty about my unhealthy breakfast.

Elspeth's house was on the outskirts of town, it looked like it might once have been the gatehouse for a long since demolished country house. She met me at the door, denying me the opportunity to check out the inside of her home.

'Sorry for not being able to invite you in, I've been asked to step in for a team in a lawn bowls competition. I'm a bit rusty and not nearly as good a player as Pam was, I mean is, but they need to make up the numbers, so I said I'd help out.'

I smiled, she hadn't struck me as someone who would enjoy team sports, but perhaps I hadn't got her sussed out fully yet.

'No problem, I'll get these back to you as soon as I can.'

'No rush,' she said as she put her bag of bowls in the boot of her Toyota Yaris.

I was halfway back to my car when something that had been bothering me finally fell into place. I hurried back to where she was preparing to reverse out of the driveway.

'I almost didn't see you there,' she said.

'Sorry I didn't mean to startle you, it was just when you said you were filling in for Pam, did you mean Pamela Blackstock, the woman who was assaulted on Aberdour Beach?'

She frowned, 'yes, how do you know Pam?'

'I don't. My friend in the police is leading up the case and I didn't realise that you might be connected.'

'I'd hardly say we're connected. I knew Pam a very long time ago from secretarial studies. Strange thing was I lost touch with her completely after that. I think she must have moved, then one day I'm at the bowls and in walks Pam. I don't think she recognised me at first, and she'd obviously changed her name, but it was unmistakeably her.'

'That must've been nice for you both.'

'Hmm, like I said we weren't close, she was a few years younger than me. I got the impression she wasn't that pleased to see me.'

'Why would that be?' I asked.

'Lord knows, women can be strange creatures especially when they're trying to recreate a new identity for themselves post-divorce, I've seen it with other pals. Listen, was there anything else, only I need to be on my way, they'll have my guts if I'm late.'

'Sorry, I was curious that was all, good luck,' I said as I waved her off.

Chapter Seven

I pondered for a minute whether I should mention to George that my client knew his victim, but decided for now, at least, it was circumstantial and was unlikely to be of any concern to him, the link was tenuous at best.

The storage container was in an industrial estate next door to a Screwfix and opposite a factory. The man at the reception desk appeared to double as a security guard. He gave me a bit of an odd look when I told him the unit I was visiting. Still, he said nothing further other than to ask for my ID and telling me to sign in on the visitor book. When he turned his back to place my driver's licence under the photocopier, I took the opportunity to cast my eye over the previous entries and was shocked when I saw Elspeth's name near the top of the page. According to this log she had been here two weeks ago.

I knocked the book to the floor, apologising as I stooped to pick it up whilst taking a quick photo on my phone that I hoped would be legible when I came to look at it later. The man glared.

'You brought your key?' The man asked.

I pulled it from my pocket, for some reason compelled to dangle it in front of him. 'Good, go down this first corridor and then turn right, the unit you're looking for is about halfway along on the right.'

I thanked him and walked in that direction. The large metal rooms on either side made the space cold and I felt myself shiver.

After I turned right as instructed, I followed the numbers until I reached 474 and put my key in the padlock. I slipped the padlock into my pocket, I'd watched too many crime dramas where people ended up locked in tiny spaces because they left the key in the door. It was an unlikely scenario, I knew that, but I had no desire to end up accidentally locked in.

I looked at my phone annoyed to see that I had no signal and only 'E' for my internet connection, if I'd thought about it earlier, I would've let Sonya know where I was. I told myself to get a grip and stepped inside the small rectangular space.

Stewart had, it seemed, done a good job of packing things away neatly and if I hadn't seen the visitors register I wouldn't have guessed that anyone had been in recently. I began looking for boxes where the dust had been disturbed. That was where I planned to start, with whatever Elspeth had been looking at. Why hadn't she told me she'd been here recently?

At the back of the room there were two boxes with lids that looked like they didn't close properly. I pulled one forwards being careful not to disturb the top of the box. There were definite handprints. Trying very hard not to drop the box I manoeuvred it off the shelf to the floor where I took some pictures of the lid before I removed it and set it to one side.

It looked like the contents had been returned to the box in a hurry, as though the last person had been interrupted part way through their search. I began lifting each item out and placing it on the ground next to me, trying to figure out what it was that someone would've been looking for.

At the bottom of the box were about twenty envelopes containing photographs, taken at a time when people still had to take a roll of film somewhere to get the pictures developed before they knew whether they had taken a brilliant shot or just a picture of their thumb. I didn't want to spend too much time here, so I popped them into an evidence bag and slipped them into the canvas bag I'd brought with me.

There were several empty photo frames, I wondered if they had contained photographs and this was what Elspeth had been looking for? I found one of a couple and two small boys, it looked like it had been taken in the sixties. I assumed this must be her parents and brothers, I wondered why she wasn't in the shot but perhaps she was the one behind the camera. The frame was old and as I turned it over I could see that the card backing was cracked slightly. I lifted the metal tabs that held it in place and eased off the back. As I did, another much smaller picture slipped out of the space and into the box.

I put the family photo to one side and delved inside to pick out the one that had fallen. It was the type of photograph that was taken with a polaroid camera, one of the few ways before digital photography that let you instantly see your handywork. It was a couple, they're both smiling, he has what would be considered these days as a dodgy moustache but in the early 80s would've been the height of fashion in facial hair. She's wearing a white knee length dress, cowboy boots and a denim jacket, her hair tightly curled into a perm. Could this be Iain and the woman he would marry only months before disappearing. I turned it over in the hopes that some clue would be scribbled on the back, but there was nothing, I added it to the evidence bag.

If there had been something other than the photographs in that box, it was gone now. I slid it back onto the shelf before taking down the one next to it. It was heavy and when I lifted the lid I realised why, it was full of paperwork. I wasn't sure why

Stewart had decided these documents were worth keeping, but I imagined it would be hard to decide what Elspeth might've wanted.

I flipped through, there was probably at least an hour of sorting to get through this box and I had no desire to sit here and do that. I decided the best option would be to take the whole box home. Another hour of lifting boxes from shelves and rooting through them had kicked up nothing but dust. My throat felt dry and I had sneezed more in these couple of hours than I think I have in the last year.

The final box I opened looked older than the others. I hoped that I might finally have got to one that contained something from Iain's life. Inside there was a small wooden box, it was locked, and I couldn't immediately see the key. I shook it gently and heard something move from side to side. I placed it on top of the box of paperwork that I had already set aside. There was also; an old-fashioned alarm clock, the sort that folds away into its stand for travel; a pair of black lace gloves, the type that Madonna wore; and a small stack of magazines and letters.

It was a strange eclectic bunch of things to have kept. Perhaps when Iain first went missing they had retained more of his belongings and over time they had been whittled down to this group of items. I hadn't noticed the key for the wooden box, but it could be inside the pages of a magazine.

It was already 2pm, my stomach rumbled. I placed the smaller box containing Iain's possessions on top of the box of paperwork and picked them up. I closed up the unit making sure the padlock was fully fastened before heading back towards the reception area.

'You get everything you need then?' The man asked nodding towards the boxes.

'Yes thanks.'

'Would you like me to give you a hand to your car?'

'No, I'm alright thanks,' the boxes were heavy, but there was something about this man that made me feel a little uneasy.

'Okay dokey, have a nice rest of your day then.'

'Actually, before I go are you able to tell me if Elspeth took anything with her when she came last time?'

He frowned, 'I can't tell you who's been here I'm afraid.'

'I'm not asking *if* she's been here, I know she came a little while ago, I was wondering if she took anything, that's all.'

'Again, I can't tell you what other people may or may not have done.'

I tried to hide my disappointment, 'Okay, thanks anyway.'

I was glad I hadn't parked too far away from the building and was relieved to get the boxes in my boot. Dust had left marks all over my black top and as I wiped my hand across them in an attempt to clean myself up, I only succeeded in spreading it around further. When I walked round to the driver's door I looked up and noticed the receptionist/security guard standing just outside the doorway, his mobile phone held up and pointing in my direction. I couldn't be one hundred percent sure, but it looked like he was taking photographs of me and my car.

I took out my phone and began taking pictures of him, I was deliberately trying to catch his attention so that he would know that I had seen what he was up to. He lowered the phone slowly and then glanced left and right before heading back inside. I got in the car and locked the doors. I sat for a few moments, was it my questions about Elspeth's visit that had triggered this response or was there something more sinister going on?

Chapter Eight

I used the living room floor to lay out Iain's belongings and despite having a good look, I had not been able to find the key to the little wooden box. I spent the afternoon going through the paperwork, trying to organise it into piles. It had taken ages, worse still nothing had jumped out at me as being relevant, still I hoped that as I examined every page something might come up.

The only things I hadn't made a start on yet were the wallets of photographs. They were a less dusty job that I would save for when I was sitting comfortably in my office.

My phone buzzed announcing that Alana was trying to FaceTime me, I answered.

'Hey, how are things going?' I asked.

She smiled, 'lectures are good, I'm learning lots of new things and I like getting in the lab.'

'That's great, what else have you been up to?'

She looked away for a moment and then shrugged, 'not much.'

'Are you okay?'

'Yeah, just wanted to check in with you that's all.'

'I'm good, working on my new case, I turned the phone so she could see the piles of evidence I had arranged across the floor.'

'Looks like you're keeping busy.'

'Uh-huh, only just getting started though.'

'You'll stay safe though, right?'

'You know me,' I smiled.

'I do, that's why I'm reminding you.'

'Gran came by the other day and brought me food, so the fridge is well stocked.'

'I'm jealous.'

'I'm surprised that she's not been up for a visit armed with supplies.'

'It would be nice to see her.' Alana said.

She looked sad, I'd never been to Uni and had no idea how she might be feeling, 'the house is quiet without you.'

'Are you missing me?'

'Of course, there's no one nagging me about staying safe and eating properly or persuading me to buy them outrageously expensive books.'

'I miss you too.'

'Where are your friends from last year living?'

Alana had started university last year, but with the pandemic it had been a year of living at home and online learning. Now she was adjusting to university life and living in halls.

'Nicholas and Bert are flat sharing, but Nicky, Zoe and Belinda are all in halls as well, not this building though.'

'We should see if we could get you all in one flat next year maybe?'

She nodded, 'that would be nice.'

'Have you made some new friends?'

'Yeah I have. Izzy, she's the girl in the dorm next to mine, is really nice, but she has her boyfriend over a lot and he's a bit of a dick, the one on the other side is meant to be for an American student, but they haven't turned up yet.

'It doesn't sound too bad.'

'This from the woman who doesn't like sharing her space with anyone,' she teased.

'I know, but it will get easier, it's just all new at the moment.'

'I miss the peace and quiet of my bedroom.'

I opened my mouth to speak and then paused for a moment. 'You don't have to stay there if you don't want to, you could always come home and travel up for lectures.' We'd discussed this option before she started, her best friend Becky did this, but she was at Edinburgh Uni and the commute was considerably shorter.

'I thought about it,' she said. 'But...'

'you want your own space and to experience living there.' I finished; it was what she had said when we had spoken about it previously.

'Something like that.'

'Dundee is only up the road, I can come and visit any time you like, or you could come back for a weekend if you wanted?'

'That would be nice, maybe you could come up and we could go for dinner or something?'

We made arrangements for my visit, and she seemed a bit perkier when she hung up. I felt momentarily enveloped in sadness, I wanted Alana to live away from home and feel secure and happy but given everything that had happened over the last few years it was no wonder that she was finding it challenging. When Alana had first been accepted to Dundee, Sonya had volunteered to speak to her friend who lectured on Alana's course to keep an eye on her. I considered taking her up on the offer but I knew Alana wouldn't appreciate it.

I decided that instead of continuing to root through magazines and paperwork I would have a quick shower, put some of Maureen's food in the microwave and spend the evening going through the old photographs I had found. When I got out, I had a missed call from George.

I phoned him back, 'everything okay,' I said as soon as he answered.

'Yeah, I was looking for a favour.'

'Okay,'

'No need to sound so suspicious, I was just wondering if you would look after Jock and Wallace for me at the weekend, I'm taking Mel away for a couple of nights and when I booked it I didn't know we'd have become dog keepers.'

'And you thought I would be a good stand in?' I asked. 'I've never had a dog I wouldn't know what to do and besides my house isn't dog friendly, isn't there someone more suitable you could ask?'

'If there was do you think I would be on the phone to you?'

'Ah, so I'm your last resort, am I? Couldn't you just take them to kennels like normal people?'

'Do you have any idea how much those places cost, I would be paying almost as much for this pair to have a night away as I would for me and Mel.'

I laughed, 'fine. But it's for two nights only, and you collect them on the way home and bring all the food and whatever they need to me.'

'Thank you, you never know, you might even enjoy the company.'

'Nope, don't get any ideas, I have no desire to have a pet and if I did it would need to be something that could fend for itself.'

He laughed at me.

'How's your case going, any leads on who attacked your woman?'

'Nothing, I'm resorting to interviewing the lawn bowling team tomorrow afternoon, so that should be fun.'

'I should probably mention then that the case I'm working, it turns out that my client knows your victim.'

I heard him try to muffle a sigh, 'why are you only just telling me this now?'

'Because I only found out this morning, I've been busy, and I didn't think it was that relevant.'

'Then why are you telling me now?'

'She's standing in for your woman on the bowls team, so you're probably going to meet her tomorrow. She says she knew Pamela when she was young, before she moved away and got married.'

'Married?'

'Yes.'

'We've no record of her being married.'

'I guess Elspeth just assumed seeing as she had changed her name.'

'We don't have a record of a name change. Are you sure your woman is right, didn't you say she was…' he paused. 'older, could she be mistaken?'

'I doubt it, she said that Pamela wasn't that thrilled to find that someone from her previous life had turned up in her current one.'

'Interesting, this woman, she's called Elspeth?'

'Yes, but please don't tell her that I told you, client confidentiality and all that.'

'Is this you asking me to stay out of your cases now?'

'Something like that.'

'I'll do my best.' He replied.

'You'd better, otherwise you'll be looking for someone else to look after your pooches.'

We said goodbye, George promising that he wouldn't tell Elspeth we'd talked. Sitting in the kitchen, my stomach now full of casserole, I opened the first of the photo wallets and began looking through them. I found half a dozen of Elspeth's graduation. Her parents were smiling and looked proud, but when I compared these to the thirty or so there was of Iain's graduation it was easy to see the difference.

This was particularly apparent in their mother's face; she looked truly joyous on the occasion stood next to her son in his gown, whereas next to Elspeth she had what could only be described as a polite smile. There was a difference in the way they'd dressed for the occasion as well. In Elspeth's photos her mother wore a dark blue skirt with a white polka dot blouse, her father in corduroy trousers and a blazer, a shirt but no tie, but next to Iain she was wearing a cerise pink dress, a white shawl and a big hat, their father in a navy-blue suit, beige shirt and blue floral patterned tie. Whatever Elspeth had told me about her father being, "pleased as punch" about her qualifications they were evidentially a lot more enthusiastic about their son's. She must have known how they felt and perhaps this is why she distanced herself from them, working abroad for so much of her career and only returning for her parents' funerals. And why she hadn't had the stomach for going through their things, maybe she was expecting that their possessions would be a shrine to their lost sons.

Whatever their feelings were about their daughter's educational choices, they clearly had no issues with their son's homosexuality. There were lots of candid shots of Rodger and Stewart at the Christmas dinner table, BBQs and even on a camping holiday in what looked like the south of France. Stewart had been embraced as part of the family, and even after Rodger's death he'd stayed close to them and hadn't appeared to settle down with anyone else.

There were also a few photographs from Elspeth's wedding. She looked like she was perhaps in Singapore, it was hard to tell exactly, but it was clear that none of her family had been in attendance. Weddings in foreign locations had been quite popular for a while now, but back in the 80s the majority of families couldn't have afforded to fly abroad for such an event. Still, Elspeth looked happy, and I made myself a note to ask about her husband. He was a tall, handsome man, with slightly long curly hair and glasses. They'd looked a well-matched couple, perhaps he was an academic as well and understood the life she had chosen for herself.

In the wallet containing Elspeth's wedding pictures there were several strips of negatives. I held them up to the light, it was hard to make out who they were of, but it also looked like a wedding scene. I would need to find someone to develop them for me, it could be as simple as Elspeth having a second ceremony when she was back in the UK, but I was keen to know for sure.

At the back of a collection of Christmas photos were a handful of pictures taken of a young woman. It was the same person that I'd seen in the polaroid with Iain earlier today. She was clearly posing in these shots, all with a similar wallpaper in the background, geometric shapes in black, grey and red as was popular on the walls of many an 80s bachelor pad. In some of the snaps she was wearing a fluorescent pink rara skirt and the black lace Madonna gloves I'd found earlier today, in others, jeans and a tie dye t-shirt.

I examined the background of the photographs and saw that on top of the white melamine chest of drawers sat a small wooden box. There was no doubt in my mind that these pictures had been taken in Iain Blair's flat.

Chapter Nine

Elspeth had been hesitant about giving me Stewart's telephone number and it had taken some persuading to change her mind. Not for the first time I wondered why clients thought they were best placed to decide who I spoke to in the course of an investigation that they had asked me to carry out. I'd been baffled by her resistance, in the end I told her that not giving me his number would only delay the inevitable, that I intended on speaking with her brother in law despite her protestations and giving me the information would at least speed the process up and ultimately cost her less money in the long run.

It had been 8.30pm last night when I'd tried phoning Stewart, but there had been no reply. This morning I was hoping that he'd phone me back without my needing to call again. To pass the time I began searching through the piles of paperwork I'd left all over the living room floor. An hour in and I was beginning to lose hope that I'd uncover anything of any use when I found a bundle of letters. They were all from Elspeth and all from 1983. I sorted them into date order.

16th April 1983
Dear Mum & Dad
I hope you are well. I understand that you are worried about Iain but he is a grown man, if he says he needs a break and he will go back to his

studies at a later date then I think you should
accept that and support him.
I can't come home from Singapore to talk to him,
I'm very busy here. As I told you in my last letter I
am the archaeologist in charge and there is no way
I can just 'pop home' for a couple of weeks. I will
write to Iain and if he wants, he can write back.
Surely you would be better getting Rodger to have a
chat anyway as they've always got along better.
Love Elspeth
Xx

I could understand her frustration, imagining how I would feel if I had been expected to abandon my job and travel halfway across the world to tell my brother to stay at uni. It certainly didn't seem like they had understood the problems this would create for their daughter.

I wished I could see both sides of the correspondence, I doubted Elspeth would've kept the letters, she'd already said she preferred to have few possessions and even if she had, there would be little likelihood that she would be happy giving them to me to read.

30ᵗʰ April 1983
Dear Mum & Dad
I cannot come home just now, I truly wish you
would understand that I have a life here in
Singapore, with a husband and a job. I cannot
afford the flights back to the UK even if I wanted to
leave which I don't.

If Iain has fallen in love and wants to get married then I am very happy for him and I really don't think it's anyone else's business who he's marrying. And no, I don't think you should tell him "your thoughts on the girl."

Max and I will not be able to come back to the UK for the wedding for the same reasons none of you came to Singapore for ours.

I understand you are upset but please stop writing to me as if it is somehow my responsibility to make Iain do anything.

Elspeth x

I assumed the same reasons were financial, but it could easily be through bloody mindedness, and that she had felt bitter about the reception her wedding was given, much like her graduation, I expected.

My letter reading was interrupted by my phone ringing, I quickly unearthed it from beneath a pile of papers.

'Hello, Rowan speaking,' I answered.

'Hi, you left me a message last night, this is Stewart Blair.'

'Thanks for calling me back, I was hoping we could meet in person?'

'What's this all about, your message said something about Iain Blair.'

I had tried to keep my message brief, not wanting to give away too much, but making it enticing enough that he would want to call back. 'Yes, that's right,'

'I've got a pretty busy schedule, over the phone would be better.'

He must be retired by now, I wondered what he was doing that meant he was so busy. 'I'm happy to be flexible,' I said.

I heard a sigh, 'do you know the sailing club in Dalgety Bay?'

'I've never been before, but it can't be too hard to find.'

'Okay, well I have a small boat, I intend to be there all afternoon completing some repairs, if you're happy to talk whilst I work then you can meet me there.'

'That sounds great, thank you – how will I find you?'

'There won't be many people around, and if it's not immediately obvious where I am my boat is called 'Mary-Beth',,'

'Fantastic, I look forward to seeing you later on today.'

When he hung up, I thought about his reluctance to see me in person, it could've been as simple as he didn't think it was worth it but then again it might be that he had something to hide.

Dalgety Bay Sailing Club was completely different to what I had envisaged. It had an open area filled with boats of all sizes and the clubhouse's elevated position gave it an amazing view across the River Forth and beyond. There were plenty of people around, despite it being cold. I hadn't realised that this was here, practically on my doorstep. I'd parked in a nearby residential street and walked round to where most of the boats were. Stewart was right, it wasn't hard to spot him, he was wearing jeans and a faded red body warmer.

He looked up as I approached. 'Rowan?'

I nodded, 'I like your boat,' I said. I knew nothing about boats or sailing.

'Thanks, I got her when I retired.'

'Why's she called Mary-Beth?'

'It was the name of my dog when I was little,'

I wanted to say what an odd name for a dog, but restrained myself. 'Do you get out in the boat much?' I said instead.

'Not as much as I'd like.'

'Did you go sailing when Rodger was alive?'

He looked down at the oily rag in his hand, 'a fair bit, not in this boat. Sadly our last boat together ended up being a bit worse for wear.'

'What about Iain, did he have any interest in sailing?'

'No, going out on the open water wasn't for him.'

'Were you close?'

He paused a moment before answering, 'I wouldn't say we weren't close, but we didn't live in each other's pockets if that's what you mean.'

'Close enough to know if he got married.'

'Didn't you say you were working for Elspeth?'

I nodded, 'does that make a difference?'

He tilted his head to one side, 'I guess that depends on what she's told you.'

'Not very much, only that she wants to find out what happened to her brother before she dies.'

'Cheery as always, I see.'

'I'm getting the impression there's no love lost between the two of you.'

Stewart put down the rag he was holding and opened two deck chairs, 'let's sit,' he said. 'I can see this isn't going to be a quick conversation.'

I sat down, remaining silent hoping that he would continue with his thoughts.

'In many ways I understand Elspeth, her parents did put unfair expectations on her because she was the only girl. They resented her for putting her career above what they saw as her responsibility to the family, especially when it took her to the other side of the world.'

He paused to unscrew the top of a Thermos flask and poured the dark liquid. He offered me a mug and I took it, immediately taking a sip in the hopes that it would warm me up. I looked up, the taste taking me by surprise.

'Sorry I should've said, it's Bovril not coffee.'

'I actually like Bovril, my taste buds were just confused for a moment. What did they expect of Elspeth?'

'Mostly that she wouldn't live half a world away and that she would provide them with grandchildren. Whether that didn't happen through her and Max's choice or because they couldn't I don't know. Her mother, particularly, seemed to think that she had deprived them of grandchildren on purpose.'

So far everything that Stewart had told me had made me side with Elspeth, no wonder she had been so frustrated when her parents expected her to drop everything and come home to sort out her brother's life.

'Do you think they were right?' I asked.

'No, but I don't think she dealt with it very well either. When Iain went missing, we searched for him and as time went on his mother was almost inconsolable, I think Elspeth should've realised that despite everything else she needed to come home and help.'

'What was going on in Iain's life when he went missing?'

'He was working on the roads and from what I could tell he enjoyed it, manual labour agreed with him.'

'It was a bit of a divergence from his previous career path though wasn't it, any idea what triggered that change?'

'There had always been a lot of pressure on Iain to excel, not just to be successful, but overachieve. He only started to do the PhD because his mother didn't stop going on about it, she had this idea that she wanted him to be a university lecturer.'

'Would you say she was interfering in all aspects of Iain's life?'

'Absolutely, Rodger had me and Elspeth had Max, so he was the only one left where she felt she had proper leverage. We, that is Rodger and me, were shocked when he moved out at the start of the PhD. She said it was because he needed space and quiet to study but I assumed that it was part of some deal he struck with them, he'd do the PhD but he wanted his own place. She had a key of course though.'

'I'm guessing his parents took him dropping out of the PhD course badly?'

'I think that's an understatement. He promised them he'd go back and finish it, but it wasn't a shock to us, he'd been telling Rodger how awful it was for about six months, he didn't get on with his supervisor, it wasn't what he wanted for his life and then one day he had a big grin on his face, he said he'd left his course and got himself a job working on the A92 build.'

'What about the wedding?' I asked.

'What did Elspeth tell you about it?'

'Nothing, when I asked her, she said her parents hadn't mentioned it.'

He took another sip from his mug, 'that's strange.'

'In what way?'

'Just why deny knowing anything about an event you were at.'

'What? Elspeth was at Iain's wedding?' I said wondering why Elspeth had lied to me.

'He never told us when they met, but Rodger assumed that meeting Iris was a catalyst to him leaving the PhD and looking for a different life.'

'And what did his parents think of her?'

'They weren't keen, they thought she wasn't good enough for their son, though I'm not sure anyone would've been good enough for Iain. Iris was a dancer, if you know what I mean.'

I did know, he meant stripper, 'is that how they met?'

'I don't think so, she was good for him though, I'll say that. He'd never been what I'd describe as a happy person but after he met Iris he changed, laughing, smiling, looking forward to the future. Rodger was happy to see him like that so when he asked him to be best man at the wedding he was delighted to accept.'

'Did his parents come?'

'No, they weren't invited. He had mentioned the idea of marrying Iris to them, and it turned into this huge full blown family argument. They asked Rodger to talk him out of it, but he told them that Iain was a grown man and that Iris made him happy, but they wouldn't hear of it. They never knew he got married, he made us promise to keep it a secret and we did.'

'And Elspeth came to the wedding?'

'She kicked up a bit of a stink about it at the time, flights were expensive then, but she still came.'

'How long before he went missing was this?'

'I don't remember exactly, it was just a registry office job, with a meal afterwards, Iris didn't even wear a proper wedding dress, as I recall it was just some random white dress she already owned.'

'Approximately though.' I asked.

'I'd say about three or four months, it wasn't long after he left uni and it was before he got the roads job.'

When Elspeth was writing to her parents exasperated, she knew her brother was already married, no doubt adding to her resolve not to travel back to Scotland to discuss Iain's life choices with him.

'How long was Elspeth in the UK for?' I asked.

'Couldn't tell you, other than it was at least a couple of days, she arrived late in the evening a couple of days before and we saw her the day after, but no idea if she went straight back to Singapore.'

'What about when Iain went missing, did she come over then?'

He shook his head, 'no. I was surprised actually, I thought she would be over like a flash, but she didn't seem to take it seriously.'

'Why?'

'She said that she didn't believe he was missing, she figured that he'd realised that the marriage was a mistake and he wanted to go back to his old life, and he'd just sodded off somewhere and would be back in a few days. But even when weeks had passed she still didn't seem concerned.'

'What about you and Rodger, were you worried?'

'Rodger wasn't in the first few days, I think he thought there was some mistake, but he became increasingly concerned the more time went by.'

'I imagine it was Iris that was the most worried.' I said, although it had been his parents that had ultimately reported him missing.

'I've no idea.' Stewart stood up and took a few paces away from where we had been sitting and gazed out to the water. It looked grey and cold, but even then he seemed to take solace in it, I got up and walked over to him.

'What do you mean you don't know, surely you talked to her?'

'I'm afraid not, no one did, she'd vanished.'

'They both went missing?'

'We thought after Iain disappeared Iris might've gone back to her old life, or…I don't know, we assumed they'd had a row.'

'But what you're saying is that both of them were never seen again and you didn't think that was strange? Or that it might indicate they were together?'

'Of course, later, it was clear that it was the most probable explanation.'

'Why didn't anyone report Iris as missing? Weren't her family looking for her?'

'As far as we knew she didn't have family, she'd been in the foster care system, something ridiculous like twenty homes in ten years. With Iain gone, there wasn't anyone to miss her.'

'And you decided not to mention any of this to the police because?'

'It was too late. Iain had been reported as a missing person by his parents and they didn't know he was married, so what were we supposed to do when they came asking questions, just tell them?'

'Yes. Obviously, that's what you should've done, what hope had they in finding him without all the relevant information?'

'I suppose you're right, but after a while it didn't seem important.'

'Not important, in what way was her life not important?' I had tried to maintain a neutral, professional tone, but this was too much.

'I don't mean…I don't know, it was just too awkward to start mentioning her, Rodger thought it would make the police think we had something to hide, he was already concerned that they might've figured out we were a couple. Things were different in the 80s and the police weren't too friendly towards you if you were a gay couple, no matter what the circumstances were.'

'When you cleared their flat, I know you gave some of his things to his parents, what did you do with the stuff that belonged to Iris?'

'Clothes went to charity, a few other bits, jewellery etc I stuck in a box and we held onto it for a couple of years in case she came back for it, but then it went in the bin I'm afraid.'

'And you never heard from her again?'

'No, I think we were all happy to pretend she hadn't existed.' At least this time he had the decency to look sheepishly at the ground.

'Can you think of anything else that might give some indication as to where they might have gone?'

He shook his head slowly, 'sorry, that's everything.'

'Thanks for meeting with me, here's my card in case you think of something,' I was desperate to get away from this man now, his indifference to his sister-in-law had left a nasty taste in my mouth and there was nothing more to be gained by spending any more time talking to him.

Chapter Ten

It was beginning to get dark by the time I got home. The house next door was back on the market, the previous purchasers never actually moved in, the estate agent had told me that over the course of the pandemic they had discovered each other's extra marital activities and were getting a divorce. There were two cars parked out front, one emblazoned with the estate agent's name and logo, the other a red Ford Focus. All the lights were on and my hope for a normal neighbour were lifted as I watched a couple about my age standing talking with the estate agent in the large living room.

I considered calling Elspeth as soon as I got in to ask her why she'd lied about being at her brother's wedding but decided against it. If Stewart had let her know that her secret was out of the bag, then she could spend the evening wondering why I hadn't confronted her.

I warmed up another bowl of casserole and jumped when I heard the front door of the house next door slam, what was I afraid of? That Maureen would appear to chastise me using the microwave to reheat her food. I laughed, even though I knew that she would tut and usher me out of the way so she could take over.

I looked around the house, I should probably tidy up a bit before George dropped off the dogs at the weekend. Why I had agreed to this I still didn't know, I liked dogs, I just don't have the time for one, let alone two. At least it was only going to be for a couple of nights, how hard could it be?

My phone buzzed and George's name appeared on the screen, it was always a little disconcerting when someone you were thinking about suddenly contacted you.

'Hiya, I was just thinking about you,' I said.

'Really, should I be worried?'

'Well, it wasn't so much thinking about you as about your two little wards you've persuaded me to look after.'

'You've not changed your mind, have you?'

'Yeah, about a hundred times but I would never do that to Mel. Anyway, what can I do you for?'

'I interviewed your client today, she didn't mention knowing Pamela at all, which I thought given our conversation beforehand was a little odd.'

'Hmm, I'm not sure that she's the trustworthy, pillar of the community type that she's making out to be, so maybe not so strange after all.'

'Really? Anything you want to share?'

'Nah, she just omitted to tell me something and I'm not sure why.'

'Interesting, she was a bit…hostile, no, that's not the right word, more standoffish when we spoke to her, I got the impression she thought we were wasting everybody's time. I did find out something I thought you might be interested in. You mentioned that Pamela Blackstock was divorced.'

'That's right, Elspeth said she had a different name now and something about the way women behave when they've been married for a long time and then get divorced. Did you find the husband?'

'No, because there wasn't one,' George said.

'Why the change of name though?'

'Pamela was adopted around the time of her fourteenth birthday and took the surname of her adoptive parents.'

'That makes sense, did she have any other family?'

'We can't find any record of any siblings, not that that means she doesn't have any, it's really difficult when kids have been in the foster care system to keep track of them, especially if they have different fathers which it's possible was the situation in this case. And of course the fact they would've been in care in the 70s doesn't help, some of that paperwork never made it on to the archived system. Maybe you could see if your client knows, it would be good to find her some family.'

'What about the adoptive parents?'

'The family moved to France when Pamela was sixteen, it looks like she spent most of her adult life there, her adoptive parents retired and died there. It was just the three of them, so no one left on that side.'

Perhaps Elspeth had been mistaken and that's why she hadn't mentioned knowing Pamela when George had spoken to her earlier. Somehow I doubted that though.

'How is she doing? Any closer to waking up and telling you who attacked her?'

'Unfortunately not, but the hospital say she's stable.'

'Any new leads?'

'None, I've been up to the house with the search team and there's not much, a few photos, some of them pretty old, some from her time in France but nothing recent. I'm trying to liaise with the French police to see if they have any information, family links to organised crime etc. It's a stretch, but given what little information we've got it seemed worth a shot.'

I said goodbye to George and walked through to the living room lifting a pile of papers and taking them back to the kitchen. It was too late to have coffee really, but I'd had trouble sticking to a sensible bedtime since Alana left. I only used half a scoop in the machine telling myself that it wouldn't keep me awake too late.

The first couple of pages were letters from the university, addressed to Iain, but at his parent's address. It would've been interesting to know if they had handed them over to him or if they'd opened them. Given that they were amongst letters from Elspeth my money would be on Iain's mother opening them. Maybe in the hope that it was news of him coming to his senses and finishing his PhD. Instead, they were simply enquiring if he would like to come back and complete the outstanding section of his course in the coming academic year.

Then there was a letter from Elspeth.

20th June 1983
Dear Mum and Dad,
I think jumping to the conclusion that Iain is dead simply because his car was found at the side of the road is a bit over the top. There are lots of reasons that he might've needed to abandon it there and I'm sure he'll turn up soon with a perfectly reasonable explanation.
Is he still with the girl you mentioned previously, has anyone asked her if she knows where he is?

I understand you would like me to come home, but I've explained before, my work here is important and the cost of flights to the UK from Singapore is very high. Also, I'm not sure why you think I would be any more successful at finding him than the police.

Please do try not to worry as much. Iain is a grown up, if he needs some space to clear his head then let him have it.

Love
Elspeth
Xx

I wondered if she ever regretted taking this attitude with her parents, she was clearly fishing to see if they knew about the wedding. Letters were all well and good, but without the other side of the correspondence it was hard to decide if her responses were reasonable or if she was a bit of a cow to her family.

The next letter was written in early July.

3rd July 1983
Dear Mum & Dad
I am sorry you are so upset, it is very inconsiderate of Iain to not let you know that he is okay, but I am sure that he is.

I still don't know what good you think having me home would be. I'm not a detective and if the police are telling you they're doing all that they can then I'm not sure what else can be done.

I'm glad that Rodger and Stewart are checking in on you regularly, I 'm sure it is nice to have that kind of support. Having them close to home must make a difference. As I mentioned before I can't do my job from Scotland, because the dig I'm working on is here in Singapore and I must stay here.

Let me know when Iain turns up,

Love Elspeth

Xxx

Elspeth clearly thought her parents were over-reacting and that her brother had just buggered off somewhere, she expected him to turn up at some point and be greeted like the prodigal son. Perhaps she was right, but I knew that it wouldn't matter what age Alana was, I would be out of my mind with worry if her car was found abandoned on the side of the road and she was nowhere to be seen. I imagined my friends and family would rally round me, to look for her and to support me. Elspeth was in a tricky position, her job required her to be thousands of miles away, I understood that she couldn't literally down tools and head home, but that didn't mean she needed to be so coldly dismissive of her parent's concerns.

Chapter Eleven

Despite trying to convince myself that the half scoop of coffee would not keep me awake, I stayed up until 3.30am looking through paperwork. I'd found a half a dozen or so more letters from Elspeth, some newspaper cut outs reporting Iain's disappearance and a couple of letters from Iain's university. The rest was of no interest, just some bills, Mr & Mrs Blair's wills, which given a cursory glance didn't seem to contain anything earth shattering and a couple of random newspapers.

The more I'd searched through the paperwork the more irritated I had become by Elspeth lying to me. I was used to people lying, it was an occupational hazard, I couldn't put my finger on what it was about this lie or liar that was bothering me more than usual. Perhaps I had succumbed to the bias that old, polite ladies were honest and trustworthy. Whatever it was, talking to her this morning wasn't likely to be a good idea. Instead, I decided to take a drive to the address that Deborah Marchmont had lived at when Iain went missing.

The A921 as it was now would've been a much busier road in the 1980s, the building of the A92 had cut the volume of traffic significantly, which is just as well I thought while I weaved my way through some of the narrower villages.

It would've been easy to miss the small turning off the main road which was barely more than a farm track. I parked on a grass verge at the side of the road, pulling my car just out of the way enough that another car could get passed, not that I imagined that it was used very much. The house itself looked well maintained from the outside and I could see raised beds around the side and a small green house.

I knocked on the door and took a half step back.

I was about to give up and leave when I heard a creak from the dormer window above me. I took another couple of steps back so I could see the person leaning out.

'I'm looking for Deborah Marchmont,' I said, shielding my eyes from the autumnal glare of the sun. It was hard to be sure but the woman in the window looked the right age to be Deborah.

'Why?'

'My name is Rowan McFarlane and I'm a private detective. I'm looking into a cold case from 1983. She gave a statement to the police.'

'That was a long time ago. I don't remember anything from then.' She started to close the window.

'You are Deborah Marchmont then?'

She paused. 'I'd like you to go away now.'

'I just want to ask a few questions, I'm trying to help an old lady find her brother before she dies.' It was an exaggeration of the truth, but close enough.

Deborah closed the window without replying.

I waited on her doorstep for close to five minutes before I heard several chains being unhooked on the other side.

Moments later the door was cracked open revealing a sliver of the woman behind it, she had dark hair heavily streaked with grey, her plump figure accentuated by the shapeless skirt and jumper she wore. On her feet were a pair of tatty green wellington boots.

'Do you like bees?' She asked.

'Yes.'

She nodded slowly looking me up and down. 'okay then come with me.' She stepped out of the house turning to close and lock the door behind her.

She walked round the side of the house towards the back garden, I followed. There at the back of the house were three beehives. She stopped a couple of metres away and sat down on a wooden bench.

'Sit down,' she said.

I sat next to her wondering why she had brought me around here.

'Without bees the world will end,' she said. 'We need pollinators you know, people often overlook insects, or treat them like they don't matter, but they do. Just because they're small or ugly they're looked on as disposable when really they hold the key to keeping everything going.'

'I suppose that's true.'

'Why did you come here?' Deborah said.

'Because I think you might've seen something really important that day and I want to find out more.'

'The police didn't come back to ask me any other questions you know.'

I thought back to the note at the side of the interview writing her off as 'a nutter'. 'I know.'

'So they mustn't have thought what I saw was important, what makes you think it was after all this time?'

'I don't think they took you very seriously and that wasn't very nice or professional of them. I think you might have been the last person to see Iain and it's just possible that you know more than you told the officer that came that day.'

'He refused to come and sit with the bees you know; said he didn't have time. Insisted on coming inside my home and I didn't like that, I don't like strangers in my space.'

That I truly did understand, when Jack's death was being investigated I hated the intrusion of the police into my home. 'That was rude,' I said.

'Yes. I think he thought I was lying.'

'Why would he think that?'

'I'm not like most people, I like my own space. I don't like attention or drama. It was a big deal for me speaking to the police and he made out that I was making it up. Kept asking if I was sure and why I needed to write everything down. He even said to me it was a bit strange to keep a note of things, acted like I had done something wrong.'

'What a dickhead.'

She laughed and it was a joyous sound. 'I like you,' she said.

'Thank you, I like you too,' and it was true. Deborah was a little unusual, but I didn't think that was equal to unreliable or not trustworthy.

'Would you like to come inside and have some tea?'

Understanding what an honour had been extended to me I quickly agreed. I'm not sure what I was expecting of the inside of the house, but it was probably one of the cleanest spaces I had ever been in. Not that she didn't have things, she did, books that overflowed from shelves and stood in neat piles, pictures, and ornaments, it's just that there wasn't any dust, not a speck.

I sat at her kitchen table as she boiled the kettle and readied the teapot. I watched as she organised everything, moving the cups into the perfect position on each individual saucer. I waited in silence, this routine felt like it was something she needed to do without me overwhelming her with questions.

'I'm sorry I don't have any biscuits,' she said as she poured the tea.

'That's okay.'

'Milk?'

'Yes please.'

'Sugar?'

'No thanks.'

She smiled and stirred the cup three full rotations with the decoratively engraved silver teaspoon and then placed the cup in front of me. I waited until she had served herself, noting that she took her tea without milk.

'What is it you would like to know?' Deborah asked.

I took a sip of tea and carefully replaced the cup in the original spot on the saucer. 'How much do you remember about the day you saw the two people passing your house?'

'I was born in this house, you know. Then when I was older my mother decided she wanted to relocate to Glasgow, that's where my sister lives and she wanted to be near her because of the grandchildren. I didn't want children. When she moved I stayed here, and I've lived here ever since.'

I wasn't sure why she was giving me this back story, but I could tell that it was important to her to clarify so I didn't interrupt.

'Even before the A92 the little road that runs outside of the cottage wasn't busy,' she continued. 'there are people who walk their dogs in the woods, they sometimes come this way, but there's no parking here which means it's unusual for anyone to come from the road direction towards the woods and that's what made that day stand out to me.'

'The police report said you kept a diary and that detailed what happened at what times?'

'It's not a diary, not really, I write things down if I think they might be important or if something strange happens. Like last week I noticed that the person who was delivering my mail had changed, I made a little note. She was later than the previous person and a woman.' She glanced at me. 'I know to most people that sort of thing might seem…weird, but I like to keep a note of things that's all.'

'It sounds like you'd make a great detective to me.'

'Perhaps, although I think I wouldn't be very good at figuring out why people do things, I've never been very good with people.'

'People can be difficult,' I agreed. 'Is there any chance I could see your notebook from that day?'

She looked at me for a couple of moments before leaving the room, returning with a brown leather book in her hands. 'This is the one,' she said.

'Can I see?'

She opened the book to the correct page and passed it to me. The entry was just as it had been described on the police report as far as the times were concerned, but Deborah had included more detail.

'It says here they were arguing, and you heard the man say that he loved her and they would always be part of each other's lives then something about it being too late.'

'She was very upset, and they were quite loud, I was in the garden, and it was very distracting. I was going to come round to the front, but I don't like confrontation, so I stayed at the side.'

'Did you get a look at them at all?'

'I went out into the path after they'd moved on and watched them carry on up the path towards the copse of woods. I didn't see his face, but she turned around and saw me.'

'Do you think you might be able to recognise them after all this time if I showed you a photo?'

'I don't know, maybe.'

I took the photo I had found of Iain and Iris together and put it on the table in front of Deborah. She picked it up and looked intently at it, gently brushing her thumb over Iris' face.

'That was definitely the woman, I don't know about him – it could've been, he's about the right height and build.'

'How sure are you that she's the same person?'

'Completely. There was something about her look that lodged in my head that day, sometimes I see her face in my dreams and I wonder if I should've done something to help her. Do you think the man she was with did something to hurt her?'

It was possible, although I had assumed that they had run away together. 'I don't know. Without being sure it's the same man it's hard to tell. If it was then he was her husband and from everything I've been told they were very much in love, but you can never be sure.'

I took another look at the page open in front of me, a short sentence catching my eye. 'Deborah, what about this other man, the one you saw a little bit later, do you remember anything about him?'

'He threw a bag into my bin, that's why I wrote about him. So rude.'

'What was in the bag?'

'It wasn't very nice.'

'Why not?'

'I waited for him to go away before I looked, he was moving very fast so I didn't have to wait very long. Then I opened the bin lid and took the bag out. At first I thought it was just a rag but then I realised it was all bloody.'

'There was a bloody rag in the bag?'

'It was a cotton handkerchief actually, when I saw the blood I dropped the bag and that was when the ring fell out.'

'The ring?'

'Yes, it must've been wrapped in the hanky.'

'What type of ring?'

'A man's wedding ring.'

'Was there anything else?'

'A ladies glove?'

'A glove, in June?'

'It wasn't a winter glove, it was fingerless and lacy. I thought it was pretty, but I supposed the other one had been lost and that's why it was thrown out.'

'What did you do with the things in the bag.'

Deborah paused. 'I put the handkerchief back in the bag and put it in the bin – it was dirty, and I didn't want to have someone else's germs in my home.'

'That makes sense and what about the other things?

'I put them in a box.'

'And did you tell the police officer about it?'

'Yes.'

'And what did he say?'

'He was cross that I'd thrown the handkerchief in the bin, he said I should've kept it.'

'What about the other things?'

'He looked in the box and said that the person they were looking for wasn't married so it was unrelated, but he told me to keep them in case they changed their minds.'

'Does that mean you still have them?'

She nodded, 'they're still in the box.'

'Could I see them please?'

'You're not police,' she said. 'I was told to keep them in case the police wanted them.'

'I know I'm not police, but I often work with them, I have a friend called DCI George Johnston…'

'I saw him on the telly, he's looking for the person that attacked that woman at the beach.'

'That's right, he is. I can ask him to come and collect them if you'd prefer.' I could only imagine what George would say if I had to ask.

'It's okay, I think I can trust you. I'll bring them to you soon, but first let's finish the tea.' She topped up our teacups and I drank up as requested, being careful not to do it so quickly that she would think I was rushing her.

'The man who put those things in your bin, do you remember what he looked like?'

'Not really. I was upstairs and saw him out of the window, I thought it was very rude to be using someone else's dustbin, just because mine is the only house out here doesn't give people free rein to abuse my facilities.'

'Absolutely,' I replied. 'This was about half an hour after you saw the couple?'

She leant over the kitchen table and tilted her head to look at the entry in the book, 'twenty-six minutes.' She put her cup back on its saucer and stood up. 'I'll be back in a moment.' She went back outside into the garden. I tried to peer through the window to see where she was going but it was no good, she was out of sight.

A few moments later she reappeared wearing a pair of cream and green gardening style gloves and carrying a small metal container.

'Is this the box?'

'I keep it in the garden shed because it's not mine, but I want it to be safe.' She straightened her arm hovering the box a few centimetres away from me.

'Thank you,' I said, taking the box and carefully removing the lid. The gold band was tarnished after years in the container and the glove was more grey than white now but it was still unmistakeably the pair to the one I had taken from the storage unit. I took them out and put them into an evidence bag before handing the tin back to Deborah.

'Had you ever seen any of those people before or since?' I asked when Deborah sat back down.

She shook her head, 'They went to the woods and didn't come back down this way, it's rare that I see people because there's nowhere to park on this side. If you walk through the woods to the other side there's a small parking area and a few houses. That's where they probably went.'

'How long would it take to get from here to the car park on the other side do you think?'

She shrugged, 'I don't like to walk that way much.'

There was no point asking her to guess, she didn't seem the type to approximate anything. 'Do you mind if I leave my car parked here and try it myself?'

'Of course,' she paused. 'Have I been helpful?'

'Yes, really helpful.'

She smiled. 'You can come back if you need to…or want to.'

'I'd like that,' I said making a mental note to come back at least once after the case was over.

The long hill that led to the copse of trees was considerably steeper than it had looked. Once I was amongst the trees it was hard to decide what was a path and what was undergrowth. After a couple of false starts I began along what I was almost sure was the path when I met a couple walking their dog in the opposite direction, which helped assure me that I was on the right track.

I'd set my stopwatch on my phone when I'd started and I'd now walked for twenty-six minutes, so assuming that neither Iris or Iain knew these woods well and that the terrain had been roughly similar in the 80s, this was approximately where they would be when the other man made his way after them. That was, of course, if you went with the theory that it was not a coincidence and that the two sightings Deborah had that day were related.

The question was did they know they were being followed? And if they did what happened when the man caught up to them. I continued walking and after another ten minutes I came down an embankment into a horseshoe shaped carpark. It was quiet with only a car and a small motorhome. The carpark was off a narrow 'B' road with no signage to indicate that the car park even existed.

The other side of the road was mostly farmland except for a cluster of three cottages, but as far as I could tell, there was nowhere to hide. If Iris and Iain had made it this far then it was impossible to know which direction they would've taken.

I turned and walked back through the woods, occasionally stopping to take detours in the path hoping they would lead me to more information. I was cold and disappointed as I walked down the long slope back to my car. I wasn't sure what I'd expected to achieve, but I was dissatisfied with the outcome. I waved at Deborah as I passed her house, she was standing in the upstairs window, no doubt waiting for me to come by. Back in my car I phoned Sonya.

'Hey what's up?' She asked.

'Nothing, this case is doing my head in, you free for some lunch?'

'It's 2.30, I've already eaten.'

'Oh yeah.' I often forgot that my hours were so erratic in comparison to everyone else. 'In that case do you want to drink coffee and keep me company whilst I eat lunch?'

'Sure, I've not much on this afternoon. You want to meet at Sunshine?'

'Perfect, see you soon.' I replied before hanging up.

Chapter Twelve

Unsurprisingly Sonya had arrived before me. I was pleased to see, however, that she was sitting at my favourite table. I made my way to her through the tables and chairs and slumped down opposite.

'Hey, thanks for meeting me.'

'No problem, am I here in my professional capacity?'

'Not today – I just didn't fancy eating lunch alone.'

'You missing Alana?'

'I'm getting used to it, I never thought I would be the type of person who found a house too quiet.'

Mohammad made his way to us, 'before you ask, Star is fine, she was just feeling tired so I persuaded her to go home and get some rest.'

I smiled, 'I'm glad she's got you looking out for her.'

'When she lets me. What can I get you today, your usual?'

'Actually, can I get a water and a baked potato with your bean chilli please.'

'Coming right up,' he turned to Sonya. 'You sure you don't want anything to eat, I've got a great chocolate cake. It's made with beetroots, so it counts as one of your five a day.' There was a twinkle of mischief in his eye as he spoke.

'Oh alright, you've twisted my arm, bring a piece for Rowan as well, I don't want to have to share mine.'

I mocked offense at the suggestion that I would have helped myself to her cake even though we both knew it was one hundred percent accurate.

'How come the case is bothering you so much, I'd have thought you'd be in your element.'

'I know, it's just it feels like no one cared much at the time about these people, I don't think there was much attempt to investigate Iain's disappearance at all, there's so little to go on.'

'What's your working theory? Dead or alive?' Sonya asked.

'It's been so long dead seems the most likely, but then why hasn't his body been found, and if he was dead what happened to Iris? Maybe they just left,' I shrugged.

'Anything to indicate either way, other than the absence of a body?'

'He had overbearing parents who still wanted to control his life even though he was an adult and I doubt they would have approved of Iris, so it would make sense that they would want to get away, but leaving like that – abandoning the car and all their possessions, I'm not sure.'

'You think there's more to it than that?'

'I do, first off you've got the fact that he was married and despite flat out denying knowing anything about it to my face, my client was at his wedding. And then there's his wife – where the hell is she and why didn't she report him missing if they weren't together.'

Mohammed arrived with two slices of cake, my water and baked potato. 'I've brought a pot of camomile tea over, it sounded like you might need it.'

I thanked him, then greedily took a few mouthfuls of food before continuing. 'They were seen together the day he went missing, but according to the police report there was no sign of there being a passenger in Iain's car that day. And why wasn't she reported missing.'

I ate a bit more of my food.

'Why do you think your client lied about the wedding?'

'I don't know, but that's not even the most annoying part.' I sighed. 'I have a horrible feeling she knows something about the woman that was attacked on the beach the other day.'

'What makes you say that?'

'She told me she knew the woman from when she was a teenager, but when George questioned her, she didn't mention it. It's probably nothing.'

'What does George think?' Sonya asked.

'He thinks it's weird, but I don't think he believes she has anything to do with it.'

'Do you?'

'No, I suppose not,' I said not quite convincing myself that I believed my own words. 'I would like to know why she's been lying to me though.'

'Only one way to find out.'

'I know, but I couldn't face it on an empty stomach,' I said taking another mouthful of baked potato.

'How's Alana getting on?'

'Good, I think. I mean academically she's doing great, but I don't know how she's getting on with the whole living away from home part. It's still new, I'm sure she'll start to love it.'

'She's probably worried about you.'

'Why, has she said something to you?' Alana and Sonya had a close bond, and I was grateful that she always had someone else to reach out to.

'No, but she worried about you when she lived at home and now that there's no one here to remind you to be safe and check up on you, she's probably concerned. I'm up in Dundee next week for a guest lecture at the university, I'll take her out for dinner afterwards and check she's okay.'

'That would be nice, she'll be really pleased to see you.' We finished our food and went our separate ways. I considered going home, but instead decided to make an impromptu visit to Elspeth instead.

Her gravel drive announced my arrival as I pulled in and parked. She was at the door seconds after I knocked.

'I wasn't expecting you today.' She was smiling but her tone was curt.

'I was passing,' I lied. 'Thought it would be a good time to catch up and there were some things I wanted to get cleared up.'

'You'd better come in then.' She moved out of the way to let me into her hallway.

Her house had at one time been the gatehouse for a much grander house, from the outside the grey stone building looked impressive. Inside didn't disappoint with its polished wooden floors and dark reds and greens on the walls.

She closed the door. 'Let's go through to the kitchen then.' She brushed past me and led the way to the back of the house where an extension housed a large country kitchen with an AGA. 'Tea?'

'Yes please,' despite having not long had lunch I tried to make a point of always accepting beverages on my house calls. A lesson I'd learnt from Jack was that in accepting hospitality you are building trust, even with those people who are not naturally inclined to be trusting.

She made a pot with considerably less attention to detail than Deborah had. 'Help yourself,' she said whilst placing the teapot and two cups on the kitchen table.

She sat opposite and poured herself a cup slopping tea over the edge as she stirred in her milk. 'So, what is it that I can help with?'

For someone who had so politely engaged my services only a few days ago it was a very contrasting attitude from the woman I'd first met.

'I wanted to talk to you about Iris.'

'Who?'

'Your brother's wife,' I said putting the photo of Iain and Iris on the table, carefully avoiding the puddles of tea.

She gave the picture a cursory glance, 'sorry never met her, not sure how I can help. She pushed the photo back in my direction.

'They look happy don't you think?'

Elspeth shrugged, 'I suppose they do.'

'Not surprising seeing as it was their wedding day.'

'Like I told you before I didn't know anything about him getting married, I mean other than my parents telling me he was shacking up with someone they didn't approve of, but honestly I'm not sure my mother would have thought anyone was good enough for her precious Iain.'

'I went to see Stewart the other day.'

She moved uncomfortably, 'good and did he shed any light on the situation?'

'He was very informative.'

'That's good.'

'For example, he told me that you were at your brother's wedding.'

Her shoulders slumped and she rolled her eyes. 'Bloody idiot, I thought after all this time he might have more…' she trailed off.

'Have more what?' I asked.

'Respect.'

'I think respect is important too, I like to think that the people who engage my services will show enough of it to not lie to me, mostly I'm right and then there are the times I'm wrong and it's so disappointing. What I would like to know is why you bothered. Your brother has been missing for nearly forty years, if you didn't want the past to be dug up why did you hand me the shovel?'

She sighed. 'I hoped that it wouldn't come up. There were only three guests at the wedding, and I hoped that Stewart would have had the good sense not to mention it to you.'

'He didn't tell me, I already knew.'

'That's impossible, how could you know if he didn't tell you, no one else knew.'

'It's interesting that you think that Iain and Iris had no social circle or friends or anyone else in their lives.'

'What do you mean?'

'Iain had friends, men he worked with on the roads, they remembered him showing them the photo of their wedding day. Do you want to tell me why you wanted to keep the wedding and your attendance a secret?'

'She was alright, Iris I mean. Not very educated, but she was kind and Iain seemed happy. She'd not had many opportunities in life. I hate to sound like my mother, but I understood why she didn't approve.'

'Why, you just said she was kind and Iain was happy, what more could your brother have hoped for?'

'What you don't understand is that Iain wasn't just clever, he was genius level clever, and Iris was...for want of a better word, stupid. She hadn't got a qualification to her name and she'd spent her working career using her assets to get by.'

'Being a stripper doesn't make you stupid and neither does not finishing school.' I said as calmly as I could manage.

'Did I hit a nerve? I understand you were a child mother.'

'I was a teenage mother, I've worked in a strip club, and I have a degree. I don't appreciate being put in a box and I'm sure Iris didn't either.'

'I realise it's a subject you're more inclined to be sensitive about, and it would be difficult for someone like you to understand the importance of having a partner in life that is your intellectual equal.'

I said nothing for a moment, desperately resisting the urge to slap this sanctimonious cow round the face. 'I understand that it's easier for you to sit on your high horse and judge people like me and Iris, no doubt it makes you feel superior, because the idea that someone like me is intelligent or that Iain was more interested in love and kindness is so foreign to you, you think it isn't possible. That's your problem and not mine. The real question here is what do you have to hide that meant you didn't want me to find out about the wedding or your attendance at it?'

'I just want to find my brother,' she said.

'Well, I can't do that without looking into his past and if you're not going to be honest with me, I'm not sure I'm prepared to keep working on this case for you. I'm busy and in high demand, when we first met I felt sorry for you and wanted to help you get the closure you were looking for.'

She rubbed her face in her hands. 'I'm sorry. I shouldn't have said those things.'

'No, you shouldn't. I'm going to give you one opportunity to be honest with me and if you choose not to be then I'm going to go home and then I don't want to hear from you ever again.'

'Please stay. I'll tell you what I know.'

Chapter Thirteen

'When did you get back to the UK?'

'The night before the wedding, it was late but we met up and had some food. I tried to like Iris, honestly I did, but she was vacuous. Iain was besotted and looking at her I could see why, he wasn't used to attention from the opposite sex and certainly not from anyone who was as physically attractive as her.

Young people are naïve, that wasn't love, it was lust and I've seen that end badly before.'

'Maybe she made him happy.'

'Pah! I tried to talk him out of it you know, the next morning. Tried to make him see that it was a mistake, but all that happened was that he told me to piss off back to Singapore and that it had been a mistake inviting me.'

'But you still went to the wedding.'

'Yes, Iris intervened and acted as peacemaker, like I said before she was kind if nothing else.'

'I'm still curious as to why no one wondered where Iris was when Iain went missing.'

'I thought what must have happened was that he had caught her having an affair and had been heartbroken and taken himself off somewhere. There was a time I wondered if he might've, you know, hurt himself.'

'Where did you think Iris was?'

'Off with her new fancy man. I doubt she ever gave poor Iain a second thought.'

'You thought so little of her that no one bothered to mention her to the police?'

'We were angry, blamed her for my brother going missing and by the time I realised something terrible had probably happened, maybe even to them both, we decided it was too late to mention her.'

'We?'

'Me, Rodger and Stewart. We couldn't see what good it would do. Months had passed by and the police told my parents that they'd keep his file open, but they were no longer investigating due to lack of evidence.'

'But you had evidence that might have helped.'

'I'm sure it's very easy for you to judge us from the outside,' she said.

'You're right I will never know what it was like for you, but it's obvious from everything you've said so far that you didn't value Iris at all. You were more concerned with how you would look to the police after months of not mentioning it than you were with making sure she was alright, let alone the fact that finding Iris could be the key to finding your brother.'

'Did you give Stewart this lecture as well?'

'More or less, although I understand that he and Rodger were afraid of the repercussions if it became public knowledge they were gay. You on the other hand could have come back from Singapore and told the police, you could have left them out of it and then there would be a reason for the delay in the information coming out.'

'Everybody has 20:20 hindsight don't they. We panicked I suppose, and honestly if I knew at the time I wouldn't see my brother for all these years, that Rodger would die without ever seeing him again, I would have done things differently.'

I drank my tea, it was lukewarm now and not very pleasant, but it gave me time to arrange my thoughts before asking my next question.

'Do you remember anything else about Iris? Her last name perhaps?'

'No. I would've heard it at the wedding ceremony I suppose, but if I did then it hasn't stuck in my memory.'

'What about where she worked?'

'She wasn't working by then, I think she must've quit her job when she and Iain became more seriously involved.'

'Did she mention any family, brothers or sisters?'

'No, she didn't talk very much. Iain said she had a tough childhood, in foster care most of her life, never in one place for very long. I don't know if that's why she latched on to Iain so quickly.'

'What do you mean 'latched on'?'

'Well, they weren't together very long before they were engaged. To be honest I wondered if she was in the family way and that's why they were getting married so quickly. Iain was, like I said, exceptionally intelligent, but he was hardly the life and soul of the party. He preferred staying home reading to going out partying, he didn't drink, didn't have a TV in his apartment. I could see how someone steady and reliable like that would appeal to a person like Iris.'

'Did you come back to join in the search for Iain?'

'Couldn't afford it, I'd not long been home and couldn't afford the flights back again. It was hard to explain to mum and dad who I'm sure thought I was just being bloody minded.'

'Did you and Max ever have a family?' I asked.

She frowned. 'No, I wasn't interested in being a mother, much to the disappointment of my parents I wasn't remotely maternal. People said I would change my mind, but they were wrong.'

'How long were you and Max married for?'

'I'd argue we still are married. That year, 1983, Max took a job on the Bulgarian border with Kosovo, which back then was part of Yugoslavia. He went out one day and never came back. No one knew what happened to him, but the team speculated that he had accidentally crossed the border and was shot.'

'I'm sorry to hear that.'

'Later in my career I helped excavate war graves there, not driven by completely altruistic motives.'

'You were hoping you'd find Max?'

'I was, it was comforting to be able to give closure to so many families although devastating that I wasn't one of them.'

'How long after Iain disappeared did Max go missing?'

'Around the same time, although Max had been missing nearly a month when the person in charge of the dig finally got in contact with me. I think they hoped that they would find him and then there would be no point worrying me unnecessarily.'

'That must've been awful, I'm sorry.'

'You weren't to know. I didn't tell anyone for a long time, I think people assumed he had left me, and I wasn't quick to correct them. My parents went to their graves not knowing because I couldn't face being lectured about how terribly unsafe my job was. It was easy enough to keep it from them, I was barely in the country and when I was, I would make excuses for Max saying that he's been promoted and was on a lecture tour or in charge of a dig somewhere. They never followed our careers properly and news of his disappearance didn't make the papers. I suppose in this digital age that would be different, I'm lucky, perhaps, that I didn't have to contend with any of that.'

'I wish you'd told me everything at the beginning Elspeth, it's very hard to help someone who keeps key information from me. If you'd said that Max was missing, presumed dead only weeks after Iain went missing it would have put a very different light on the situation.'

'I'm a very private person and I was hoping that you might be able to locate Iain without digging into my own past. I didn't really think that one through, did I?' She gave me a half smile.

'Not so much.' I was still frustrated by the way both Elspeth and Stewart had been so casual about Iris' disappearance and neither coming forward to tell the police about the wedding but it was hard not to feel sorry for Elspeth; no one knew what she was going through, responding to her mother's pleas to come home and focus on Iain must have been beyond frustrating as she was coming to terms with the likelihood that she would never see her husband again.

'Are we back on track?' She asked.

'Yes, providing that you've told me everything, I'm not going to unearth anything else that you've omitted to tell me?'

'That's it all, all my family's sordid secrets laid out on the table for you to pick through and examine.'

I wanted to tell her as skeletons in the closet go this one was fairly innocent, but I doubted that it would bring her any comfort.

'Right, from now on if you remember anything, any detail at all no matter how insignificant you think it might be then please let me know. I'll keep you updated with any progress I make. Also if you have any old photographs of Iain, or better still of the wedding day I'd really appreciate it if you could let me have them.'

'Of course, and Rowan, I'm really sorry I lied to you.'

'Let's just draw a line under it shall we and move forward from here.'

She nodded. 'Thanks.'

Chapter Fourteen

Overnight the wind had been so strong it had knocked over something in next door's garden, startling me awake. It was 4.30am, I got up and looked out of the window to check if I could tell what had made the noise, but it was hard to see anything through the rain-streaked windows. Instinctively I headed into the hallway and towards Alana's empty bedroom, stopping just before I got to the door. I could text her, but if I sent a text at this time of day she would think there was something wrong. I headed back to bed and lay looking at the ceiling trying to empty my mind enough to encourage my body to get another couple of hours sleep.

At 5.30 I gave up and got dressed. In the kitchen I made myself a pot of coffee and turned on the heating. It was dark, wind and rain battered against the back of my house. I zipped my hoodie up around me and padded through to the office.

I looked back over my notes so far. I'd sent an email to the university Iain was doing his PhD at to see if there was anyone still around that might remember him or if they had any idea what triggered him to leave so close to completion but hadn't heard anything back. It had been a long shot so there was no surprise.

Seb had told me that Iain felt like an outsider working on the roads and that's what had drawn the two together. I had assumed that he had felt that way because he was out of his comfort zone, but what if that's how he'd felt at university as well. Everyone I'd met mentioned that Iain wasn't good with people, perhaps that was exactly why he'd fallen in love with Iris, maybe she was someone who made him feel like he wasn't on the outside looking in.

Seb had also mentioned a man called Michael Swanage. I scoured social media looking for him and had narrowed it down to three possibilities. It was 6.30, perhaps too early to be trying to contact anyone. I waited another half an hour and then sent them each this message:

> Hi, I'm a private detective and I'm looking for Iain Blair. I think you worked with him on the A92 project at the time of his disappearance in 1983. I would be grateful if you could get in touch and let me know a good time for us to talk.
> Rowan McFarlane

I got two quick – 'I'm not the man you're looking for' responses, nothing so far from the third. This could be because he didn't much use social media and hadn't seen the message; or he was the person I wanted, and he was considering his response.

My phone rang, an unrecognised number.

'Rowan McFarlane speaking.'

'Hello Rowan, this is Deborah, we met the other day at my cottage.'

'Hi, is everything okay, have you remembered something else?' I asked and then thinking about the weather added, 'the cottage wasn't damaged in the storm last night, was it?'

'No, nothing like that, it's just I saw something…and I hope you don't think I'm wasting your time, I wouldn't want to be a nuisance.' She paused.

'It's no problem, it's nice to hear from you,' I said hoping that it would encourage her to get to the point of the call.

'That's good, it's just I thought you would want to know about this because you were asking about the woods before.'

'Yes, anything you can tell me might help.'

'I've just seen two police cars, and another car, a black Volvo go past my house on the way to the woods and then a policeman came down and put tape across the road and he's stood there now guarding it so no one can go that way.'

'When did this happen.'

'Just now.'

'Thank you, I'm glad you called. Did you happen to get the Volvo's registration number,' I asked.

'Yes.'

She read it out to me, and I immediately recognised it as George's. 'That's great Deborah, I really appreciate you thinking to call me. Can you do me a favour and keep a note of everything that you see and check in with me later?'

'I would be happy to.'

I hung up after confirming my promise to come and see her again soon. George wouldn't appreciate me calling him when he was at a crime scene and even though he had no way of knowing that I knew he was there he was unlikely to be willing to talk, even if he bothered to answer my call.

I dialled Sonya's number, but it went straight to voicemail. A couple of minutes later I received a text from her.

> Can't talk now, with George, will call later to fill you in.
> Sonya x

If Sonya was with George it could only mean one thing; that a body had been found. It was doubtful that it could have anything to do with my case, but the fact that something had happened in the woods I was in just the day before made me feel uneasy.

I put the news on in the background in the hope that the media might've picked something up, but so far it was just documenting the damage done across the region by the storm last night. A tree had taken down electricity cables near Glenrothes leaving several streets without power and two schools so far had said they wouldn't be opening today due to damage.

I sent Alana a quick text to check she was okay and there had been no damage to her accommodation. She replied saying everything was fine, which at least gave me one less thing to worry about.

I tried to distract myself with research but found I couldn't concentrate for wondering what was going on, wishing that I could have gone along with George. I had no desire to be in the police but being his consultant last year on the Harmony Adams case had given me access to crime scenes and other data that I usually had to be much sneakier about obtaining.

It was 10.40, I'd drunk three cups of coffee, eaten a slice of toast and apart from sending a couple of messages I'd achieved absolutely nothing. I rested my forehead on my desk and closed my eyes, perhaps it had been a mistake to take on a case that was this old, everyone has their limitations after all. I let myself wallow for at least two minutes before going into the kitchen and splashing icy cold water onto my face.

I took the last slice of Maureen's chocolate cake and ate it straight from the container. My phone rang, Maureen's name appeared on the screen. Guilt filled me for half a second, like a naughty child who'd been caught in the act.

'Hiya, are you okay?' I said.

'Oh thank goodness, I was starting to worry when you didn't answer straight away.'

I glanced at the cake, 'sorry I was in the kitchen, my phone was in the office.'

'Not to worry I just wanted to check that you were all alright. Wasn't that weather something awful, especially for this time of year. Must be that climate change stuff I've been reading about. And thank goodness they didn't have it half as bad in Dundee, Alana said they had some rain but not much wind to speak of, which is unusual.'

'You've spoken to Alana?' I asked.

'Oh yes I phoned first thing so I would get her before lectures, she said she was doing well and not to worry. I'm sure she thinks I'm fussing about nothing, but you know me I'm just looking after everyone. So, you're okay?'

'Yes, nothing to report here either, a couple of smashed plant pots next door but nothing serious.' I paused, suddenly feeling like a bad person because it hadn't crossed my mind to phone them and check they were alright. 'And you and Eddie? And Carol?' I added trying not to make her sound like an afterthought.

'Carol is fine, she was staying at her boyfriend's house last night and hasn't been back to her flat yet, but they're both okay. And we're fine, just a couple of slates off the roofs down the street.'

'That's good then.'

'There was one thing though that I thought you'd think was strange or at least interesting.'

'Oh right, what was that.'

'Well Eddie said when you were chatting to the road gang in the club the other night that you seemed to have hit it off with Seb, or at least that he was the person that was most helpful.'

'Yeah.'

'Well, it's just that he was away walking in the hills, lord only knows why he didn't head home as soon as the weather started to turn bad. You'd think someone with his experience of hiking and camping out would've known better. Anyway, his wife can't get a hold of him, apparently it's like he's turned his mobile phone off and she's awful worried. Wullie, that's Seb's brother-in-law, he's been getting a group together to go looking for him.'

'He's probably just taken shelter somewhere,' I said.

'You'd think he'd have found a way to let someone know, it was daft him going off on his own this time of year at all if you ask me.'

'You said he was experienced though, so he probably didn't think the weather was going to come to much.'

'You're probably right. I just can't help thinking what if something bad has happened to him.'

'Why would something bad have happened to him?'

'I don't know, it's just…' she trailed off.

'Are you worried that it has something to do with him talking to me?'

'No, I don't know what I'm thinking.'

'There's got to be a reason it's bothering you Maureen, what's up.'

'Seb's a good man, part of the community. I just think everyone was shocked that he remembered so much about that man Iain you're looking for.'

'It's not that surprising, they were friends after all.'

'You're right, of course.'

'What's on your mind Maureen? I can't do much if you don't let me know,' I said trying to sound as gentle as I could.

'His wife said that he's been a bit distracted lately…'

'Since he spoke to me?'

'No, before that, for a couple of weeks. What if going up into the hills wasn't what he was doing, what if…what if he's done himself some harm.'

I thought about the man I'd met a few days ago, he'd seemed steady and calm, but you never know what's going on in someone's head. It was possible that he knew more about Iain than he'd shared, that me bringing up the past had unearthed a long-buried trauma that had impacted him, but Maureen said he'd not been right for a couple of weeks. Then for one stomach churning moment I considered if there was a corelation between the police cars in the woods and Seb's disappearance.

'I wouldn't start jumping to any conclusions, I'm sure that Seb will turn up and wonder what all the fuss is about. But on the off chance Wullie and his mates don't find him can you make sure someone reports Seb missing to the police, it's going to be another cold evening and he might be injured or something.'

'Leave it with me.'

We said our goodbyes and I finished eating my slice of cake, but I couldn't stop thinking about Seb. It would be a coincidence, it had to be. Seb had told me about Iain being married, and the others had seemed genuinely shocked that he'd known so much about a man they had given very little time to in 1983 and thought even less about since. But why would that put him at any risk now, it wasn't like he was the only person with this knowledge.

I was over thinking it, Seb had gone out for a hike, the weather had turned bad, he was probably hunkering down in a bothy somewhere with a flat mobile battery waiting for the rain to let up a bit before heading home. I would get a call from Maureen to tell me all was well; I was sure of it.

Chapter Fifteen

At 6.30pm I got a text from Sonya:

Are you home?

Yeah – everything okay?

Lots to share – I'll come to yours.
Have you eaten?

See you soon – I can order take away?

Give me 20 mins

'Is the food on the way?' Sonya asked as I opened the door. 'I'm so hungry I could eat a scabby horse.'

'Thanks for the imagery there, and yes, it is, it'll be about another ten minutes.'

'Are you going to tell me what the big news is?' I asked as I followed her through to the kitchen.

'George got a call this morning from a farmer. His farm backs on to the woods you were checking out the other day. The farmer was out checking his fields after the storm last night.' She paused to take off her coat and drape it over the back of a chair. I could feel my heart pounding harder and harder against my chest in anticipation of what she might say next.

'Anyway,' Sonya continued 'a tree was blown over in the wind, it took down one of his fences, but when he went to check how easy it would be to move he realised that tangled up in the roots was a body.'

'What? How?'

'I say body, but it was a skeleton really, and a few items of clothing that hadn't completely degraded.'

'How long has it been there do you think?'

We were interrupted by the arrival of our food, I would've happily waited to get my answer, but I didn't think Sonya would appreciate it.

'It's hard to say,' she said taking a large mouthful of curry.'

'Best guess?'

'Given the level of decomposition of the body, we're talking decades, my best guess is he died around forty or fifty years ago, his body probably helped to fertilise the soil that the tree grew on and as the roots spread, they got mixed up with his bones.'

'He, it's definitely a man?'

'No doubt about that, you can tell by the size of the pelvis. I haven't had a chance to properly examine the bones though, it's going to take a while to fully untangle it from the tree roots.'

'Any idea how he died.'

'Looks like he was shot.'

'Shot?'

'Yeah, it's not as common these days but in the 70s and 80s handguns were still legal and there was a decent amount of people who had one in their home.'

'Can you tell what kind of gun it was?'

'I'll be able to tell more when I properly look at the damage that's been done to the bones. Shot in the chest though.'

'Do you think it could've been an accident? Someone out shooting pheasants and didn't realise they'd hit someone?'

'Someone shooting pheasants would've used a shotgun, so I doubt it. I need to have a better look when I examine the remains in the lab to know more. Also if the person had been killed accidentally his body would've more likely been found at the time. Even if it was in a secluded bit of the woods and not discovered it would be highly unusual to find an intact skeleton, animal scavenging would mean that some bones would be missing or he'd certainly be spread over a larger area.'

'You thinking someone buried him?'

'I do. And I was thinking didn't your missing person disappear in the early 80s?'

'Yeah, '83. He was seen going into the woods the day he disappeared. Any chance there's another body buried in the same place?'

'Why?'

'I know it wasn't in any of the reports, but the witness that saw Iain go up that path said he was with a woman, and I'm inclined to believe her. Iain was married – his parents didn't know, and his brother and sister decided not to tell the police, so no one ever reported her missing.'

'Charming. I'll make sure the forensic team is aware to look for other remains when they're searching the area. You know though if we don't find her it might mean that she was the shooter.'

'It's possible, but there was a third person that went into the woods that day, another man.'

'I looked through the file on your missing man, that wasn't in it either.'

'The witness, Deborah, she got the impression that the police officer that interviewed her afterwards thought she was making things up for attention. She's a bit eccentric for sure, but I don't think she's a liar.'

'But Iain is the only one reported missing, even if he was followed into the woods that day there's nothing to say that the sighting of the second man had anything to do with it.'

'Has anyone contacted his sister yet?' I asked.

'No, I think George is hoping that we can find out more information first, but once we've got the bones back to the mortuary we can run some tests once I have something to run a DNA sample against.'

'Then what?'

'The whole area is being searched just now for any evidence that might've survived, ballistics aren't my area of expertise so George is sending someone to sit in on the examination of the remains with me to take some more detailed findings which might help narrow down what type of weapon was used.'

'That means I've got a little bit of time to continue investigating without George getting in my way then,' I smiled. 'Because if it turns out to be Iain Blair, my life will have just become a lot more complicated.'

'I'll have the crime scene photos available tomorrow if you want to swing by in the afternoon?'

'Sounds good, it'll need to be early afternoon though, I've got George dropping off the dogs tomorrow and I need to get the place tidied up a bit first.' I looked around, a quick Google search had informed me that there were lots of things that dogs shouldn't eat, several things that could kill them if they ate them and that dogs could be very sneaky if they had the opportunity to get their paws on something they weren't supposed to have.

'I've no idea why he thought I'd be the right person to look after them, did he ask you?'

'He did, but I need to leave Sunday afternoon to head up to Dundee for the lecture I'm giving on Monday. I've got a table booked at an Indian restaurant I like for me and Alana for after the lecture.'

'She said she was really looking forward to seeing you.'

'It's still weird coming here and not having her bombard me with questions over dinner.'

'Tell me about it.'

Sonya reached across the table and squeezed my hand. 'You'll both be fine; it takes time that's all. I'm meeting one of her lecturers on Sunday night – I'll make sure to ask him how she's getting on.'

'Thanks. I try not to let her know how much I'm missing her, don't want her thinking I can't be trusted home alone.'

'I think that ship has sailed,' Sonya laughed.

It was late by the time Sonya headed home, it had been lovely to have the distraction and for the place to be filled with the sound of chattering and laughing again. I made myself a cup of chamomile tea and checked my phone. There was a response I was hoping for.

> Hi. I was friends with Iain Blair. Not sure I know anything useful, but I would be happy to help. Mike

The message had arrived almost three hours ago, I looked at my watch, it was nearly 1am. Probably too late to reply and expect anything back, but still he'd see it when he got up in the morning.

> Thanks for coming back to me. I know it was a long time ago, but I think you were one of the people he was closest to before he disappeared. I'm just trying to get a feel for how things were for him then. Let me know when you're free for an initial chat. Thanks. Rowan.

Chapter Sixteen

The next morning I decided to give Elspeth a call, news of the discovery would be out today and whilst there was no proof that the remains did belong to her brother she deserved to hear from me first that they'd been found.

'Morning Elspeth, I wanted to catch you this morning, something has come up and it might be related to Iain,' I said.

'Okay.'

'There have been some human remains found in a wood near where Iain's car was abandoned.'

'Is it him?' she asked.

'I honestly don't know, after such a long time there's…' I paused, there really was no delicate way to say it. 'not a lot left of the person.'

'I understand, I told you before I dealt with war graves in my career, I know what happens to a body when it's left in a hole in the ground to rot.'

'At some point over the next week I imagine that DCI George Johnston will be in touch looking for a DNA sample from you so they can do the appropriate tests to determine if it is Iain.'

'That's fine.'

'If it is him then the police will open an investigation into what happened.'

'Will that be you finished then?'

'Only if you want me to be, otherwise I'll continue delving into his life to find out what was going on.'

'I'd prefer you continue to look into it, it's not that I don't trust the police you understand, it's just, well this is my brother and I need to know all the stops are being pulled out.'

'Great, I'm glad. I'd be happy to continue my investigation.'

I was getting ready to end the call when she said, 'do you know the cause of death?'

'It seems he was shot.'

'Shot?' The word broke as she tried to speak.

'Yes, I'm sorry, I can't imagine what's going through your head right now.'

'It was that little tart Iris, it had to be. You mark my words it'll turn out that she's the one you're looking for.'

Her hatred of Iain's wife had long made me uncomfortable but given the circumstances I decided not to say anything, instead promising that I would get to the bottom of what happened.

I was disappointed to find that Michael Swanage hadn't replied to my message, perhaps replying in the middle of the night had sent the wrong kind of signals. Or maybe he hadn't decided if he wanted to speak to me yet.

I spent the rest of the morning ensuring that all things poisonous to dogs had been relocated safely out of reach, though given that they were Scottie dogs that didn't have to be that high. I grabbed a quick lunch before heading across to meet Sonya in her lab.

'Perfect timing,' she smiled. 'I've just finished putting all the photos on the board.

George would have a similar board for his team, both interested in what evidence the crime scene would yield, but Sonya was already making a list of other experts that she might need to call in.

I recognised the section of wood, it was one of the wrong turns I had taken before I got to the car park on the other side, it was distinguishable by the unusually large rose bushes that I guessed had been dumped there from someone's garden because there weren't any in the rest of the undergrowth.

The skeletal remains almost looked like a convoluted Halloween decoration the way they were intertwined with the tree roots. 'Where was he shot?'

'There's damage to the rib cage where a bullet has broken bones. With the absence of any soft tissue it's obviously much harder to narrow anything down, but from my own experience I would say that whoever shot this man was at point blank range.'

'Killed instantly?' I asked.

'Again, until I get the bones here and can start working with other experts it's hard to be certain but looking at the skeleton, I would say it's probable that the bullet went close enough to the heart area to kill him quickly.'

'Do you think George will call off his weekend away?'

'Unlikely, there's going to be very little for him to go on until early next week, not much point in him assembling the troops and then everyone sitting around twiddling their thumbs. You're just trying to get out of dog sitting.'

'It's just bad timing, I was hoping to get stuff done this weekend.'

'People with dogs get things done, you never know, you might enjoy it.'

'I doubt it, anyway I'd better get going, you'll let me know if anything interesting turns up?'

'Of course,' Sonya replied.

After I left Sonya I sat in my car for a bit thinking. If the skeleton turned out to be Iain then where was Iris? The way I saw it, three people walked into those woods thirty-eight years ago and one of them didn't come out. I'd been operating under the assumption that the couple Deborah had seen were Iain and Iris, but what if Iain was in fact the second man she saw. If I believed Elspeth's assessment of her character then Iris was the type of woman to take advantage of Iain's good nature, was it possible that she was having an affair and that it had been Iain following them that day?

I rubbed my hands across my face. The thought that had been niggling in the back of my mind bubbled to the top. Whether Iain was part of the couple or the solo man, the fact remained that only one vehicle was found that day and Deborah didn't see anyone coming back down the path, so if they didn't all come together, then how did the third person arrive at that location?

Chapter Seventeen

My thoughts were disturbed by the vibration of my phone announcing I'd received a message. It was from Michael Swanage:

> Hi, I'm happy to chat but was hoping we could do it face to face.

The brevity of the message surprised me, I'd become accustomed to people being suspicious of me, wanting to know why I was going over old ground, or having them tell me they were happy to talk but doubted they'd be much help after so much time.

I replied saying that was great, asking when would be suitable for him, suggesting as I always did that we meet in the Sunshine Café.

Half an hour passed before he responded:

> I'm in Nairn, it's not so easy for me to get back down to Fife, I'm a single dad. Is there any chance you could come to me? I could meet you halfway at a push.

It wouldn't take me too long to drive to Nairn and if I met Michael early enough in the day I could detour through Dundee and visit Alana on the way home.

> I can come to you.
> When suits?

A reply pinged back almost immediately.

> How about next Friday, sorry it can't be sooner – I have commitments.

I was hoping he would've been free at the start of the week, but at least he hadn't suggested this weekend, otherwise I'd have had to take the dogs with me.

> No problem. Is 1pm okay for you?

He replied saying that it was perfect and suggesting we meet in a small café. I wouldn't be on home ground, but at least he'd agreed to talk to me and face to face which I always preferred.

George called to let me know he was on the way over with the dogs and I spent the next twenty minutes quietly cursing myself for agreeing to this.

'Thanks for this Rowan, we really do appreciate it.'

'Hmm,' I looked down at the two small black dogs.

'This one's Jock,' he said pointing at the dog on his left, 'and this one is Wallace. I think – honestly it's hard to tell. They have tags on their collars though.'

The dogs sat well behaved at either side of George, looking at me with their heads slightly cocked.

'They've been well trained and don't bark much, they do like their food though and if one of them finishes first then the other will try to barge in and get his brother's grub. I've got a bag in the car with food and dishes etc. I've been walking them properly once a day and then an additional couple of times so they can do their business.' He handed me their leads and went back out to the car to collect the bag.

'They'd better be well behaved, I'm hoping to get some work done this weekend as well,' I said.

'They'll be fine, and we'll pick them up on Sunday evening when we're on our way home.' He patted them on the head and left.

They sat on the kitchen floor looking at me expectantly. George had sheepishly told me that he'd not had a chance to walk them properly before dashing off. Once he left I stuck on my coat and boots and walked across through the houses to an area of grass where I had seen groups of dogwalkers in the past. It was quieter than usual and after half an hour we headed home.

The next morning, I went into the kitchen to find my new wards waiting next to their food bowls. 'Where shall we go for your walk today?' I asked them. Their tails flicked in excitement at the word. I wondered if they missed their owner, and I wondered if she'd ever be well enough to take them back. Thinking about Pamela had reminded me that Jock and Wallace were used to being able to run freely on the beach, although when I pulled into the car park near Silver Sands a bit later, I worried that the little dogs might remember the incident and feel distressed. Thankfully there was no sign of any PTSD on their part.

In the beginning I was nervous about letting them off the lead, imagining trying to explain to George that I had lost them, but when my arm couldn't take it any longer, I unclipped them and they zoomed off in the direction of the water. I sat back on a large rock and watched them play in the sea foam before chasing one another along the sand, sand that I would no doubt be vacuuming out of my car for weeks.

An hour later they trotted back to me and I rewarded their good behaviour with some treats. It started to rain as we walked back to the car. I dried the boys off with the towel I'd remembered to fling into the boot before we'd headed out.

All that time in the fresh air with nothing to do had got me thinking about how to track down more information on Iris. I wrote the request for Iain and Iris' marriage certificate, this at least would provide me with her maiden name and details of her parents. The website suggested that I gave as much detail as possible with regards to date, place etc so I wasn't sure how well my, sometime in April 1983 in the registry office in Cuddieford, would go down but it had to be worth a try.

Then I emailed the university asking if the professor that had supervised Iain's PhD was still working there and if not did they have forwarding details. I looked through the information I'd taken from storage, if it turned out that the body in the tree roots was Iain then I'd imagine George would be at my door expecting me to hand it all over.

Half an hour into scanning documents I'd probably never need, I decided to take a coffee break. The dogs had fallen asleep under my desk and one of them raised a sleepy head as I wandered through to the kitchen. I opened a packet of biscuits and took out two, both of which had been eaten before my coffee was brewed. I took two more and went back to the office.

Many of the documents were held together with staples, some rusty. As I picked apart a particularly seized one an envelope dislodged from between the pages and fell onto the edge of the desk. I opened it, carefully pulling out the folded cream paper. It was a letter of recommendation:

To Whom it May Concern,

I wholeheartedly recommend Iris Hatfield to you. She is a diligent young lady with an excellent sense of right and wrong. She is accomplished in touch typing, (with a 100 words per minute speed), audio typing and shorthand. She speaks French fluently and is proficient in mathematics. She would be an excellent addition to any office environment.

If you require any further information, please contact me at Cuddieford College.

Yours faithfully

Marion Stephens

If Marion Stephens had been a young teacher in the early 80s, say in her twenties then, she would be in her sixties now, unlikely to still be teaching but hopefully she should still be alive. And now I had Iris' full name. I sent a quick email to the admin department of the college asking after Marion and claiming to be a previous student.

Marion's letter painted quite a different picture to the one I'd been given by Elspeth and Stewart. They had told me that Iris was uneducated and unskilled, that she'd been a stripper with no prospects who'd latched on to their brother in the hopes that he would be her meal ticket to a better life. But it seemed that Iris had skills, and ones that would've been in high demand.

If Iris was, as I'd been told, a stripper, was it for financial reasons? They made good money, likely more than she could make working 9-5. Not that it mattered what Iris had done for a living, someone should've cared what happened to her.

My social media search had turned up no sign of the woman who hadn't been seen for thirty-eight years. I wouldn't have minded the sloth like pace this case had been taking if it weren't for the remains sitting in the mortuary awaiting identification. If I didn't uncover something soon I would have to stand back and investigate from the side lines as George and his team put their resources into finding out what happened. I thought about asking if he would arrange for me to be a consultant to the police again, we'd mostly worked well together when Harmony Adams had gone missing last year. But that had been different, I'd practically had to beg him to investigate.

The dogs stirred as I got up to go to the kitchen, they trotted after me looking longingly at the front door.

'You can't want walked again, surely. Are you not knackered after your run around this morning?' I asked.

They stood steadfast, clearly communicating that they were not, as I hoped, exhausted.

'Fine, you win. But only a short walk mind.' I hadn't imagined myself the type of person that spoke to dogs, perhaps I was a dog person after all.

The field near the house had been alright for our first walk but it had been quite dull so I decided to drive out to the coast. I could park in Dalgety Bay and walk along the coastal path, the sea air would help arrange my thoughts. It was windy on the exposed pathway, and I was glad I'd stuck a woolly hat in my pocket before we set off. I hadn't been down here since I'd briefly stayed in Mark's apartment. I looked up at the block that had been his and wondered who lived their now. Finding Jack's killer felt like it happened a lifetime ago and almost as though it had happened to someone else.

A deep throaty growl from Jock brought me back to the present. 'What are you complaining about?' I looked around to see if I could see something that might have upset him. The path was quiet, the only other person was a fair distance away. 'Behave or I'll take you back home,' I told him sternly.

We walked on for a little bit before they both started barking, Wallace pulled on his harness. The wind was wild, it rustled through the bushes and trees casting strange shadows on the concrete path. I tried to get them to move forward but they had other ideas, I was in the middle of negotiating with them offering treats for movement when I heard someone say my name.

I looked up. Elspeth was stood in front of me. 'Oh, hello,' I said a little embarrassed that she might've overheard my conversation.

'I didn't know you had dogs,' she said giving them an odd look.

'I don't. I'm dog sitting for a friend, they're being a bit obstinate though, I don't think they're fans of the wind.'

'Hmm, not for me, dogs can be so tying, can't they?'

'I only have them for the weekend.'

'I've been along visiting Stewart at the sailing club.'

'I didn't realise you were close,' I said, thinking back to my meeting with him where I got the impression that there wasn't a lot of love lost between them.

'I wouldn't say close, I think with you looking for Iain it's brought back a lot of old memories and I thought it was time I reached out to him, after all it's only the two of us left now. Have you come across any new information?'

'I'm tracking down a couple of new leads but nothing to report at the moment.'

'I understand, I've braced myself for the fact the remains the police found recently are Iain's.'

'We'll know more in the next couple of weeks.' DNA results could take anything up to twenty-eight days to come through, although I had a feeling that George would be keen to push the lab for a swift turnover on this, so he at least knew who his victim was. 'Right, I'd better be getting this pair back.'

We said our goodbyes and I led the dogs up the steps into the nearest car park, I'd take them back to the car through the houses otherwise I'd likely end up carrying them or taking all evening at the rate they were going. Jock and Wallace were happy to trot along beside me, encouraged by regular treat intervals.

If *they* weren't knackered by the time we got home *I* certainly was. I was grateful for the food Maureen had delivered earlier in the week and took my plate of food through to the office being careful not to fall over the dogs who seemed to enjoy following me everywhere. I made myself comfortable at the desk whilst they curled up in the foot space beneath it. I took a mouthful of food and opened the file mark Iain and Iris and was checking through my notes when my phone vibrated.

It was Maureen. 'Hiya, is everything okay?' I asked.

'Not really. Seb's still not come home, and no one's been able to get in touch with him.'

I thought back to when she'd first told me about him going missing. 'Is that two nights he's been missing?'

'Yes, his wife Donna called the mountain rescue people, and they've been out and had a look but not found any trace of him. The police have said they're going to look into it but not to worry.'

'That's good.'

'I was thinking would you mind asking George if he could do something, make them take it more seriously, his wife is beside herself with worry.'

'He'll be here tomorrow, I'll speak to him then,' I said. I was sure that George wouldn't appreciate me asking him to meddle, but he owed me a favour for this weekend and I was happy to cash it in to help put Maureen's mind at rest.

'Thank you, I'll let Donna know.'

After our call I gave up doing more work, my eyelids were heavy and there wasn't much more I'd be able to do this evening, besides Jock and Wallace were early risers, if I wanted to get anything close to a decent amount of sleep, I'd need an early night.

Chapter Eighteen

The next morning I took the dogs for a long walk and then a run on the beach hoping that they would be tired out when George came to pick them up. I felt restless all afternoon, I'd reached out to anyone who might be able to tell me more and now it was just a waiting game.

By the time George arrived at just after six pm I was both looking forward to seeing him and feeling a little sad that my two companions were leaving.

'How have they been?' He asked as I opened the door.

'Fine, although I've probably been spoiling them with treats, Mel not with you?'

'She said to say she'll call you tomorrow and arrange a proper catch up. I dropped her home first. One of her regular clients has just bought a holiday home in Cornwall and she's already sent half a dozen emails, so she thought she'd better get back to it straight away.'

'Fair enough,' I said, although I was a little disappointed not to see her.

Jock and Wallace had been at my heels when I'd gone to the door and had seemed pleased to see George. He bent down scratching them both behind the ears, a dog at each hand. 'Have you fellas been missing me?'

'I took them for a super long walk earlier on so hopefully they won't need much this evening.'

'Thanks.'

'Did you have a nice time?'

'It was great, especially seeing as I'm expecting work to get very busy in the coming weeks.'

'Any idea when you'll get the DNA results?' I asked.

'I've asked for them to be expedited, the boss doesn't want this one sitting around for too long before we get going and I sent someone to Elspeth Blair's house to get a sample from her for comparison. How's your investigation been going?'

'Slowly, 1983 was a really long time ago and it's been challenging hunting people down, and even when I have, their memories have been a bit vague. Actually, that reminds me, I was hoping you could do me a favour.' I looked at him hopefully.

'What?'

'I met some of the guys that worked with Iain on the roads, there was one he was particularly friendly with, a man called Sebastian Wojcik, Seb, anyway he was really helpful, told me about Iain being married.'

'I'll need you to give me his details if this turns out to be Iain Blair's remains,' George interrupted.

'Yeah of course, the trouble is he's gone missing.'

'What do you mean missing?' George asked.

'He went out for a hike four days ago and didn't come back, his wife is worried sick according to Maureen...'

'How's Maureen involved in all of this?' George asked. He was one of her people, the small circle that she fussed around and enjoyed taking care of and even if he didn't like to admit it, George had grown fond of her.

'Eddie introduced me to Seb and Maureen is friendly with his wife.'

'And has she, the wife I mean, reported it to the police?'

'Yep, and mountain rescue but there's been no sign of him. I'm worried that it might have something to do with Iain Blair and these missing remains. I was hoping you might be able to use your influence and get it looked at more seriously?'

He nodded, 'I'll bring his disappearance in as part of the murder investigation. Even if it turns out not to be Iain, it's still too much of a coincidence this Seb bloke going missing right after the skeleton was discovered.'

'Thanks, I appreciate it.'

'Right, I better get this pair out of your hair.'

Jock and Wallace trotted off to George's car without even a backward glance to me and when I shut the front door my house once again felt too empty and too quiet. I spent the next forty-five minutes Googling dog ownership before I came to the realisation that my lifestyle and a high dependency pet like a dog were not a good fit.

With precious little else to do I opened one of Jack's old cases and began to read through. It was something I'd started doing to fill the time and keep my mind occupied during lockdown and it had become a habit. I felt like I was walking in his shadow, trying to see if I would've reached the same conclusions as him.

In 1996 he was investigating a theft at a local university, not much was taken but they had wanted to know if there was any way of discovering how it happened. I scanned my eyes down Jack's report, stopping to more thoroughly read the list of missing items; an amulet, some pottery fragments, the complete skeletal remains of a rodent of some sort – I wasn't familiar with the Latin name, and three journals belonging to Max Thorogood.

The items were never recovered, and Jack had concluded that they were likely taken by a student or a member of the faculty.

There had been a surprising lack of any evidence. In the file was a note from a police officer stating that the university only noticed the items were missing when they were doing an annual inventory.

Jack had recommended the university improve its security measures and consider checking on items more frequently than once a year. His report was brief, and the university seemed to accept his conclusions.

I sat back in my chair, what were the chances of me opening that file and coming across a name linked to my case. Jack hadn't like coincidences and neither did I. How hard would it be to get a list of faculty members from 1996? And who else would I find on the list.

Chapter Nineteen

Monday morning and I finally had something to be working with, the college had replied saying they would forward my contact details to Marion Stephens, who had now retired. By 10.30 I'd already had a reply, saying she didn't recognise my name could I jog her memory. I explained who I was in a follow up email and she replied saying she'd be happy to meet later today – she had been particularly fond of Iris and was happy to do anything she could to help with my investigations.

An email from the university told me that Iain's PhD supervisor died in 2003 and they didn't have access to any records dating back to the 1980s. My separate request for the list of faculty members for the academic year starting September 1996 had been provided though, it was more extensive than I expected. Thankfully it had been produced in alphabetical order by course subject making archaeology near the beginning.

I wasn't surprised to see Dr Elspeth Blair on the list. It made sense that she had come back home to lecture, even if it was only for a little while. Did she and Jack cross paths, did anyone make the connection between the stolen journals and her? I would never know.

Elspeth had given me the impression that she had spent all her career travelling, only returning to the UK to finally retire. There had been no reason for me to know where she was in 1996. It was thirteen years after her brother's disappearance and highly unlikely to be connected, still I found myself wondering what else she'd glossed over. The veneer of her as a polite, well-educated academic with nothing to hide had completely cracked days ago. In my experience when someone lied or omitted the truth about one thing then they generally had more skeletons in the closet.

I'd arranged to meet Marion Stephens in the Sunshine Café at 2.30pm. It should be quieter by then, the lunchtime rush normally finishing around 2pm. An exhausted looking Star was at the counter when I arrived.

'I thought you said you were going to be resting,' I said.

She put her hand on her pregnancy bump, 'I know but I want to keep going as long as I can. They say it's good for you to try to keep your normal routine.'

'I don't think that counts when your normal routine is being on your feet all day for at least eight hours.'

'I've promised Billy I'm going to cut it down to only a couple of days a week soon, Mohammed has already taken over a lot of the day-to-day stuff. Anyway, what can I do for you today?'

'Just my usual please, I'm expecting someone any minute now.'

'No problem, I'll bring it over in a couple of minutes.'

I made my way to the back of the café seeking out my favourite table, positioned ideally for privacy from fellow patrons but with an excellent view of the front door. A few minutes later the chimes above the door jingled. I looked up and saw a woman in dark denim jeans and a roll neck cream jumper, her grey hair swooped up in a bun on the top of her head. She scanned the room.

Star appeared from the kitchen with my order, almost colliding with my guest. It was impossible to make out their conversation from where I was sitting but it was clear the pair knew each other. The short interaction concluded with a hug and Star pointing and waving at me. The two came across together.

'I didn't know you knew Marion,' Star said.

'I don't, she's going to be helping me with my case, I hope. How do you two know each other then?'

'Marion used to live along the road from my auntie back in the day. Right, I'll let you get on with it then.'

'Thanks for coming Marion,' I said.

'I'm happy to help. I haven't heard from Iris in a long time though so I'm not sure what use I'll be.'

I spent a couple of minutes explaining that I'd been hired to find Iain Blair and through my investigations I had discovered that he had married Iris. 'The thing is, I'm really struggling to find out who Iris was as a person. The people I've been speaking to so far have all been connected to Iain and I'm struggling to find anyone who knew Iris back then.'

'She was a bright girl, could've done anything. I'm surprised she married so young, actually.'

'Why's that?' I asked.

'She was a very self-sufficient young woman, she'd had a hard life and she wasn't the sort of person who needed or relied on anyone else, I had a heck of a job trying to get her to trust me.'

'What do you mean she had a hard life?'

'You know she was in care most of her childhood, I suppose?' She glanced at me for confirmation.

'I didn't know that, do you know why?' I didn't really consider it a lie, Elspeth and Stewart had said Iris had been in care but I hadn't taken anything they'd told me about Iris to be truthful.

'Her mother was murdered, not that she had it easy before that, Iris was the eldest of three, she had a younger sister and brother. Their mother had a drink problem, and she was…a lady of the night, if you understand me.'

I nodded. Star appeared at the table with our cups and cake but didn't stay to chat this time.

'How old was Iris when her mum died?' I asked.

'Ten, and it hit her hard in more ways than losing a mother, she had practically been the surrogate parent to her siblings and when her mother died the girls went into the foster system, back then there wasn't much done to keep children together. Her brother's father was still around so she said he went with him and after that they lost contact. She was close with her sister and there wasn't much in their ages.' Marion paused to drink her tea.

'What about their father, where was he?'

'As far as I could tell, Iris wasn't sure they had the same one, but either way he was nowhere to be found. I saw her birth certificate once when I was helping her fill out forms, it said 'Father Unknown'. It broke her heart to lose her siblings. I'm not sure what happened to the sister, but Iris never settled in any of the homes she went to, I think the social work people eventually gave up trying and she spent the rest of her youth in a group home.'

'That's a shame.'

'Yes, like I said she was a very resilient person, the only thing she seemed interested in was finding her brother and sister and bringing her family back together. When did you say she went missing?'

'I don't know exactly.' Marion clearly cared for Iris and I was sure she would have a similar reaction to me when I told her no one had bothered to report Iris' disappearance. 'From what I gather she married Iain in April 1983, and I haven't been able to find any records of her after he went missing.'

'What about the police, did they have any luck finding out anything at the time?'

'Iain's family didn't report Iris missing, only Iain. The marriage had been kept a secret from his parents and the rest of the family didn't think it was important to mention to the police.'

Marion wiped her mouth on a napkin, 'you mean they didn't think *she* was important enough.'

'Yes, it does appear that way. You're the first person I've spoken to who has had anything good to say about Iris, it seems like Iain's family thought she was beneath him. His sister told me that Iris was working as a dancer in a gentlemen's club, does that sound likely?'

'No.'

'What about if she needed the money?'

'Iris wanted her family back, she wanted them to be proud of what she'd made of her life when she met them, and I'm not saying that young ladies that choose that profession shouldn't be proud of themselves, I just know that Iris was all about having a squeaky-clean image, especially after her mother, you understand.'

'What was she planning on doing?'

'I assumed secretarial work.'

'I saw the letter of recommendation you wrote for her, that's how I tracked you down.'

'I did several for her, I was happy to help.'

'Do you know if she secured a position with anyone?'

'Last I heard she was working as a secretary for a solicitor and doing well. It's not unusual for me to lose contact with students, it's what you expect really, you get them on to the next stage of their lives and then…' she paused, 'and then you think about them from time to time and hope they're doing well.'

'Do you remember the names of any of her friends from back then?'

'She was quite friendly with a girl called Joyce Brown, but I've no idea if they stayed in contact. I liked Joyce too, she had a big family, there was about ten of them I think and maybe that's why Iris was drawn to her, you know the life she never had. Joyce lived on the Robert the Bruce estate, not sure if she's still there though.'

'Thanks.' Everyone knew everyone on the estate and even if she'd moved on it shouldn't be too difficult to find someone who could tell me where to find her. There was a time that I would have been apprehensive about going there, but since Jimmy Murray's demise it had calmed down a lot. 'What were her brother and sister's names?' I asked.

'No idea about the brother, her sister was Paula I think, but I'm not a hundred percent sure. I should be off,' she said looking at her watch. 'If you find out what happened to Iris, you'll let me know?'

'Of course, and thanks for your help.

Chapter Twenty

I was awake before George called, sitting in the kitchen trying to see if I could find any sign of Joyce Brown on social media.

'Morning George, how are things?'

'Bad news I'm afraid. Your friend Seb, his body was found last night. I thought you'd want to know.'

'Oh God that's awful, was it an accident or…' I trailed off.

'It's a bit early to have all the details, Sonya will be doing the post mortem this afternoon, he'd been dead for several days she thinks.'

'So he died the day he went for his hike then, do you know what the cause of death was?'

'Blunt force trauma.'

'The question is did he fall or was he hit?' I asked.

There was silence on George's side of the conversation for a few moments. 'You know I shouldn't give you any more details, but you're going to find out soon enough anyway so I might as well tell you, it was murder. His body had been moved, shoved under a bush. A couple of guys coming back from their hike found him, they only noticed because one of them was going to use the bush to take a piss.'

'Can I tell Maureen?'

'Yeah, we've informed his wife last night so she might already know.'

'Thanks for telling me, you'll keep me updated?'

'I suspect I will,' he said before hanging up.

I was grateful that it was Eddie that answered the phone. "Hey Eddie, it's Rowan.'

'Do you want me to get Maureen?'

'No, I don't think so.'

'What's wrong?' He asked.

I explained about Seb, 'I wondered if it would be okay for you to tell Maureen?' I asked, I felt like a coward, but I always felt so entirely useless when someone cried, and I knew that she would.

'Of course.'

'Listen Eddie, did Seb have any problems with anyone that you know of?'

'He was an outspoken bloke, happy to give you his opinion, wasn't afraid of what people thought, but not so much that someone would want to kill him over it. He's always been that way.'

'Did he often go out hiking by himself?'

'As far as I know, he liked to get out into nature, he said it helped him hit the reset button, but I know that he'd met some folks on his walks.'

'You don't remember him mentioning anyone by name?'

'Sorry pet I don't, I'll keep my ear to the ground and let you know if I hear anything though.'

'Thanks, but don't put yourself in any danger though,' I said.

'I'd say the same to you, but I think I'd be wasting my breath.'

After our call I made myself a fresh cup of coffee, it felt like it was going to be a very long day. I'd reached out to Robbie to see if he knew Joyce. He had spent most of his life living on that estate and if there was anyone who could help me out it was him. He'd messaged me back to say he went to school with a girl and Joyce was her aunt, he'd see if he could arrange a meeting.

Who would want Seb dead, and did it have anything to do with Iain and Iris and if so, what? It had been Seb that had told me about Iris and the wedding, if he hadn't let that slip then perhaps neither Elspeth nor Stewart would've been honest enough to tell me, but there would be no guarantee that I wouldn't uncover it anyway, besides why would someone kill him for that, it's not like it would change anything.

I suppose the question really was, if he knew about the wedding then did that mean that he knew Iain a lot better than anyone realised, and could that mean he knew more than he'd told, more than he'd been willing to share with me in the pub in front of his friends?

Sonya finished the post mortem at just after 3.30pm and I headed over to see her.

'Do you want a coffee?' She asked as I went through to her office.

'Go on then, I've already had a vat of the stuff today but I'm sure one more won't hurt. How's Alana?' I'd had intended on texting Sonya this morning but after the call about Seb I decided I should wait.

'She's doing really good you know, you should be proud. She's doing well in all her classes, studying, handing assignments in on time.'

'That's good, does she seem happy?' I wanted her to do well academically of course, but none of that mattered if she was miserable.

'I think she's found the adjustment harder than she anticipated, but from what she told me she has a good core group of friends, they hang out together, eat way too much pizza, but nothing too wild.'

'That's good. I'm having to go up to Nairn to interview someone for this case I'm working, so I'm going to detour past Dundee on the way home and have a catch up with her.'

'She mentioned that. I think she's really looking forward to seeing you.'

'Thanks for checking in on her,' I said.

'It was my pleasure, I actually miss having her about and taking her to lectures and talks.' Sonya smiled. 'Soon I'll be going to hers if she carries on the way she's going.'

'I feel like I'm at one every time she talks about the course, last time it was something about markers that help you know where a person is from.'

'She's going to go on and get her PhD isn't she?'

'That's the plan, Dundee for 4 years, then a masters somewhere, then the PhD – I just hope she's got the stamina for that much studying.'

Sonya smiled, 'she'll be fine. Right would you like me to tell you about Seb?'

'That would be good, thanks.'

'He was hit on the back of his head by someone standing to his left, which I would say means they were right-handed. The weapon was something with a rounded end, looks like it was made from some sort of bone.'

'Bone?' I questioned.

'I've sent it off for testing to get more information, but there were tiny fragments in the wound.'

'What the hell is made of bone?'

'I was wondering about the top of a walking stick, perhaps. If so it might be easy enough to identify and if I can get it into the lab there's likely to be Seb's DNA no matter how well it was cleaned up.'

'Do you think he was walking along with someone, and they hit him or that someone came up from behind and attacked him?'

'Impossible to tell for sure but given the force of the blow and the fact he has no defensive wounds I would suggest that he was stationary when he was struck and either he knew the person and wasn't afraid of them or it was a surprise attack.'

'George said they had hidden his body in a bush.'

'He'd been moved post mortem, I doubt it was very far from where he fell, it would have been challenging to move him far in that terrain if you were by yourself.'

'Are you thinking the killer rolled Seb under the closest bush to where he fell?'

'That's my thoughts, I've got a forensic team up there examining the area around where the body was discovered to see if we can find the actual murder site.'

'I keep thinking that if he hadn't talked to me about my case then this might not have happened.'

'Don't be daft, how could this have anything to do with what you're working on?'

'I don't know I just don't like it when things like this happen, you know how I feel about coincidences.'

'You sound more like George every time we talk,' she smiled. 'Even if it was connected there's no way you could have possibly prevented this.'

'Any news on the skeleton from the woods?'

'Still waiting for DNA results. He might potentially need to take a back burner whilst George is looking into this latest murder though.'

I decided to pop round to see Maureen on my way home. Eddie answered the door.

'I thought I'd come round and see how she is,' I said.

'That's good of you, she's through in the sitting room if you want to stick your head round the door.'

Maureen stood to hug me as I entered the room, as a rule I wasn't really one for hugs, but for her it was easy to make an exception.

'Thank you for calling this morning, such sad news, isn't it, I'm glad it's George in charge though, I told Donna that he was the best.'

It was nice to see the blind faith that she had in George.

'Now you *will* stay for dinner, won't you?' She'd posed it as a question, but I knew only too well that it was more like a statement of fact. I was happy to stay and be cooked for and by the time I left she'd boxed me up the leftovers and half the coffee and walnut cake she'd made earlier in the day. And that's what I was tucking into now as I scanned through my notes on this case.

Debbie had certainly been the last person to see Iain and Iris, I was sure of that. Elspeth was adamant that Iris had killed her brother, but after speaking to Marion this afternoon I was inclined to believe that was unlikely. Sonya had the forensic team scan the area near the tree to see if there was any sign of a second body, but nothing had turned up.

Chapter Twenty-One

'Our body in the woods is not Iain Blair,' Sonya said.

This was not what I'd been expecting when she'd called to tell me the results of the DNA tests were in. I'd headed over to her lab to see her report convinced that Iain had at last been found.

'What do you mean?' I asked.

'Well on the assumption that Iain and Elspeth are in fact full biological siblings, which all evidence tells me they are, then the remains we found tangled up in the roots of that tree cannot be that of Iain Blair.'

'They have to be the other man then. The one the witness said she saw head up the path a little while after she saw Iain and Iris.'

'Are you sure she's a reliable witness?'

'She was a bit odd, but that doesn't mean she was lying about what she saw.'

'Do you have any clue who he might be?'

'None,' I rubbed my hand across my face. 'It's almost impossible to know at this point.'

'Was your witness able to give you a decent description of the man she saw?'

'Not really, tallish with dark hair. He threw some things away in her bin.'

'What kind of things?' Sonya asked.

'Well there was a bloody handkerchief, but before you get too excited it was never collected and it would've gone to landfill, but she kept a lace glove and a man's wedding ring.'

'Any chance she'd give them to you?'

'I have them already actually, I'd forgotten all about them with Seb's body being found, do you think you might be able to get anything from them?'

'It's a long shot, and it will depend if she cleaned them or how they've been stored.'

'In a metal tin in a shed.'

'Not ideal, but we can see.'

I rooted around in my bag and pulled out the 2 small evidence bags, handing them over to Sonya.

She held the bags up, 'why would a man be throwing away a lady's lace glove?'

'I think it was Iris'.'

'What makes you think that?' Sonya asked.

'I have its pair at home, took it out of a storage unit kept by Iain's sister and brother-in-law, it was in a box of stuff that belonged to Iain.'

'Even if we can get anything off of these things, how much use they will be is dependent on whether any matches ping up in the system.'

'Have you got anything to go on for identifying the remains?' I asked.

'He'd had a few teeth removed and had previously broken his arm, it was fully healed. If you can get me any possible names, then there's a chance I can find a match from dental and medical records.'

'I'm hoping that this bloke I'm going to see tomorrow might be able to shed some light on the matter.'

'Fingers crossed. Listen, whilst I remember, George said to tell you he needs to speak to you about Seb, I think he just wants to get an understanding of the conversation you had with him.'

'Okay dokey, I'll head over to see him just now.'

'Let me know when you get to Nairn tomorrow.'

'Why, are you checking up on me?' I laughed.

'Of course,' she responded as I left.

The drive from Sonya's lab to the police station took way longer than the distance would have implied. I must've got stuck at every red light en route not to mention the fact the council had decided to dig up the roundabout I would normally exit off, providing me instead with a diversion that took me half a mile in the wrong direction before I could get back on track.

By the time I arrived at the front desk I was fed up. 'I'm here to see DCI Johnston.' I said to the desk sergeant.

'Name?'

'Rowan McFarlane.'

At this she stopped writing, her pen hovering above the paper, and looked up and smiled. 'I don't think we've had the pleasure. I'm Natasha Findlay, you can call me Nat.'

'I take it my reputation precedes me?'

'It most certainly does, I must say I'm always impressed by a woman who's prepared to get out there and get the job done.'

'Thanks.' I was aware that I was like marmite in the station, there were plenty of officers who thought being a private detective was a bit of a joke, but they couldn't deny the cases I'd solved.

'I'll take you up.' Nat indicated to someone to take over from her as she pressed the buzzer that let me beyond the point civilians usually got to tread. 'I like George, he's one of the good ones, if I ever get into plain clothes, he's the sort of person I'd like as my boss.'

'Is that what you'd like to do, become a detective?' I asked.

'That's the plan.'

We reached the top of the stairs. 'I know where I'm going from here,' I said. 'And good luck with the career progression.'

'Thanks, um…can I give you my card. I mean I know I'm not a detective or anything, but if you were ever in a situation where you needed help and perhaps George wasn't available – well I'd be happy to step in.'

'It's always good to have back up,' I said taking her card and putting it into my jeans pocket. 'See you later Nat.'

George was old school, despite being able to track the case on computer he still preferred to have it detailed on the wall – he was stood in front of it as I walked through the door. Amadeus raised his hand in a brief wave before turning back to his screen. Hargreaves was staring at his screen, it looked like he was watching CCTV.

Liz looked up, trying not to look annoyed to see me, after her behaviour towards me last year George had considered moving her to a different team, but she was new to the role and he'd decided to give her a second chance.

'Boss, your friend is here,' she said.

George turned around, 'Hi Rowan, come on through to my office.' Then he turned to Liz, 'can you fetch us a couple of coffees please.'

Liz forced a smile and got up out of her chair.

Once the door to his office was closed, I said, 'I don't think I'll be drinking anything she's been in charge of making for me.'

'Perhaps that's wise, although she is trying very hard to make a good impression.'

'Sonya said you wanted to see me.'

'I wanted to ask you about Seb, find out a little bit more about him.'

'I only met him the once but I would've liked to talk to him more. I thought he might have been holding back some information.'

'What made you think that?'

'I met him in the working men's club, Eddie arranged it for me and there was a group of them. Seb was definitely the one with the most insight on Iain. He said he understood him because he knew what it felt like to be an outsider.'

'Did it seem like any of the others were angry about him saying so much?'

'I got the impression that he was known for being outspoken. Iain had found an error in the plans and Seb's brother-in-law Wullie, he was the supervisor – he told the people in charge and from what I gathered he made out that it was him that figured it out. It made me wonder if this was the sort of behaviour Seb saw all the time from Wullie. But I didn't get the feeling that there was proper bad blood. How's the investigation going?'

'Badly, everyone who knew him says he was a great bloke, the type that was happy to help a neighbour out, really friendly. His wife said that he liked to go out hill walking, said it helped his mental health and that as far as she knew he always went alone. She did mention that he'd made some acquaintances in the passing, fellow walkers, ones he saw regularly, but that he preferred to keep himself to himself. He had been known to stay out all night, set up camp in a bothy if the weather was good and he'd walked further than he intended, but that at this time of year he always came back because it was too cold otherwise.'

'Was anything stolen from him?' I asked.

'His mobile phone is missing, could have been taken by the killer, or it could've rolled out of his pocket and got lost when they moved his body.'

'Is it possible that it was a mugging gone wrong?'

'I've not completely ruled it out, but the idea that someone would hike up there to steal a mobile phone is a bit far-fetched, especially since his wife said it was an older model and the screen was already quite badly cracked.'

'Do you think it's related to your other body?'

'I don't know, if it had turned out to be Iain Blair's remains then I would have thought it more likely, but until we find out whose skeleton that is down in the morgue it's going to be impossible to know if there's any connection.'

'How did Elspeth take the news that it wasn't her brother?'

'Actually, that was one of the things I wanted to talk to you about.'

'How come?'

'I just wanted to check what you said to her.'

'I just told her that some human remains had been found near the last place Iain was seen and that you would be collecting a DNA sample to see if it might be him.'

'Okay, it's just that she implied that you had given an assurance that you already knew it was him and when I said there was no match she wasn't happy, and that's an understatement.'

'Perhaps she was really hopeful that she might get to bury her brother?'

'Maybe, it seemed more than that though, it was more like she was angry.'

'I wouldn't read too much into it if I were you, she'll have just been in shock. Was that all you wanted to talk to me about?' I asked.

'Yeah, that's it for now.'

'Good, I need to get home and pack.'

'Aren't you staying for your coffee?'

'Probably safer not to.'

'Where are you going?'

'I'm going to Nairn to interview someone who was friendly with Iain back in the day and then I'm staying overnight in Dundee and having dinner with Alana.'

'Okay, and I know you hate it when I say this, but be careful, and tell Alana I said hi.'

'Will do.' I stood up to leave, catching my bag on one of the folders stacked on George's desk sending it toppling on to the floor. 'Oh God, sorry.' I said, quickly crouching down to pick up its contents. 'Who's this?' I asked picking up a polaroid picture that had come out of the file. It was of two girls in their teens.

'This one is Pamela, you know, the woman who was attacked on the beach and we don't know the identity of the other woman, but given how much they look alike I'm guessing it was a biological sister.'

I stared at it, 'I know who it is,' I said sitting back down and pulling a small file out of my bag. I took out the photo of Iain and Iris on what I assumed was their wedding day. 'It's Iris Blair, or Hatfield as she would've been then. I recently found out she was separated from her siblings when they went into foster care, there was a brother as well.' I lay my photograph next to the one that had fallen out of George's file, and we looked at them together.

'No mistaking that it's the same young woman, although I suppose given how similar they look it could be either of them in your picture.'

'Except that you said that Pamela was living in France when her sister went missing. Do you know if she kept in touch with her sister at all?'

'Not that we've found any evidence of so far, but if Iris didn't know Pamela had been adopted then she would've struggled to find her sister once she had a new name.' George said.

'It makes you think though, if they looked so similar when they were young, maybe Pamela was mistaken for Iris and that's why she was attacked.'

George picked up the picture, 'people change as they get old, don't they?' He opened the folder and took out a current photo of Pamela and held the two side by side. He turned them so I could see. 'Although I would suggest that the resemblance is good enough that if you'd known her as a teenager you might recognise her now. What do you think?'

'You're right, listen I've got to go.' I stood up, this time careful not to knock anything else over. 'Can I take this with me, I promise I'll return it.' I said holding the photograph of the sisters in my hand.

'Where are you dashing off to?'

'There's someone I need to talk to before I head off tomorrow.'

'You want to share with me what's going through your mind?'

'Not yet. I promise if my hunch turns out to be correct you'll be the first person I tell.'

'Fine.' George tutted.
'Thanks.'

Chapter Twenty-Two

It was starting to get dark as I pulled onto the gravel driveway outside Elspeth's house, the crunch under my wheels once again alerting her to my arrival as she was at the front door by the time I got out of my car.

'If you've come to tell me it's not Iain you're wasting your time, that buffoon of a policeman told me earlier. I suggested they run further tests and perhaps actually get an expert to look at the bones.' Elspeth called towards me.

'I know it was probably a shock, but the DNA wasn't a match.'

'I said to that policeman DCI something or other...'

'Johnston.' I interrupted.

'Yes him, that I want to get my own independent tests done, I'll have someone in the forensic anthropology community sort it out for me, but he had the audacity to tell me that wasn't going to be possible.'

'You need to let them do their job,' I replied.

'If that's not why you're here then what do you want?'

'I've come to talk to you about Pamela Blackstock.'

'Why?'

'Can I come inside?' I asked.

'I suppose.' She led me through to the kitchen and indicated for me to sit down. She had a half-drunk cup of coffee that she took a sip of but didn't offer me anything. 'Why do you want to talk to me about her?'

'You said you recognised her from secretarial college that you both attended.'

'That's right, although that wasn't her name then.'

'I think you're lying,' I said.

'What? Why would I lie about something like that? I think it's time you left.' Her voice reached a shriek as she finished the sentence.

I didn't move. 'I think you did recognise Pamela and I think you thought you'd found Iris.'

Elspeth's face paled. 'I had found her. It didn't hit me right away, there was just something every time I saw her that niggled in my brain, and I knew that I knew her from somewhere. Then one night as I was getting into bed it hit me. I felt stupid.'

'What did you do?'

'The next time I saw her I suggested that we went out for drinks afterwards and she agreed. Then I confronted her. I told her I knew who she was and that I wanted her to tell me what she'd done to Iain.'

'She said that I was mad, that she didn't know anyone called Iain. I wanted to know why she'd changed her name – seemed to me like that was the sort of thing you did if you had something to hide. She said that it was none of my business why she'd changed her name. She got up and left. I followed her into the car park but she just drove off. And after that she was very standoffish with me at the club, she would barely speak to me, but I knew. I knew that she must know where Iain was, all I wanted her to do was tell me what happened that day.'

'Is that why you attacked her on the beach?'

'How dare you – I have never attacked anyone in all my life. How would trying to kill her have helped me? She can't answer my questions now can she.'

'She can't answer your questions because she's not Iris…'

'I told you I recognised her.'

'You were mistaken, Pamela is exactly who she says she is and when you confronted her about changing her name, she thought you meant her surname which happened when she'd been adopted as a teenager. Pamela is Iris' little sister.' I said taking the photograph of the two girls out of my bag and pushing it up the table towards her.

Elspeth picked up the picture, her jaw slackening in shock.

'They do look very alike, I couldn't believe it myself when I saw them together. They were separated when the three children went into foster care after their mother died. I doubt there are terribly many photos of them together and it was just by chance I saw this one,' I continued.

Elspeth covered her mouth with her hand. 'Oh no, what have I done?'

'You tell me.'

'I was so horrible to her. I went to the hospital, pretended to be her friend and they let me sit with her for a while, I told her I hoped she died. What if she could understand me?'

'Are you sure that's all you did?'

'You think I'm capable of attacking her like that, look at me.'

For all Elspeth was trying to play the fragile old woman routine I did think she was capable of the assault. 'I do actually. Since I took this case, you have lied to me, misdirected me and been downright difficult to deal with. I'm going to call DCI

Johnston and let him know; he can come and take a statement from you and decide what happens next.'

'Is that necessary – I haven't done anything wrong.'

I stood up and began walking toward the door. Elspeth hurried after me grabbing my arm, proving that she was much stronger than she looked. 'Let go of me.'

'I can't let you leave like this. I need you to understand, you have to promise you won't tell the police.'

'Elspeth, there's a woman in a coma in the hospital, and you thought she was your missing brother's wife, they need to know. If you haven't done anything wrong, then you have nothing to worry about.'

'The thing is I was on the beach that morning, but I didn't attack her I swear. I knew she went there to walk her dogs. I thought that if I could catch her there alone, it would be easier to talk to her, get her to open up about Iain. But I slept in and by the time I got there it was too late. She was lying on the beach with those bloody dogs sitting there just yapping. I thought she was dead.'

'Why didn't you phone for help?'

'I couldn't, how would I explain being there, besides I thought it was too late. It wasn't until later when I heard about it on the news that I realised that she was still alive. I didn't see anything.'

'That's even more reason for you to speak to the police. Either you can phone them and tell them, or I will.'

'Alright, but not that Johnston man, I don't like him.'

I took my phone out of my pocket and it caught on Nat's card. I called her and she agreed she would grab another officer and come out and take the statement.

By the time I got home it was late and I was tired. I considered waiting until tomorrow morning to pack, after all I was only going to be away one night, but I needed to make an early start if I was going to make my meeting with Michael.

Chapter Twenty-Three

George's name appeared on my phone as I closed my car door. I rejected the call, I'd intended to phone back when I was on my way, but I didn't have to wait long before he called again.

'Morning.'

'Are you ignoring me?' He asked.

'Nope, I was just getting in the car, I was going to call you back. What's up?'

'You want to explain yesterday evening to me? One minute you're in my office and then you dash off to follow a hunch, the next thing I know I've got a uniformed officer popping her head round my office door saying you'd called and asked her to go and take a statement from a witness in my case.'

'You seem to have a pretty good handle on what happened already.'

'Rowan.'

'Alright, calm down. When I saw the photo of Pamela and Iris I wondered if Elspeth had thought she had found her brother's wife so I went to confront her. She wasn't keen on speaking to the police, you in particular – she really doesn't like you. I'd met Nat earlier on and her card was in my pocket, and I thought she'd be ideal. What's the problem with that?'

'You don't think calling and giving me a heads up might've been nice?'

I sighed. He was right, if the shoe was on the other foot I wouldn't have been happy. 'Sorry. I should've called and let you know. I was tired, it had been a long day and I just wanted to get home and packed for today. I knew Nat would tell you what was going on, I didn't think you would mind.'

'A bit of collaboration next time, isn't that what you're always banging on about?'

'Fair. Anyway, I thought what Elspeth had to say might be of interest to you. What did you think about her statement? Do you think she was telling the truth when she said that she's not involved in the incident on the beach?'

'Hard to say, I've got the team checking CCTV and traffic cameras to see when she pops up on them to see if any of them corroborate her timeline. It feels a bit like too much of a coincidence to me. I'm going to get Liz to go and pick her up later today so I can ask her a few questions and I don't give a rat's arse if she doesn't like me.'

'Probably wise. In my opinion I think she's physically capable of it, I'm just not sure thwacking someone over the head and leaving them for dead is her style.'

'Even if it's not her it's possible that she did see something or someone, might just be that she hasn't realised the significance of what she saw.'

'Hopefully you make some kind of breakthrough. How is Pamela?'

'Doctors say she should be conscious by next week, signs are very positive for a full and complete recovery, all things considered she's been very lucky.'

'I imagine Jock and Wallace will be pleased to go back home eventually.'

'Yeah,' he sounded wistful. 'I think I'll miss them you know.'

'You're getting soft in your old age,' I laughed.

'Whatever. Drive safe and give me a shout when you get back.'

'Will do.'

We hung up. It was raining, that light misty type of rain, the sort that you don't think much about because it doesn't batter against your windows but will have you soaked to your skin in minutes if you go out in it. It was making the road feel greasy and my windscreen was soaked.

Thankfully the weather had improved by the time I got to Nairn and all I needed to contend with was a strong wind. I pulled my hair into a quick ponytail before getting out of the car so I would still look at least half presentable by the time I got to the café. It was only a short walk although I was thankful to Google Maps without which I would have had difficulty finding it so easily.

Once inside I looked around the occupied tables to see if there was anyone who looked like the small photograph of Michael that I'd seen on the internet.

'Table for one, is it?' The woman behind the counter asked as I reached the head of the queue.

'I'm meeting someone actually, I was just trying to see if he was here already, but I think I must be the first.'

She smiled and took me to a small table in the corner near the large window at the front of the café. I had to make my way through the maze of chairs being used to make sure each occupied table was the correct distance from one another to get to my seat. When I sat down I had the uneasy feeling of being trapped.

About five minutes later a man came in, his eyes darting around the room. I stood up, almost knocking my chair over in the process. 'Michael,' I called out, hoping that it was him as several people turned to look at me.

'Rowan?' He said.

I nodded and he began picking his way through the chairs towards me.

'Thanks for coming all this way to meet me, I'm sorry I couldn't be more flexible,' he took off his face mask and stuffed it into his pocket. 'I still can't get used to this,' he said.

'At least we can meet face to face, I think I'm over having Zoom calls.'

Michael was tall, easily over 6' and he looked like he either spent a lot of time in the gym or did a physical job. He was dressed in jeans and a dark bomber style jacket, everything about his appearance was youthful for a man who must at least be in his late sixties, only his grey hair and weather worn face gave him away.

The waitress came over and took our order. There were a couple of moments of awkward silence before I said, 'How well do you remember Iain?'

'I liked him. He was smart, properly intelligent. I liked that, you could talk to him about more than the footie.'

'Did he mention why he dropped out of his PhD?'

'He'd had enough studying, enough of only ever doing what everyone else expected or wanted him to do. His parents were the controlling type, always wanting to know where he was, what he was doing, and he was a grown man.'

'Did Iris have anything to do with his decision?'

Michael smiled, 'she was lovely…'

'You met her?' I interrupted.

'Yeah, we – me and my then Mrs, we went out to dinner a few times, had them round the house, that sort of thing.'

The waitress arrived with our lunch and we momentarily paused the conversation.

'What was she like?'

'She was feisty, I think she brought Iain out of his shell, she'd had a tough time being in the care system. They were like – what's that thing, you know the black and white thing that links together?'

'Yin and Yang?'

'Yeah, that's it. They were different from each other, but that's what made it work. But to answer your earlier question, yeah I'd say Iris had a hand in Iain's decision. She showed him that he didn't have to do what other people wanted and gave him a reason to make a different choice.'

'Was she working when they were together?'

Michael took a bite out of his sandwich and I took the opportunity to do the same. 'Yeah, secretary, I want to say for a lawyer, but it could be any type of office, it was a long time ago.'

'Not a dancer or a stripper then?'

He laughed, 'no, what would make you think that?'

'His sister and brother-in-law both said that she was a stripper who'd latched on to Iain as a way out of her life.'

'Bloody hell, that family is vicious. I was surprised he invited them to the wedding you know, I wouldn't have had any of them there. I guess he thought it was important to try to maintain some family relations.'

'You were at the wedding?'

'Yeah, he invited me and the wife and Seb, another bloke from work, and his Mrs were there too and there were a couple of people from his uni days that came along but I don't remember much about them. It was a small wedding.'

I wondered why Seb had told me about Iain being married but not about him being one of the guests. I wondered if Michael knew about Seb's death.

'I was under the impression that it was only Iain's siblings in attendance.'

Michael frowned, 'No I mean his brother and his partner were there and his sister but not her hubby – no idea why though.'

'Any idea what happened to them, was it was out of character for them to disappear like that?'

He shook his head slowly. 'Iain and Iris are good people, they were building a life together, so all I can say is that if they left that day then there would've been a reason for it.'

'It seems like you were close with them, did you ever hear from either of them after that day in June?'

'No, I was due to be moving up here the July of 83. I got a job up this way because my ex moved here with my son – it was going to be a right pain to see him if I stayed and when I thought about it there was nothing keeping me in Cuddieford. She actually asked for the divorce only a couple of weeks after Iain's wedding and I didn't want to mess her about, my parents stayed together for the kids, and it was horrible growing up with all that tension. I didn't want that for my boy. I only got pissed off when she said she was moving all the blooming way up here. I suppose it made sense, this is where she was from originally, moved down to Fife to be with me. It was actually Iain that made me see sense, he said I could tarmac roads anywhere but there was only one place I could be a real dad and he was right, best decision I ever made.'

'I'm glad you've been happy, I've always liked Nairn, your son was lucky to grow up somewhere with the beach on his doorstep. Is he still living locally.'

'Aye, he went away to uni, but he came back, has a family of his own and I have a couple of wee grandkids, so it all worked out in the end.'

'That's good. When Iain went missing did the police contact you or speak to any of his friends?'

'Nah.'

'Did you know that Iain's family didn't mention Iris at all when he went missing? Didn't even tell the police that he was married.'

'That's weird, why not?'

'Wanted to spare their parents the upset apparently.'

'But they knew. He told me he'd taken Iris to meet them, it didn't go well as you can imagine, but he wasn't keeping Iris a secret. Does that mean the police were never looking for Iris?'

'Only Iain, and even then, they didn't do an awful lot of investigation. From the notes there was speculation that Iain was gay for some reason, and you know what things were like for gay men in the early 80s'

'Not personally, but I knew Iain's brother Stewart was gay and that he'd been attacked a couple of times because of it, now *that* was a secret from the parents.'

We were finishing our lunch when I decided I needed to tell him about Seb. 'I'm not sure if you keep in touch with many people from Cuddieford, but I thought you'd want to know that Seb died recently.'

'Bloody hell, what a shame – we've not spoken in a while, but I kept in contact with him, birthdays, Christmas that kind of thing. What happened?'

'He was murdered.'

'What? Why? Have they caught the bastard who did it?'

'I don't know why. The DCI in charge thought it might have something to do with Iain.'

'How could it possibly.'

'Human remains were found in woods near to where Iain's car was last seen, the police thought that it might be Iain, but it turned out it wasn't.'

'Who's body was it?'

'They don't know – no matches in the system so it's a bit of a mystery.'

'It's grim isn't it, imagine getting shot and then no one finding your body until it's nothing more than remains.'

I froze, I hadn't mentioned anyone getting shot. 'Well there were more guns then I suppose,' I said hoping that he might say more.

'I suppose the nearest farmer assumed they were poaching, maybe fired a warning shot to scare them off and got it wrong,' Michael replied.

There was something about the way he'd replied that left me feeling like he was trying to cover up his previous comment. I thought about challenging him about it, but instead decided to keep it to myself. Michael knew much more than he was letting on.

Chapter Twenty-Four

How did Michael know the man in the tree roots had been shot? I was sure his story of the farmer had been his way of covering his tracks, but did that also mean that he knew who the remains belonged to? My mind raced as I drove towards Dundee, trying to think of all the statements released by the police, I couldn't remember George saying that the person had been shot. He was usually particularly vague in the beginning – not wanting to muddy the waters before an investigation had got going properly. I considered phoning him and asking but instead I decided I'd wait and double check when I got home. For now all I wanted to think about was spending some time with Alana.

Her dorm room was immaculate, unlike me she'd always been relatively tidy. It was basic but she'd made it her own by adding pictures to the walls. On her desk there was a framed photograph of Jack, me, and her with the firepit in the background. We all looked happy. I was glad that we'd taken so many photos that night, I'd have taken more if I'd known it was going to be the last time the three of us were going to be together.

Alana was busy telling me about her course when we were interrupted by the sound of two people having an increasingly loud argument in the corridor outside. She sighed, 'I wish I could just tell them to shut up and sod off.'

'I'll tell them if you like,' I smiled.

'Don't you dare – I've got to live here.'

'I think we should see about getting you a flat next year, I'm sure you can get enough of your friends together to make it doable.'

'That would be amazing. It's only been one term and I'm already fed up.'

'You're not that far from home, you can always come back a few nights a week if you want.'

'It's not really practical, I try and schedule extra lab time on my non-lesson days to make up for missing so much of it last year.'

'No problem, it was just a suggestion.'

'I'm sure I can survive this year and then yes, a flat would be amazing.'

'I've made dinner reservations at the hotel. If you want you can grab an overnight bag and stay with me.'

'That would be nice, are you sure that will be allowed.'

'I'll tell them at reception when we get there, I'm sure it'll be fine if I pay for an extra person.'

After a little confusion at the front desk, explaining that Alana was my daughter, we dropped our bags in the room before heading to the hotel restaurant. After dinner we sat on the bed and watched TV, eating snacks I'd brought with me to avoid paying the inflated room service prices. It reminded me of the time four years ago when we'd been forced to stay in a hotel after our house was broken into. Alana had grown up so much since then, I was proud of her in more ways than she would ever know.

The next morning we ate breakfast, a full Scottish with haggis, black pudding and tattie scone, in bed.

'I've been thinking about your case,' Alana said, her mouth full of toast. 'This man you met yesterday, could he have been the third person your witness saw? I mean what if Iain pulled his car off the road because he was having a row with his wife or because she was feeling sick or something – maybe this Michael bloke was travelling with them and then when they hadn't come straight back he went to find them.'

'Possibly, but that doesn't explain the remains though.' I dipped the corner of my toast into my fried egg and then narrowly avoided spilling the yolk on to the white bed sheets.

'It could be a coincidence that the remains were found there, I know you don't like the idea of that, but you should at least not rule it out.'

'It just feels wrong, that's all – the last place Iain and probably Iris were ever seen, and it also happens to be where someone was shot at approximately the same time?'

'True, although it's possible that body was already there and had nothing to do with what might've happened to Iain.'

I wrinkled my nose, she was right of course – it was possible, it was also highly unlikely.

"Okay, but what if the three of them witnessed something they shouldn't have? What if Michael caught up to his friends and they saw this man being shot and that's the real reason they all disappeared or moved away.'

'That's possible, but then how would the man and his killer have gotten there, Deborah said she didn't see anyone else going that way.'

'Maybe they came a different way, didn't you say that there was a car park round the other side of the woods where dog walkers would stop sometimes.'

I nodded.

'Then what's to say they didn't come from that entrance.'

'But why wouldn't they report what they'd seen to the police?'

'I guess that would depend on who the person doing the shooting was – you're the detective,' she smiled. 'I'm just giving you options.'

I missed having her home to bounce ideas off of like this, I even missed having her tell me to be careful every time I went out, not that I would admit that to her. We both seemed to be dragging our heels getting packed up to check out.

'I could stay a few more days if you'd like,' I said.

'I would like, but you can't really – you need to get home and solve this case and I need to get my head down and do some work.'

She was right. 'Come home soon for a long weekend, I'm sure you don't need to be in the lab every day.'

She agreed that once she had finished what she was working on she'd come back for a visit. It had been nice to spend some quality time with Alana. Driving home my car felt quiet. I turned on the radio, the music filling up the background space and helping me to focus on the case.

Mentally I worked through my thoughts: Iris hadn't been a stripper, I didn't know why Iain's family had lied about that, but I was planning on confronting Elspeth about it when I next saw her. I was sure she was lying about the day Pamela was attacked, but had she simply seen more than she was letting on or was she involved? I was certain the remains discovered in the tree roots were connected to Iain and Iris' disappearance, but if it wasn't Iain then it had to be the mysterious third person. And lastly, was whoever killed Seb also responsible for attacking Pamela? How any of these things were connected though, was anyone's guess.

As I got closer to home I changed the radio channel in time to pick up the latest news broadcast:

Police have released a description of a man they want to talk to in relation to their investigation into the murdered hill walker Sebastian Wojcik. They are hoping to speak to a potential witness seen in the area at around the time they believe Mr Wojcik was attacked. The man was described as tall, grey hair, red jacket, and dark trousers.

The description was vague, it could match a number of older men, it could match the description of Michael Swanage if he had a red jacket, but what would he have been doing in Cuddieford, would he have known where Seb liked to go walking? He might, they'd been friends once. And I only had Michael's word for it that Christmas and Birthday cards had been the extent of their communications. Why kill Seb though? The only reason would be if you thought he knew something that you didn't want to get out.

As promised, I phoned George once I was back home. 'How did you get on questioning Elspeth yesterday?' I asked.

'Well you were right, she wasn't too pleased to be sitting opposite me, she said she was sorry for not reporting it when she found Pamela. She said pretty much the same thing she told you – she thought Pamela was Iris and had wanted to meet up with her to ask her about it.'

'Did she see anything?'

'Nothing useful, or so she says.'

'You don't believe her?' I asked.

'I don't know, she's lying about something, but what that is remains to be seen.'

'Are you any closer to finding out who your human remains belong to yet?'

'No, Sonya has drafted in some specialist help, so with a bit of luck we might have a bit more to go on soon.'

'What about Seb, has your person of interest come forward?'

'No, but that can take a couple of days, weeks even and that's assuming the person is local enough to hear the request. How was your trip north, you find out anything you want to share?'

I thought about my interaction with Michael for a moments. 'You know in all your press releases about the remains, have you mentioned how the person died?'

'No. You know me, I like to keep my cards close at this stage, why do you ask?'

'Something Michael said, he said, "imagine being shot and then no one finding you for all these years" and no before you ask, I did not let it slip during our conversation.'

'How did he know then?' George replied.

'Well either he saw it happen, he shot the person or someone in your team knows him and has told him more than they should.'

'Did you press him on it?'

'Only gently, I didn't want to spook him, he started talking about accidental shootings by farmers when they find people poaching. I got the impression he was trying to cover his tracks though.

'How did he come across to you?'

'He seemed like a nice bloke, his move up north had been planned for a while, he was moving to be closer to his son, so there was nothing suspicious in that. He was friends with Iain, Iris, and Seb, they socialised together. But if you're asking me if

I think he shot someone and hid their body in the woods then I don't know. He's another one that's hiding something.'

'Interesting, I might have a wee follow up with him myself.'

'Well do me a favour and don't tell him I sent you his way.'

'I'll keep your name out of it, don't worry. Right, I'd better be going, and try and stay out of bother.'

'I'll do my best, but before you go, I don't suppose you know if there was any damage to Iain's car – any reason he might've needed to pull off the road, a burst tyre or something?'

'I'm honestly not sure the records go back that far, but I'll get your best friend DC Collins to look them out for you.'

'Yay, I'll expect them sometime never then.'

Hanging up on George I noticed that I'd missed a call from Robbie, he'd quickly followed up with a text message meaning I didn't need to call him back. It read:

> Joyce Brown died a few years ago, heart attack her daughter says. I asked if anyone else remembered Iris but no joy. Sorry I couldn't help any more. Hope you're having better luck. Let me know if you need help with anything else.
>
> Love Robbie x

It would've been nice to have spoken to a friend of Iris', although I doubted that Joyce could've shed any light on her disappearance. I scored her off my list of people to talk to then text Robbie a thank you and a promise to get together soon.

Chapter Twenty-Five

I wasn't sure where I stood with Elspeth, I couldn't imagine that she had been thrilled to have been brought into the police station and interviewed by George, but I had little sympathy. I decided it would be best to turn up on her doorstep unannounced, it would be harder for her to fob me off in person.

The driveway was empty, and no one answered the door, typical that I had come at a time she was out. I sat in the car waiting for her to return. I thought about my conversation with Michael, there was a lot that he'd told me that I wanted to confront Elspeth about, the only thing I had to decide was in what order.

After thirty minutes I was contemplating giving up and heading home, there had to be more useful things I could do with my time. I'd just buckled my seat belt when her car came into sight. I got out of the car.

'I wasn't expecting to see you today,' she said as she shut her car door. 'I wasn't aware that we had an appointment.'

'We don't, there's some things come up in my investigation that I wanted to ask you about, that's all.'

'Oh. Alright, I hope you didn't have to wait long for me, you'd have been better calling ahead and I'd have made sure I was in.'

'That's okay, I was passing this way and I only arrived a moment or so before you.' I followed her into the house.

'Do you want a coffee?'

'That would be great, thanks.'

'It'll have to be instant I'm afraid, I broke the machine yesterday,' she put the kettle on. 'What was it you wanted to ask me about?'

'There's a couple of things, but I'd like to start with Rodger and Stewart's relationship. How did you parents take it when Rodger told them he was gay?'

Elspeth stirred the coffee, the spoon clanking loudly off the sides of the mug. 'They were fine about it,' she said eventually.

'When did he tell them, would they have known about that before Iain went missing?'

'Of course, he was living with Stewart by then, why the interest?'

'The 80s weren't that tolerant of a time, and your parents would've been from a generation that struggled with homosexuality. I'm just surprised that Rodger felt so able to be open with them, but Iain didn't want to introduce Iris to them.'

She sighed, 'alright, they didn't know, not then anyway. They thought that Stewart was Rodger's flat mate, I think Dad suspected but he didn't want to ask Rodger in case he was right. And that's how it went on, a not so secret, secret, I suppose you'd call it. Then eventually Rodger told them and by then they were older and had already lost one son, I think they were always embarrassed to tell people they knew, but for the most part they accepted Stewart and after Rodger died, they stayed in close contact. They probably spent more time with him than me, what with me being out of the country.'

'In the original police report, one of the investigating officers noted that he thought Iain might be gay, do you think your parents were concerned about that?'

'Maybe but if they were they didn't tell me, and for what it's worth I never thought Iain was gay, I thought he didn't want to take his girlfriends around our parents because mum was so over the top controlling with him, she'd have scared them off without even trying.'

'What did they think of Iris?'

'They never met her.'

'I think they did, from what I've been told Iain took her to meet them not long before they went missing.'

For a few moments she was silent. 'He told me he was going to, but I didn't know if he had, and after he went missing they didn't mention it so I said nothing.'

'Why?'

'Their son was missing, the last thing they needed to know on top of that was that he'd married some…some…'

'Some what?' I interrupted.

'Stripper, hooker, god knows what she was.'

'She was a secretary for a legal firm.'

'No, that's not right she was a stripper.'

'You're wrong, she wasn't, I haven't found one shred of evidence to back that up. What made you think that's what she did for a living?'

'I was told.'

'By who?'

'It doesn't matter now, does it?'

'It matters to me. Was it Iain?' I asked wondering if for some reason the two of them had decided to make up this story to shock his family?

Elspeth frowned, 'no. It was Stewart, he said he'd been to a stag do with some straight friends, they'd ended up in a strip club in Edinburgh and he'd seen her there.'

'Did you ever talk to Iain about it?'

'No, of course not. What would I say – I heard your wife's a stripper; how would that conversation even go?'

She had a point, 'but wasn't it on this basis that you decided you didn't like her, because you thought she was using Iain to get away from that lifestyle?'

'Yes it was and in retrospect I should've done more to get to know my new sister in law.'

'Why wasn't your husband at the wedding?'

'Who told you he wasn't?'

'Another wedding guest.'

'Stewart?'

'No, one of Iain's work friends, I didn't realise till recently that there were more people at the wedding than you'd mentioned.'

'It was a long time ago, I forgot.'

'You forgot your husband didn't go to your brother's wedding?'

'I'm an old woman, I forget things sometimes, Max usually would've come with me to this sort of thing but looking back I'm guessing we didn't have the spare money for both of us to fly back to watch my brother get married in the registry office and then go out for a meal.'

I finished my coffee and thought for a moment about what Elspeth had just said, she had been very dismissive of her brother's relationship and subsequent marriage, I was beginning to suspect that it was her that was so against telling the police about it, I just didn't understand why.

'Missing person's cases of this age are notoriously hard to solve, I explained all this when we first met,' I put my hand up as Elspeth opened her mouth to interrupt. 'And yes, I'm aware you believe that he isn't missing, that he's dead. Either way this case was never going to be easy…'

'You're giving up, is that what you're saying? Admitting defeat, this case is too hard for the great Rowan McFarlane!'

I took a deep breath in and let it out slowly, I was tired and she was making it very difficult for me to not lose my patience. 'No, that's not what I'm saying. If you'd shut up and let me finish, please. Because they're already complicated it's always difficult to solve, but what makes it next to impossible is not how long it's been since Iain was last seen, it's all the bloody lying. You lied then to the police about Iris, you've constantly lied to me about it all. How can I believe anything you tell me when your story changes all the time? If you truly want me to find out what happened to Iain then you need to be truthful with me, otherwise I'm going to call it a day, not because I don't believe I can solve this case, but because I cannot be bothered dealing with a client who seems to tell a new lie every time she opens her mouth.'

Elspeth's cheeks were flushed a reddy-purple colour. 'I find that very offensive…'

'I find your lies offensive, to me, to the police, but more importantly to your brother. You told me that you wanted closure, to know what happened to Iain whilst you still had time to find out. If any of that is true, then I can't understand why you've been making my job so bloody difficult,' I paused. 'I'm going to go. I'd like you to have a proper think about what you want to get out of this investigation and when you're ready to tell the truth you can let me know.' I walked to the front door. Elspeth made no attempt to follow me.

Chapter Twenty-Six

Still no news from DC Collins about Iain's car, it was a long shot anyway, but I would've liked to know what made him pull off the road and head up the hill.

I'd left Elspeth's this morning frustrated, with more questions than answers. Driving home I'd wondered had Stewart been wrong when he thought he'd seen Iris in the strip club? After all he barely knew her, it could easily have been a case of mistaken identity. I made a mental note to check where Pamela had been living then. But why did he tell Elspeth? Why didn't he speak to Iain about it and then there would've been the opportunity to set him straight? The other possibility was that Stewart had made up the whole thing because for some reason he just didn't like his new sister in law.

Back home I made myself a coffee and went through to the office and began making notes, trying to find a new line of enquiry.

Iris had been an enigma from the start of this case and if I hadn't seen the photographs and heard from other people that she existed I might've been persuaded that she wasn't real. There was something odd about the way that Iain's family had wanted me to think badly of her, that she had been taking advantage of their brother, that she wasn't worth reporting to the police as missing.

I wrote Iris' name in the middle of my page and circled it with my pen. What if none of what happened that day had anything to do with Iain and instead it was all about Iris? Iain loved her and if something happened that meant she needed to get away I believed he would have dropped everything and gone.

I phoned Marion Stephens and asked her if she had any recollection of where Iris was living when she did her secretarial course. She was very apologetic, but it wasn't something she'd kept a note of.

I searched the National Archives for information, which took me to the Care Leavers Association, they might have the details of Iris' list of homes during her time in care, but they weren't going to give them to me. The woman on the other end of the phone line had sounded appalled by my request, and when I asked if I could make a Freedom of Information request, she said I could try but it would be unlikely that I would meet the necessary criteria for being given the information and that if there were grounds to believe it was necessary in connection with the detection of a crime then the police were the only ones able to make that request.

I dialled George's number.

'Hey George, how's it going?' I asked before he had the opportunity to get in a dig about me bothering him.

'I'm very busy, what can I help you with?'

'I need to know the list of foster homes that Iris Hatfield lived in.'

'Why?'

'Because I think we've been looking at this all wrong, it's not about Iain, it's about Iris.'

'Maybe your case is, but I don't see what that's got to do with mine.'

'Your case started with Pamela Blackstock being assaulted, right?'

'Assuming that there is any link between the three, then yes.'

'Okay, now we know that Elspeth wanted to confront Pamela because she thought she was Iris. That wasn't an unreasonable assumption on Elspeth's part because certainly when they were young the two girls really looked alike. What if Elspeth wasn't the only person to think that, and Pamela was in fact attacked because someone thought she was Iris.'

'But why?'

'I'm not sure about why, but to me this is the only thing that makes sense. Iris disappears off the face of the planet, she's not reported missing by anyone, literally no one seems to miss her.'

'Okay but why would Iain's family not mention her?'

'Maybe he asked them not to, he might've been trying to protect her?'

'But why would Elspeth think her brother is dead then, why would she have any need to hire you at all if she'd known what was going on?'

I thought for a moment, George had a point. 'I don't know, but I really believe that this case is all about Iris' disappearance and if we find out what happened to her then all of our other questions will be answered.'

'We?' George asked.

'Yes, we. Surely you agree that at this point it makes sense for us to work together on this, pool resources?'

'Am I going to live to regret this?' He sighed.

'When have you ever regretted working with me?'

'Do you want a list?'

I laughed, 'come on, you know you want to really.'

'Fine, but this time Rowan you need to tell me what you're doing and not because I want to control you or anything, but because that's how working together actually works, not me giving you all my information and then you dashing off on your own without letting me know what's going on and ending up getting into who knows what kind of trouble.'

'I promise.'

'Fine, I'll get a request put through to get a list of addresses.'

'Did you find an address book or anything like that at Pamela's house?' I asked.

'I don't think so, but we weren't looking for one.'

'Any chance I can get the keys and have a nosey about myself?'

'Only if I send one of my people to go with you.'

'As long as it's not Liz Collins.'

'How about your pal Natasha?'

'That would work, get her to give me a buzz when she's ready to go and I'll come by the station and pick her up.'

'It'll probably be tomorrow morning,'

'Thanks George.' I said before hanging up.

Chapter Twenty-Seven

Natasha texted me at 8am, saying she was ready when I was. Thankfully I was already eating my breakfast when it came in which meant for once I wasn't rushing out the door with a piece of toast in my hand. She was waiting in the car park when I arrived, dressed in plain clothes – jeans and a long-sleeved top.

'Thanks for this,' she said as she got into the car.'

'George seemed to think I needed babysat and I'm glad it's you that's coming along.'

Natasha smiled, 'it's weird hearing you call the DCI, George. Anyway, I'm not sure I was even on his radar before I got chatting to you, and now I'm getting involved in a major investigation and I really appreciate it.'

'Have you been out to Pamela's house before?'

'Once, my partner and I did perimeter duty when she was first attacked, you know stopping anyone coming near the house, keeping an eye out for journalists or anyone who shouldn't be there.'

'How long have you been in the police?'

'Eight years, I dropped out of Uni when I was twenty, I'd been studying accountancy, but I hated it. I started imagining my career sitting in an office and I knew I had to find something else. I applied for the police and passed all the tests and as soon as I got my start date I left university and yeah, it was the best decision. What about you how long have you been a PI?'

'Almost four years.'

'Wow, you've done a lot in that time, you're a bit infamous around the station.'

'Is that a polite way of telling me that some of your colleagues could see me far enough?'

'Let's just say you're a bit marmite,' she laughed, before continuing giving me directions. 'You want to take the next left by the way, otherwise you'll end up going a long way for a short cut.'

I followed her directions which took us into a cul-de-sac at the far edge of a small estate of houses. They'd been built in the 80s when every housing estate seemed to have a lot of bungalows. Pamela's house looked identical to every one of its neighbours, faded sandstone façade with a small square of grass at the front and a long drive up the left-hand side of the building which led to a small single car prefab garage.

'Do we have keys for the garage as well?' I asked as we got out the car.

Natasha looked down at the bundle, 'I think so,' she said holding up a couple of keys that didn't look like house keys. 'Where do you want to start?'

I half considered starting in the garage, that's where people often stored things from their past, but I wanted to get a feel for the type of person Pamela was first.

'Let's open the front door and see what takes our fancy.'

Inside the scent of dog hit me as soon as the door was opened. But then it had taken a few days for my house to stop smelling like Jock and Wallace and they'd only been there for a couple of days. The hall had laminate flooring, pale wood-effect. I opened the first door on the left and walked into a large living room –

dining room space. The walls were cream and the carpet a dark grey. One wall was given over entirely to bookshelves, and I couldn't see a tv anywhere.

'I wish I could keep my place this tidy,' Natasha said from behind me.

I nodded, 'me too.'

I opened the drawers along the top half of the sideboard, napkins, tablecloths, and placemats were all I found though. I picked up the first of three framed photographs that sat along the top. It was a picture of Pamela as a young woman and what I assumed were her adoptive parents, the second was one of Jock and Wallace as puppies, the third was much more interesting, two young girls and a boy. The girls were clearly Iris and Pamela, was the boy their brother? Iris' secretarial teacher had mentioned her having a brother. He looked strangely familiar, but I couldn't place him, perhaps it was that he looked like his sisters.

'I'm going to take this,' I said waving the framed photo in the air before I placed it in an evidence bag.

'Okay, DCI Johnston wants me to keep a record of everything you take away with you.' She took a picture on her phone.

The kitchen and bathroom didn't have anything out of the ordinary, although I had been relieved that someone had taken away any food that had gone bad, which at least meant the kitchen smelt fresh.

Of the two bedrooms, one had been made into a sewing room, with a machine that looked more complicated to use than anything I'd seen before. I moved on to her bedroom and sat down at the large dressing table. Opening the drawers it was clear to see that Pamela had expensive tastes in moisturiser and make up, one of the drawers had a little stack of letters, a five year diary and a small address book.

'Bingo,' I said.

'Oh, what have you found?'

I opened the address book, Pamela's handwriting was full of loops and curls and not easy to read right away but she'd clearly had the book for a long time, some of the pages were barely attached. I flipped gently forward to 'H' hoping to find Iris but she wasn't there.

'Try 'I',' Natasha said from behind me. 'Perhaps there was a time when Hatfield wasn't Iris' surname, or she might've thought it could change, didn't you say Pamela changed her last name when she was adopted?'

I turned to the next page and sure enough Iris was the first entry. There was a page and half of addresses for Iris, all but one crossed out. 'This must've been the last address that she had for her sister.' I ran my finger across the list of addresses, a wave of sadness pricking my insides. I imagined Iris was happy for her sister to find a forever family, but it must have been heart breaking to be left behind.

'I can run that address when I'm back at the station if you like, see who lives there.'

'That would be great.'

I put all three items in evidence bags, I'd take my time looking through the diary and letters later on, at home. We headed out to the garage. There were a few boxes, but it mostly looked like things that had been put there in readiness for taking to a charity shop or to the tip.

'Did you see an attic hatch in the house?' I asked.

'No, but I wasn't really looking.'

'Let's go back in and check.'

We found the hatch in the ceiling outside the sewing room but couldn't find a ladder in any of the cupboards. I dragged a chair out from the dining room and stood on it to make myself tall enough to open the hatch. I peered my head through, shining my torch into the space.

'I need to get in here, do you think you could give me a leg up?'

'Probably,'

After a couple of failed attempts which left us half collapsed on the floor, Natasha finally succeeded in getting me high enough that I could pull myself the rest of the way in. The attic space had been crudely floored. I walked carefully over to the far side where there were a stack of cardboard boxes. The first one had Pamela's old school work and report cards, some were in French which I could barely understand but it looked like she'd been a good student. There were a couple of boxes of books, the final box though was much more interesting. It appeared that Pamela had kept a diary for a long time. Along with the diaries was a small biscuit tin, inside were old photographs taken when Pamela and her siblings were small, some of them with a woman that I suspected was their biological mother.

'One box coming down,' I said. 'And be careful, it's heavy.'

The bottom of the box almost gave way as I passed it to Natasha but we managed to get it out in one piece.

'How are you going to get out?' She asked.

'If you put the chair under I should be able to lower myself down.' Climbing out of the loft hatch I made a mental note to get back to the gym, my forearms shook as I descended, I half thought I was going to end up embarrassing myself by collapsing out the space and onto the floor.

'You got everything you need, do you think?' Natasha asked.

'Hopefully, if I can just shed some light on who Iris was then hopefully we can find out why she went missing.'

'DCI Johnston said you think this whole case is about her.'

'I really do, I mean I know at the moment he's just humouring me, but that's because he knows I've been right before.'

'And because he knows you're going to do all this stuff anyway and he might as well be involved now as deal with it later?' Natasha said.

'Yeah. It's good though, I know people think it's weird, but we do work well together.'

Natasha took a couple of moments to photograph everything in the box before we loaded it all into the boot of my car. 'Am I dropping you back at the station?'

'That would be great, then I'll get on to looking into that address for you.'

Chapter Twenty-Eight

Back home I laid the diaries out in date order, her current version was a five-year diary that she'd started in January last year, the previous one covered the last five years. There were gaps in between where either she hadn't kept one or it had got lost in one of her moves. The oldest one dated back to 2002, by which point Iris had been missing for almost twenty years.

I scanned through the entries looking for Iris' name, stopping occasionally to read snippets of Pamela's life. She'd lived in France until she was in her fifties, never married although she'd been engaged to a French man called Gabriel, but he had died from anaphylactic shock after being stung by a wasp. At fifty-four she moved to Belgium where she worked as a pastry chef before returning to the UK six years ago.

Iris' name had come up quite a few times on birthday's and at Christmas. She missed her older sister and brother and it seemed she'd never stopped feeling guilty about being adopted and having a better life.

The Christmas entry from last year read:

Merry Christmas my dearest sister Iris, I hope you are somewhere happy and loved, I will never stop looking for you. And to my dear Moran I miss your postcards and news of your adventures. I'd like to believe you found your happy place at last and made peace with it all. To my darling Gabriel, I miss you every day.

Could Moran be their brother, it was an unusual name, but who knows where their mother had taken her inspiration from. I'd ask George to see if he could trace a Moran Hatfield, although it did occur to me that they might not all have the same surname.

There had been a dozen or so photographs of the children when they were very small and only two had what appeared to be a father figure in them. The woman I'd taken to be their mother had gone from looking happy and healthy to looking gaunt and sickly, I'd seen that type of deterioration before, and I wondered at what point she'd started to take drugs and if that was why she ended up becoming a prostitute. How much did her children know and how long had they remained in her care before they were taken away? And what became of the mother, that was something else I'd like to know, not that it was likely that she'd still be alive now, but I felt the need to know if she ever got herself sorted out and went looking for her children.

The bundle of letters included postcards from Moran from all around the world. The last one was dated 1978 and was from Gdansk in Poland. I wondered why he stopped writing, maybe he hadn't but along the way these were the only postcards Pamela had managed to save. Where was Moran now?

The letters were a mixed bunch, there were some from Iris, always saying that she was well and that her new foster family or group home was lovely, that she was being well taken care of and had lots of friends. I doubted that for the most part this was true, instead suspecting that Iris had chosen to let her sister believe that she was okay. The oldest of the three children, Iris had the odds stacked against her that she would find a permanent home at all and in the 1970s it was even less likely that she would be able to stay with her siblings.

The remainder of the letters were mostly from Gabriel, it was clear how much they'd loved each other, but other than opening a window into Pamela's personal life they did little to help move my case forward.

My phone rang, a local number I didn't recognise.

'Hello, Rowan McFarlane speaking.'

'Is that your posh phone voice?' Natasha asked.

'I wouldn't have bothered if I'd known it was you.'

'It's because I'm using the landline. Anyway, I'm calling about that address you asked me to check up on.'

'Did you find out much about it?'

'It was Max Thorogood's family home.'

'Elspeth's husband?'

'Yep, weird right?'

'His parent's fostered Iris?'

'I cross referenced it with the information that the boss had already got on all Iris' foster homes and it was the last family placement she had while in foster care and that's not all, it gets stranger. You'd think as she was almost at the age to be discharged from care that she would've spent the last few months at the same place, wouldn't you?'

'But she didn't?'

'No, with three months left she was moved into a small group home.'

'Do we know why?'

'There's not a lot of information about it, the only records from that time say that she requested the move, but it doesn't say why, and here's something else; she put in the request to move on a Thursday morning and she was moved on the Sunday evening. That's not the normal sort of turn around I would've expected from the system, especially back then.'

'Did the family continue to foster after Iris?'

'Looks like they had placements for another ten years or so afterwards and then nothing.'

'What sort of thing would have them move a teenage girl within a couple of days like that?'

'Nothing good,' Natasha replied.

'Hmm, I can understand that Elspeth might not have made the connection, but you'd think Max would recognise the name and even if he didn't, he would surely have recognised his new sister-in-law in photographs.'

'Maybe Elspeth didn't take any?'

'That would be odd though wouldn't it,' Natasha replied.

'I think I'm going to have to have another chat with Elspeth, have you given all this information to George yet?'

'I wanted to let you know first.'

I smiled, George would be less than amused by that, 'thanks, can I ask another favour whilst I've got you on.'

'Sure.'

'Pamela mentions someone called 'Moran' in her diary and there are some postcards signed 'Moran', I think it might be her brother.'

'I can run a check for the name Moran Hatfield, see if it turns anything up.'

'Thanks.'

I looked back over my notes, Max Thorogood had been away on his fateful archaeology trip when Iain and Iris went missing.

After a couple of hours of research and phone calls I had managed to track down one of the people who'd overseen the expedition, Christopher Phillips. While he had given up digging and lecturing a long time ago, he now made a living writing books about his experiences. I'd managed to get his contact details from his agent and had sent him a message asking if he would have some time to talk to me about Max and what actually happened.

Chapter Twenty-Nine

At 8am the next morning I was sitting at the kitchen table drinking coffee and planning out my day. I wanted to do a bit more investigation into Max Thorogood before I next spoke to Elspeth. He'd published a few academic papers in the late 1970s and early 1980s but nothing other than that.

My phone rang at 8.45am.

'Hello is that Rowan McFarlane?'

'It is, who is this?' I asked.

'Chris Phillips, you sent me a message to get in touch.'

'I really appreciate you coming back to me so soon, I'm interested in finding out what you remember about Max Thorogood when you worked together in Bulgaria.'

'I don't know if you've ever heard of the Borovo Treasure?'

'No, I haven't'

'In the interests of brevity, it was a treasure trove, very interesting and accidentally dug up in 1974 by some farmers. Anyway, there was a belief that this was only the tip of the iceberg and archaeologists spent a fair bit of time in the late 1970s-80s digging around to see if we could find any other examples.'

'And that's what you were doing in 1983?'

'In part, but in 1982 the Sveshtari Tomb was discovered, of course I had known there were tombs in Bulgaria, you may know of the Kazanlak Tomb discovered in 1944?'

'I'm sorry, not my area of expertise.'

'Of course, and I'm waffling. What I mean to say is that Bulgaria was very rich in history with a lot to fascinate an archaeologist. And when I put together the dig team, I was delighted to have Max on board. He had a great reputation for this kind of speculative dig, and it helped that he'd done a fair bit of work out in Egypt.'

'How long were you there before he went missing?'

'Myself and the main team had been on site for about a fortnight when Max joined us and we worked together for almost six weeks.'

'Was it unusual for him to go off and work by himself?'

'He liked to go for a look about, get the lie of the land so to speak, see if there were any areas he thought we should be looking at in more detail.'

'And when he didn't come back you weren't immediately concerned?'

'He always took a pack with him, and a small one man tent just in case something happened and he couldn't get back. After a couple of days with no sign of him though we contacted the local police, went to the embassy, checked hospitals.'

'But no sign of him?'

'Unfortunately not.'

'Why did you wait so long to inform his wife?'

'I don't know what you mean?'

'She said Max had been missing almost a month by the time you let her know.'

'I'm not sure why she would say that. I telephoned the emergency contact number from Max's file the same day I went to the embassy, there was no answer and as it was hard to get to a phone in those days, I sent an urgent telegram to let her know.'

'And did you hear back from her?'

'A few weeks later yes, she got in contact to ask that Max's possessions be sent home. I couldn't manage to get them to Singapore but, I had a post-grad student that was heading back to the UK, and we agreed that he would take Max's things. There wasn't very much you see, he would deposit them at Edinburgh University which is where Max was affiliated at the time, and she could collect from them on her next trip back.'

'What do you think happened to Max?'

'Very difficult to say, Bulgaria wasn't a particularly dangerous place then and although Kosovo wasn't exactly stable, I'm not sure I was ever satisfied with the idea that Max was shot merely for an accidental border crossing, honestly I would've thought a fine would have been more likely'

'But that was the official line?'

'I don't think there was one, he was missing. I submitted all my reports to the local police and embassy and that was all I could do.'

'But he was later declared dead?'

'I believe so, not that I was involved in that at all.'

'What was Max like?'

'Intelligent, diligent, adventurous. Not sure any of that helps you though.'

'Did you notice anything unusual about his behaviour?'

'He was one of those hyper-focused types, once he was locked in on something he wasn't interested in outside distractions. There were a couple of unopened letters from his wife, which was unusual in general, but it didn't feel like that was out of character for him.'

'Did he speak about her at all?'

'No. In fact I remember questioning if they were still together…I don't like hanky-panky going on amongst the team, it throws the dynamic off completely and I happened to walk in on him and one of my under-grad students in a compromising position, he had only been at the dig a couple of days by then. I had to have a word with him, he apologised, I think he said he'd got carried away or something, it was a long time ago, I don't remember exactly what was said.'

'The student, she was a willing participant?'

'Oh yes, head turned by experienced archaeologist, not that I blamed her, I could see how he might've swept her off her feet, I told her it wasn't a wise move, but I held him responsible for the situation, not her.'

'Did you like him?'

'It didn't really matter, more important to have the right people on site than to have your friends there.'

'So you didn't like him?'

'Archaeology is a team game, it's about the preservation of history, not personal glory. Max was arrogant, opinionated, and occasionally rude. He had to be reminded on more than one occasion that he wasn't the one in charge.'

'How did he take that?'

'Didn't appear to make the slightest bit of difference to him.'

'Before Max disappeared did anything out of the ordinary happen at the site?'

'You mean like arguments?'

'Not necessarily, just anything you remember, even if you don't think it's connected.'

'We had one of our Jeeps stolen.'

'Was that the sort of thing that often happened at digs?'

'It wasn't uncommon, it had never happened on one of my digs before, but the sites can be magnets for thieves, we carry a lot of equipment, some of which is valuable, often we store artifacts before they're taken off site for safe keeping and we live in tents so it's not difficult to break in.'

'Was it ever recovered?'

'A couple of towns over, sitting in a car park with the keys in the ignition.'

'Was it damaged?'

'Not at all, the fuel tank was empty, but apart from that it was untouched.'

'Thank you for all your help today, Chris.'

'I'm not sure if you can tell me, but is it Max's disappearance you're investigating?'

'No, I've been asked to find his brother-in-law, they went missing within weeks of each other, albeit in two separate countries.'

'Do you think they're connected?'

'No idea, probably not, it just bothered me that the two things happened so close together and I thought it warranted more investigation.'

'If in the course of your work you discover what happened with Max would you mind letting me know?'

'Of course not.'

After the phone call I thought about the way Chris had described Max and then I spent what felt like hours trying to discover travel routes from Bulgaria to the UK in the 1980s. Flights weren't as frequent and would've been expensive, and even then it would probably have been multiple flights. If I were attempting the same journey today without flying I could do it in a couple of days taking a combination of buses, trains, and ferries.

The abandoned stolen Jeep a few towns over might've been how Max started his journey. If he'd wanted to get back to the UK then my guess is this would be how he'd done it. I knew I was clutching at straws and worse still drawing conclusions from the very flimsiest of evidence, but it was just too much of a coincidence that Iris had lived in Max's home.

I sent Natasha a text asking her if she could find any other women who had been teenage foster children that also had a placement with the Thorogood's around the same time as Iris.

Chapter Thirty

I drove across to Sonya's lab in the hopes that she would be in, and it wouldn't be a wasted trip. I had to wait whilst she finished giving a live online lecture, but twenty minutes after I arrived, I was sitting in her office drinking coffee.

'Is there any way of telling if our skeleton man ever lived abroad?' I asked.

'Not easily, why, do you have someone in mind?'

'It's a weird one, Elspeth's husband, Max, disappeared from an archaeological dig in Bulgaria not long before Iain and Iris disappeared.'

'What happened to him?'

'They think he accidentally crossed into Kosovo and got shot, but there's a lot that doesn't feel right about that story, not least that his family were Iris' last family foster home.'

'You think he might be our man in the tree roots?'

'Maybe, have you got any other suggestions?'

'We're drawing a blank, have you told George your theory yet?'

'No, he'll tell me to come back to him with something more concrete.'

'I'd be happy to run some tests, even if all it does is rule Max out, but you know what I'm going to say don't you?'

'Speak to George first.'

'It is his investigation, at least as far as the police are concerned and they are the ones I'm meant to be working for,' Sonya laughed.

'Alright I'll talk to him and when he agrees, which he will, do you think it will take long to know if I'm right?'

'We'll use dental records, hopefully they'll still be available because whoever our man is he's had a few fillings.'

'Perfect, you'll let me know when you get the results?' I asked.

'Assuming I get the go ahead from George. But don't be expecting it to be a 2 minute job. First, I have to get the dental files and then they need to be looked at by a forensic odontologist.'

'Okay, I'll try to be patient.'

After leaving Sonya I drove to the hospital and found my way to Pamela Blackstock's ward.

'You said you were with the police?' The nurse asked.

'Yes, I'm a consultant. DCI Johnston tells me that you're planning to bring Pamela out of the coma next week?'

'That's right, she had some swelling in the brain after the attack but that's gone down nicely now, the doctors are confident that she'll make a full recovery, she's very lucky someone found her when they did.'

'Could she have died from her injuries?'

'Possibly, or at least have been left with long term damage to her brain. You don't expect it do you, I mean of course I know people get attacked, we see the worst of it in here sometimes, but you think you should be able to walk your dogs on the beach in the morning without this happening. Are the police any closer to finding out who's responsible?'

'We're hoping that she might be able to remember something when she wakes up that helps us.'

'And then that man was killed out for a walk in the hills,' the nurse continued.

'I know it's dreadful isn't it.'

'I'll leave you to sit with Pamela for a bit.' She pulled the curtain around the bed for privacy.

Pamela could've just been sleeping if it wasn't for the tubes and machines, I hoped the nurse was right and she did make a full recovery. She would be pleased to be reunited with Jock and Wallace, and I suspected they would be glad to be back with their owner.

Sitting in silence felt weird so I began to talk to Pamela, telling her that I thought Iris had been in some sort of trouble and I wondered if she'd confided in her sister. Then I told her about how Jock and Wallace were being spoilt by George and Mel, and about my dog sitting weekend and how upset they'd both got on our walk.

I paused mid-sentence, they had been fine until Elspeth had been nearby, it had been her scent that had triggered their behaviour.

'Now why would Elspeth cause such a reaction?' I asked Pamela. 'Had she ever interacted with them? If only you could answer that, I wonder if you ever took them to the bowling?' I patted Pamela on the hand. 'Only one way to find out – it's about time I met the rest of your team. Thank you Pamela, this has been most enlightening.'

A quick telephone call to the club later and I was on my way to the green to meet up with them. I'd driven past countless lawn bowling clubs, they seemed to be the mainstay in most Fife villages, but never had cause to go to one. Esther Smyth, the club secretary was waiting for me in the doorway.

'I've got everyone gathered in the club house, come on in and I'll get you a wee cup of tea.'

She led me through to an area that reminded me of a church hall turned into a café, – there were a couple of large metal urns over on a table. I was pleased to see a biscuit tin next to them.

'Right everyone, this is Rowan McFarlane,' Esther said. 'She's a private detective working with the police, and she's asked to have a chat with us today to help with the investigation into finding out what happened with our Pamela.'

There were collective hellos and then Esther brought me a cup of tea and the tin of biscuits and put them on the small table to my side. I would have preferred to sit down and talk to everyone on a one-to-one basis but Esther had stood me at the end of the room so I could address everyone like it was a lecture.

'Thank you for taking time away from practice, I really appreciate it. Like Esther said I'm looking to get a bit more information about Pamela, the dynamics of the team that sort of thing and I know that some of you have given statements to the police already, but there are some other angles I'm investigating, and I know that you're going to be able to help.'

'How's she doing?' A voice from the furthest away table asked.

'I've just come from the hospital – she looks comfortable, and the doctors are looking to bring her round soon, they're very hopeful she'll make a full recovery. Were you close?'

'Aye, we were.'

'What's your name?'

'Yvonne.'

'Thanks Yvonne, did you see much of each other outside of the bowling?'

'Pamela doesnae live that far away fae me, we normally walk oor dogs together morning and night.'

'Is that something you do every day?'

'Aye?'

'She's asking you if you should've been there that morning with Pamela,' Esther interjected.

'I had intended tae but then I got a call tae say that ma son, Bert had been in a prang in his car.'

'Who was the call from?'

'A man, said he was fae the AA, and that Bert had been taken tae the hospital for a check-up tae make sure he wasnae concussed.'

'What did you do?'

'Went tae the hospital right away of course. I called Pam and telt her I wasnae going to be able to make it.'

'And when you got to the hospital was Bert alright?'

'That was the weird thing, he wasnae there. The woman looked at me like I was daft. I was panicking because I'd tanked it along the road quick as I could and it had still taken me nearly twenty minutes, I got stuck behind a tractor.'

'What had happened, was your son okay?'

'Aye, there was nothing wrong wi' him, after I left the hospital I called the polis and they said they didnae know anything about an accident, so I drove to Bert's hoose and his car was still in the drive and it didnae look like it had been hit, I chapped his door and let me tell you he wasnae best pleased that I'd got him oot o' bed at that time on a Sunday morning, he was hanging oot his arse.'

There were muffled laughs from around the room.

'Did you tell the police all of this?

'No, they've no got tae me yet. I was looking after ma grandbairns when they came and spoke tae most o' the team.'

'Did you recognise the voice?'

'Naw, someone local though.'

'Thanks Yvonne, that's been really helpful. One more thing, where Pamela walked on Sunday morning, was that the route you usually took?'

'In the mornings aye, in the evenings we vary it.'

'Who else would know that?'

'We sometimes seen other dog walkers, you tend tae see the same folk over and over, and the team probably.'

I would get George to follow up the phone number that had sent Yvonne on a fool's errand.

'Did you all get on with Pamela?'

There was collective agreement.

'Anyone not get on so well with her, not that I'm saying anyone would hurt her but it helps me to get a picture of her life.'

'I didn't really know her that well, I tried talking to her a couple of times, but I don't think we had a lot in common apart from the bowling, but we'd say hello and pass the time of day and stuff, it's not like there was any hard feelings.' A blonde woman sitting nearest me said.

'Thanks, what's your name,' I said.

'Hazel

I made a note of it and then noticing her look of concern added, 'no one ever gets on with everyone,' so that she didn't feel too bad.

'There was a falling out between Elspeth and Pamela a few weeks back,' Esther said.

'Do you know what that was about?'

Esther shrugged, 'Elspeth can be a bit touchy, she has been part of the team a while, she's the type that likes to organise everyone and then Pamela joined, and she was popular, friendly, good at bowling. Better than Elspeth and I don't think she liked that.'

'So Pamela hadn't been on the team long then?'

'No, I persuaded her to come,' Yvonne replied. 'We were good neighbours, and I knew she'd played before in France or at least some version of it and I suggested she come along.'

'Do you get a lot of new members?'

'From time to time,' Esther replied. 'We have people who like to come as much for the social element, and we play at all different levels of course, and we mostly play in fours and the club has a men's team also.'

The rules of bowls were still beyond me, not that they were important. 'No one knows what Elspeth and Pamela fell out over though?'

Hazel said, 'Elspeth was a snooty cow. I might not've been best friends with Pam, but I can't stand Elspeth, she's always telling me what to do, I think it's because I'm the youngest in the group, but I've been playing since my teens, I had lots more experience than her and she doesn't like it if you speak back to her or disagree with her.'

'Elspeth has her good points as well though, she does a very good job of organising the fundraiser every year, she's on the events committee and I have to say things get done. But Hazel's right she does like things to be done her way and heaven help you if you don't like it.'

'Do you think it was Pamela replacing Elspeth on some of the teams that caused the problem between them?'

'I don't like to speak ill of people who aren't here to speak for themselves,' Esther said.

I hadn't specifically asked them to exclude Elspeth, I hadn't wanted to cast any suspicion on her. 'Where is Elspeth today?'

'I called her and said, someone from the police is coming to ask us a few more questions about Pamela and she said, I'm busy this morning and they know where to find me if it's important.'

'Is there anyone else who isn't here?'

'Cathy and Gillian, but that's because they're away down to York, they go this time every year.'

'Did Pamela ever bring her dogs to events here?'

'Dogs aren't allowed at the club, we need to make sure we keep the greens immaculate,' Esther said.

'She said Pamela was a liar,' a voice from one of the middle tables said.

I looked around for the person who had been speaking. She waved her hand.

'Hiya, I'm Susan. I was here one day and we were talking about the next fundraiser, I forget what it is and I said something about how Pamela used to be a pastry chef when she lived in France and she could maybe make use some nice cakes to sell and Elspeth sort of scoffed at it and said she doubted if Pamela could make a sandwich, and when I asked her what she meant, she said that Pamela was a liar and couldn't be trusted. She said she wasn't about to let a jumped-up secretary ruin her fundraiser.

I didn't know what she meant but I didn't want to argue so I just left it.'

I finished my tea as she spoke. 'Thank you, Susan, that's also helpful. Did anyone else know much about Pamela's life before she came to live here.'

There was a collective acknowledgement that everyone knew some things, the fact that she had been a pastry chef in France seemed to be the most prevalent.

'Thanks everyone for your time, I've left some of my business cards with Esther so if you think of anything else or you would like to talk to me privately, just call.'

Esther walked me to the door. 'Elspeth's not as bad as that sounded. She's difficult but until Pamela arrived there wasn't much disagreement amongst the team, Elspeth played well and in the confines of the game she had good team relations, yes she got a bit carried away with events and such but never anything vicious. It was when Pamela arrived that she got really riled up, if it hadn't been for the fact that Pamela seemed genuinely blind-sided by Elspeth's behaviour towards her, I would've sworn they had known each other at some point.' Esther paused, 'what I'm saying is, on Elspeth's part at least, this felt like a deeper issue than pastries and bowling, do you know what I mean?'

'I think so, let me know if you think of anything else.'

She smiled and stood in the doorway until I began to drive out of the car park, then she gave me a raised hand wave and went back inside.

Chapter Thirty-One

I was about to call George when my phone buzzed announcing that Natasha was calling.

'Hey, I just wanted to let you know that I couldn't find a Moran Hatfield on any database. I checked birth records at the hospital where Pamela was born, but I couldn't see any others with the same mother, not to say she didn't give birth there because I didn't find any record of Iris being born there either and for all we know she might've been married or divorced and changed her name in between times.'

'Okay, well it was a long shot anyway, but thanks for trying. Is George in the office just now?'

'He is, do you want me to buzz you through?'

'Yes please.'

'No worries, speak later.'

I listened to a couple of moments of hold music before hearing George's voice. 'How's it going?' He asked.

'I've had an interesting couple of days. You free for a chat, I could come to you if it's easier?'

'Sunshine Café, half an hour?' He replied.

'Honestly George, sometimes I get the distinct impression that you don't want people to know you're working with me,' I laughed. 'See you soon.'

It only took me twenty minutes to get to the Sunshine Café, the windchimes at the door jangled and the familiar and comforting smell of incense and baking hit my senses.

'Rowan, it's so nice to see you,' Mohammed came round the counter and hugged me.

'You too, don't tell me Star has finally decided to go home and get some rest before this baby arrives?'

'I've persuaded her to leave it to me now, but you know her, she still pops in just to check everything is running smoothly. We laughed. 'Are you here for business or pleasure today?'

'Business, George should be along soon.'

'No problem, I'll get your tea sorted, listen do you fancy trying this apricot and cardamon cake I'm experimenting with?'

'That sounds amazing, I'd love to.'

Mohammed had just delivered my order when George arrived, sitting down at the table across from me.

'Don't worry, your coffee is on its way,' I said.

'Thanks. Have you got any information to share or were you just missing me?'

'Yes and maybe to the information and always to the missing you,' I laughed.

'Can we start with the yes.'

'Obviously, I need to butter you up so that when I get to the maybe you agree with me.'

'Why do I already feel like I'm regretting meeting you?'

I smiled, 'So I went to see the lawn bowling ladies today and discovered that one of them, Yvonne Peterson, was really pally with Pamela, she said they walk their dogs together most days.'

'Then why weren't they together the day Pamela was attacked?'

Mohammed came across with George's coffee after which I relayed everything that Yvonne had told me. 'I've told her you'll be in touch, and someone will probably want to come and check out her phone to see if there's any details they can get about the caller.'

'Thanks Rowan, I can't believe we could've missed this. It changes things completely now doesn't it. Because now we know that the attack on Pamela was deliberate and planned.'

'Also, there must only be a very small pool of people who would know enough about their routine to be aware that they need to get Yvonne out of the way.'

'Good work. Now are you going to hit me with this maybe?'

'Okay, but you have to promise to let me finish before you say anything.'

'Fine.'

'As you know, I think this whole case, Pamela, the body in the tree and Seb are all connected somehow to Iris disappearing.'

George nodded.

I explained what Christopher Phillips had told me about Max's apparent death, the stolen car, and my theory of how Max would have returned to the UK. 'I think we, well you, should get Sonya to check Max's dental records against the skeletal remains.'

'Because you think that for some reason, Max Thorogood was prepared to risk his career, and his marriage to fake his own death and travel back to the UK to speak to some woman who used to be in foster care at his home?'

'Yes.'

'And you don't think that's clutching at straws?'

'The connections are there, I might not know exactly how they all link up yet, but I'm convinced I'm right.'

'When are you not?'

'How many times have I been wrong?'

George sighed.

'Look at it this way, you don't know who those remains belong to, it's not Iain and I'm guessing there aren't any other missing persons who match the general description. Max's body was never found, he was declared dead on the probability that he was but that doesn't mean he couldn't have done exactly what I've suggested and if I'm right we'll be so much further forward.'

'Or we'll have lots more questions and suspects.'

'At least they'll be the right questions and suspects though.'

George leaned back in his chair. 'Only you could come to these conclusions.'

'Aren't you lucky that I'm sharing them with you then.'

'Like you didn't already ask Sonya,' he said.

'I mean can you blame me, I'm a little offended she said I had to get your approval to be honest.' I laughed.

'Alright, I'll authorise it, but if you're wrong you don't get a do over.'

'Agreed.'

'Natasha said that you had her looking for a Moran Hatfield?'

'Yeah, I found some stuff, letters, diaries that sort of thing at Pamela's house, in her diaries she refers to someone named Moran and she has postcards from all over Europe from someone who signs themselves as Moran. I thought it was likely that it was her brother. The only other people in those entries are Iris and Gabriel.'

'Who's Gabriel?'

'He was her fiancé, he died though, looking through her diaries I don't think she ever really got over it.'

'I'll get Natasha to start digging into the mother's background, see if we can find out if she changed her name, and then track down birth records, hopefully that will help.'

'She's good, isn't she?'

'Natasha, she's keen.'

'But also good, I think she'd make a good detective, don't you?'

'Christ, next you'll be offering to write her a letter of recommendation.'

'I would but I have a feeling that might go against her.'

'She's good, and I know you like her, she's still got a lot to learn, but if there's an opportunity for Detective Constable, I'll put in a good word for her. Are you satisfied now?'

'Thank you.'

'What are you doing for the rest of the day, anything I need to know about?'

'I'm going home to FaceTime with Alana.'

'How's she getting on?'

'Good, but I think we're going to look at getting her a flat for next year.'

'Yeah, I can't say living in halls was something I enjoyed.'

'Didn't know you went to university.'

'Only for a year, couldn't stand it. Dropped out and worked on a building site for a year, then joined up. Right, I'd better get back to it, I'll give Sonya a call and no doubt she'll let you know when the results are in.' George finished his coffee in one gulp and left.

I was about to go when Mohammed came over, 'so what did you think of the cake?'

'It was lovely, it tasted warming and fresh, a definite winner.'

'Hopefully Star will agree, I don't want her to think I'm taking over whilst she's on maternity, but it's nice to be able to bring something new as well.'

'I'm sure she'll be delighted, tell her I said hello won't you.'

I was home with plenty of time before Alana was due to call me. It was great to see her face appear on the screen in front of me.

'Hey mum, good to see you're managing a case without someone trying to kill you for a change.'

I laughed, 'for now anyway.' I heard someone cough, 'is someone with you?'

'Umm, yes, I wanted to introduce you,' Alana looked away from the screen and made a motioning with her hand to make them come over. 'Mum, this is Xavier and we've been on a few dates so I thought it might be time for you guys to meet.'

Xavier smiled awkwardly, his cheeks colouring. 'Hi Mrs McFarlane,' he waved at me.

'Mrs McFarlane, what's wrong with you,' Alana teased. 'She's not you're primary one teacher and I already told you she wasn't married.'

'Sorry,'

'It's fine Xavier, but please for everyone's sake just call me Rowan. So how long have you two been going out.'

'Not long, but I told him I don't keep secrets from you and if he didn't want to meet you then I wasn't interested, luckily he passed the test.'

'As long as you are good to each other and safe,' I said.

'Ew mum, not now please.'

I held up my hands, 'I didn't say anything.'

'How's the case going?' Alana asked.

'I think it's slowly coming together, at least some things are starting to make more sense.'

'And the skeleton in the tree roots, any closer to knowing who he is yet.'

'Possibly, I'm waiting on Sonya coming back to me with some test results and if it is who I think it is then that makes everything much more interesting.'

'You had any luck tracking down the missing woman's family?'

'I found her sister, she's the woman that was attacked on the beach just before I took this case, do you remember?'

'I heard George talking about it on the radio, I think.'

'Anyway, now I need to try and find out where their brother is.'

'Why don't you just ask the sister?' Xavier asked.

'Because she's in a coma,' Alana and I said in unison.

Xavier blushed again and looked down at his knees.

'All I've got to go on is a first name, Moran, which is really unusual.'

'You mean like the Colonel?' Xavier asked.

'What do you mean?' I asked.

'Colonel Sebastian Moran, he was one of Sherlock Holmes' arch enemies, second only to Moriarty.'

'Xavier is studying English and English Literature,' Alana explained.

'Did you say Sebastian Moran?'

'Yeah, why, is that important?'

'I think it might be very important.'

'Why would you name your child after the villain in Sherlock Holmes, and not even the super famous one?' Xavier asked.

'I don't think she did – I think it was a nick-name, the question is why would that be your childhood nickname?'

Xavier shrugged, 'don't think I can help you with that one. I can send you some information on the character if you like.'

'Okay thanks, Alana will give you my details.'

'Right, I'm going to leave you to catch up properly,' Xavier said. 'I'll see you after,' he said to Alana before kissing her on the head and leaving.

'He seems nice,' I said, trying to process how I felt about her having a boyfriend.

'He is, he's sweet and I like that he's studying something different from me, all the guys on my course act like it's a competition and frankly they aren't taking very kindly to losing to a girl! Which is so outdated and pathetic, they're not all like that but there's a group who think they're something special.'

'I've known plenty of grown men like that, and I know I don't need to tell you to not let it bother you, but you keep doing what you're doing and don't even give them a second thought.'

'You've figured out who the brother, is haven't you?' Alana asked.

'I think so, I met a man called Sebastian a while ago, he had a Polish last name so I assumed he couldn't be anything other than a friend, but there's nothing to say that he didn't just change it.'

'Or maybe his father was Polish.'

'That's also a possibility.'

'You should ask him,' Alana said.

'I wish I could, he was murdered a few days ago, when he was out walking in the hills.'

'This means that whoever attacked that woman…'

'Pamela,' I interjected.

'Whoever attacked Pamela,' Alana said, 'probably killed Sebastian.'

'That's what I'm thinking as well, and I think it's the same reason that Iris and Iain vanished. The question is how did anyone know that they were related and what was it they knew that meant someone felt the need to kill them.' I told Alana about my suspicion the human remains belonged to Elspeth's husband and about the foster care connection.

'You have to go back to the foster home thing, it's the only thing that makes any sense to me,' Alana said.

'Me too, but you've no idea how hard it is to find people who were in the same foster placements as Iris.'

'Then don't focus on Iris, see if you can find anyone who was in care with Sebastian, it's possible that she confided in her brother and that in turn he might have told someone.'

She had a point, first I had to confirm my suspicions that Sebastian was in fact Pamela and Iris' brother.

Chapter Thirty-Two

When George knocked on my door I was on the verge of calling it a night and head to bed. Since Alana left for uni I'd found myself going to bed earlier to avoid sitting in a quiet house by myself.

'Hi Rowan, I hope this isn't too late?' He asked.

'Not at all, is everything alright?'

'Yeah, all good.'

'Is it something with the case?'

He shuffled awkwardly on the doorstep making me concerned for him. 'Are you going to come in?'

'Is that okay.'

'Of course, what's going on George, you're acting very weird.' I led him through to the kitchen.

'Sorry. I wanted to ask you something and now that I'm here I'm worried you'll think that I'm overstepping the mark.'

'Just spit it out, I'd rather know and be pissed off at you than we carry on like this.'

'It's about Mel…I'm going to ask her to marry me.'

'I don't know whether to hug you or hit you, I was starting to think there was something seriously wrong.'

'I wanted to show you the ring I got, I'm not sure if I should've waited and let her pick something herself, but I couldn't get down on one knee and have no ring, anyway I bought something I thought she'd like and then this afternoon I was looking at wedding websites and I began panicking that I'd got it wrong.'

'Let me see then,' I replied.

He reached into his inside jacket pocket and pulled out a black ring box and handed it to me. I carefully opened the lid and looked down on the stunning single ruby, set in gold.

'This is perfect,' I said smiling. 'You've made a really good choice, she will absolutely love this.'

'You think so?'

'I know so, ruby is her favourite stone. Have you told Becky yet?'

'You're the only person that knows, so if you could keep it to yourself.'

I ran my fingers across my lips and pretended to lock them at the other side the way primary school children do. 'Your secret is safe with me, what's the plan for asking her?'

'I'm going to wait until after this case is over, because I don't want to be interrupted by a call mid proposal.'

'Are you taking her somewhere special?'

'We had our first date at this really nice Moroccan restaurant, so I'm planning on taking her there.'

'Don't do it in the restaurant.'

'No?'

'No, you want it to be somewhere intimate. I mean I've never been proposed to so I could be wrong, but maybe go for a walk in the afternoon and stop somewhere pretty and do it, then the meal can be a celebration. And make sure you speak to Becky first, I know you two get on, but it'll be important to Mel that you've got Becky's blessing.'

'See this is the reason I came here. Thank you.' He paused. 'You don't mind, do you?'

'You asking my advice? Not at all.'

'No, I mean about me and Mel.'

'Of course not. Just don't ever hurt her or I will have to hunt you down and kill you,' I laughed.

'Sounds reasonable.'

'Right, I better get off home, unless you've solved the case this afternoon.'

'Well…'

'That's not even possible.'

'Not solved, but I think I've figured something out. I think Sebastian Wojcik is Pamela and Iris' brother.'

'There's absolutely nothing that ties them together – how have you got to that conclusion.'

'You remember that I told you about the postcards and the note in Pamela's diary?'

'Yes, they were signed Moran so we've been trying to find someone with that name.'

'Well, when I was talking to Alana earlier, her boyfriend, Xavier, who's studying English…'

'Alana has a boyfriend and you're alright with that?' George interrupted.

'Conversation for another time. Anyway, he said that there's a character in Sherlock Holmes called Sebastian Moran and it got me thinking – what if Moran was a nickname? Then someone killing Sebastian would make more sense.'

'I thought you said he was Polish.'

'Everyone said he was Polish, and he had a little bit of an accent and a Polish name.'

'And now you think he was faking being Polish?' George sounded unconvinced.

'No, I don't think he was faking it. I think that Sebastian's father was probably Polish, Pamela has postcards from Moran from Poland, maybe he was looking for his father. I don't know, anyway I was going to call you tomorrow to suggest that we do a familial DNA test on Sebastian's remains against the profile you hold for Pamela. What do you think?'

George moved his head, cracking his neck in the process. 'I think it's another long shot.'

'Doesn't mean I'm wrong though, does it?'

'I'll tell you what, I'll set Natasha on looking into Pamela and Iris' mother and finding out if she ever married someone with the surname Wojcik and if there's any chance your theory can be backed up by solid evidence I will arrange the DNA test, so you'd better hope your mate is as good a detective as you keep telling me she is.'

'Alright.'

'I've got to get home, thanks for your help with the ring and stuff,' he put the box back in his pocket and patted it.

Chapter Thirty-Three

> I've got the dental results, if
> you want to come over to
> the lab whilst I open them.

Sonya's text was brief but had me up and out the door quicker than most other things. I took a glance at myself in the rear-view mirror once I had parked. I looked more like I'd just done the walk of shame than was going to a meeting.

'Thanks for the heads up,' I said when Sonya met me at the door.

She smiled, 'couldn't bear to listen to you complain if you had to hear it from George. Speaking of him, he's also on the way. It only seemed fair that you were both here.'

'Any chance of a coffee?' I asked.

'I'll put the kettle on, have you had breakfast yet?'

'I had a slice of toast in the car, why what were you going to offer?'

'I have some muffins that Mohammed dropped round on his way into the café this morning. He's trying out some new things and I agreed to be his guinea pig.'

'Ooh fancy.'

'I'll take that as yes then.'

The door buzzed announcing George's arrival. He took off his coat and draped it over the back of one of the chairs in

Sonya's office and took a large gulp of the coffee that Sonya had made for him.

'Right, are you going to put us out of our misery?' George said to Sonya before turning to me, 'time to see if your hunch has paid off or if I'm going to have an uncomfortable chat with my boss explaining why I wasted so much money on a pointless test.'

I smiled, quietly confident.

Sonya opened the envelope, 'It came old school because the records are so old and haven't been digitised.' She paused for a moment whilst she read the file and looked at the x-rays that had accompanied it. 'Okay, we have a match. The dental records show an exact match to Max Thorogood.'

'I knew it!'

'God help me, are you going to be smug all day?'

'Probably. What will you do about telling Elspeth?'

'Have you got the details of the bloke you spoke to that Max was working with when he went missing in Bulgaria?'

'Christopher Phillips, yeah I'll email them to you.'

'I want to do a bit of digging before I bring the widow in, do you really think it's possible that she had no idea that he'd come back to the UK?'

'At this point I think anything is possible with her, she's given lies and half-truths at best, even the story she gave me about Max going missing was different from Christopher's account of it. I know it was a long time ago, but you'd think the disappearance of your husband would stick in your mind.'

'Maybe she's telling the truth and this Christopher bloke is lying.'

'What would he have to gain from lying to me?'

'What if he had Max smuggling artifacts out of the site to sell on the black market?' George said.

'Unlikely, he was part of a group that campaigned for repatriation of lots of artifacts that were taken during the time of the Empire.'

'That could be a cover.'

'It's possible,' I conceded without any real conviction.

Sonya had been sat sipping her coffee quietly watching our exchange. 'Shall I get the familial DNA organised for Sebastian Wojcik now?'

'Yes,' George and I said in unison.

'You do know it's me that makes these decisions, don't you?' He said.

'I like to let you think that,' I said smiling.

'If Sebastian is Pamela and Iris' brother doesn't that make it much more likely that it's Elspeth that's lying about Max's death? Where was she when he went missing?' Sonya said.

'Singapore.'

'Can we be 100% sure of that?' Sonya asked.

'I found letters amongst her parent's things when Iain went missing where she was replying to them saying that she couldn't come home just now and being very dismissive of the thought that anything bad had happened to Iain.'

'Could she have written them in advance and left them for someone else to post?'

'No, these were all responses, so if she wasn't in Singapore, she wouldn't receive the letter from them to respond to.'

'But she did eventually come back home?' George asked.

'Yes, she did. Although by then it looks like the missing persons case on Iain was already cold.'

'Was she ever interviewed by the police about her brother's disappearance?'

'There was nothing in the file that you gave me, I suspect they wouldn't have thought there to be very much point seeing as she was out of the country at the time and honestly, I think that they thought that Iain was gay, and I believe that had an impact on how hard he was looked for.' I said, glad that it had been before George's time in the force.

'Right, well we're not going to get to the bottom of this chatting through theories here are we,' George said. 'I need to be getting back to the station, see how Natasha is getting on locating Sebastian's birth record. What are you going to do with yourself?' He said to me.

'I'm going to go home and get tidied up and then I'm going to go and visit Mrs Wojcik and see what she knows about her husband's background.'

'How long for the DNA results?' George asked Sonya.

'A day or so, I'll ask for them to be put to the front of the queue, just a reminder though familial DNA isn't as cut and dry as parental DNA, if they're full brother and sister then it'll be a stronger match, with half siblings it will still be higher than unrelated people, but it's not the 99.9% that you see in paternity cases and it could mean that they are related but doesn't necessarily mean siblings.'

We both nodded.

'Good, I just wanted to set your expectations.'

Back home I phoned Maureen and after half an hour of catch up I asked if she would be willing to speak to Mrs Wojcik and ask her if I could come and see her this morning. I could have made the arrangement myself, but I knew that Maureen was friendly with the woman and a recommendation from her would probably stand me in good stead for getting Sebastian's wife to open up.

Chapter Thirty-Four

An hour later I was being shown into Mrs Wojcik's living room. There were photographs on the walls, several of which I presumed were of their children. Both it looked like had gone to university, and there were also pictures of younger children, probably their grandchildren.

'Do you want a cup of tea? I'm sorry I don't keep coffee, neither me nor Sebastian like…liked it.'

'Tea would be lovely Mrs Wojcik.'

'Please call me Donna.'

I sat on the brown leather sofa whilst she was in the kitchen, it was worn but still in very good condition. Looking around the room I thought it had probably been redecorated in the early 2000's with its colour scheme of chocolate browns and beiges.

'I only keep rich teas in the house,' Donna said as she put the cup of tea on the table in front of the sofa.

'That's lovely.' I replied.

'I don't have a sweet tooth you see, never have had. I'd rather eat a packet of crisps than a bar of chocolate, but sometimes a rich tea hits the spot, do you know what I mean?'

I smiled.

'Sorry, look at me, I'm rambling about biscuits when you have a job to do.'

'Don't worry about it, we can take as much time as you need.'

'What would you like to know?'

'When did you and Sebastian meet?

'1978. Me and some girlfriends were out for a night in Edinburgh, going to see something at the Playhouse, and in the interval I was in the queue for an ice-cream, I don't know if they still do that these days, have the ice-cream sellers down the front near the stage, anyway they did then. I'd been waiting for ages and starting to think that the second half would come on before I had got to the front of the line. Sebastian was in front of me, and I'd noticed him, of course, he was very handsome. Anyway, we get to the front of the line and he buys the last ice-cream. The woman says she's sorry but she's all out and the second half is due to start, and he looked at me and smiled and gave me his.' Donna was looking at her cup of tea her eyes watery at the memory.

'That was nice.'

'It was, he walked me back to my seat and we arranged to meet outside after the show, and then him and his friends walked me and mine to the train station. He took me on our first proper date a couple of days later and the rest as they say is history.'

'And you've got a couple of children,' I said pointing at the wall.

She beamed, 'Yes, Luca and Sasha and five grandchildren too.'

'That's lovely, were you all close?'

'Oh yes, Seb loved being a granddad and they worshipped him. He was a good father too, different from other dads.'

'How so?'

'Well take my brother Wullie, you've met him?'

'I did, the same day I met Sebastian.'

'Well him and Paula, they've got three kids and I don't think he ever did bath time or read them a story when they were little, but Seb, if he wasn't working lates, sometimes he had to with the roads, he'd say to me to take the load off and have a rest and he would play with them in the bath and then read stories. He took time off for school plays and parent's night. When they got older he went to all their games. It wasn't what I was used to, I loved my dad, and he was a good man, but you only got him in short bursts, like I used to help with the veg garden and him and Wullie went to the football, but you wouldn't have caught him doing the every day stuff. Wullie used to tease Seb and say he was doing women's work and Seb would say it's family work and ignore him.'

'What do you know about Seb's childhood?'

'Not very much, he didn't like to talk about it. When I met him, he'd not long come from Poland to find work. He'd travelled all over, we could never afford to go abroad with the children, it was so expensive then. Not like it is now.'

'Did his family come for the wedding?'

'No, his side was mostly friends. He said his parents were dead and he didn't know where his sisters were. It sounds bad but it was much more common then, not so easy to keep in contact with one another, no FaceTime then and if you didn't get a new address for someone then you'd lost contact.'

'Where abouts in Poland did he come from?'

'This is going to sound terrible, but I don't know. All I know is he was born in the UK and then moved to Poland to live later. I always figured that's why his English was so good, although Wullie always poked fun at his accent, not that it was very strong and my dad was unsure about me marrying him on the account of him being foreign,' she rolled her eyes. 'But I told him I was a grown woman, and I would marry Seb with or without his blessing. By the time we got married they'd made peace with one another, although they were never close.'

'This might sound like a strange question, but did Seb read a lot of Sherlock Holmes?'

Donna frowned, 'it's weird that you say that, after Seb's death was in the news I got a call from a man sending me his condolences, he said that he'd been friends with Seb when they were kids and his name was Jim Moriarty and I thought that's odd, just like in Sherlock, but I didn't say anything to him because, well he was the baddy wasn't he and it sounds awfully impolite to call someone a villain, even if it's just in fiction. Seb did like to read though, I'd never known anyone read as much as him. Wullie once told him to tone it down when he was at work because it made the other lads think he was weird.'

'Did Jim leave a contact number?'

'No, I'm afraid not.'

'Did Seb and your brother get along?'

'So-so, Wullie looked out for him on site, and I was grateful for that, my brother was a big bruiser of a man in his younger days and those that would've been likely to bully Seb wouldn't have risked crossing Wullie. I'm not saying that Seb was soft or couldn't look after himself, it just wasn't his nature, he always said why throw a punch if instead you can walk away.'

'That sounds like a pretty sensible way to live.'

'I agree, but back then if you weren't willing to get into a brawl you were seen as a bit limp wristed and I know that's not an okay thing to say, I don't want you to think that I have any prejudices, I don't. Our oldest grandchild, he's called Seb after his granddad, he came out as gay last year, he's only fourteen. Seb told him it was all good, being happy and safe was the most important thing.'

'Do you remember Seb's friend Iain?'

'Oh yes, thick as thieves those two, he was a reader too, an academic, no idea what he ended up doing on the roads, they were close, them and another man, Mark maybe…no I think it was Michael.'

'And Seb went to Iain's wedding?'

'We both did, his wife Iris was stunning, proper hippy type, but with her feet on the ground. They made a good match I thought. He went missing not long after that. No idea what happened to her though.'

'They both went missing,' I said.

'How strange. And you're looking for them, are you?'

'I'm trying, but it was a very long time ago and that makes it harder.'

'Maureen's your gran, is that right.'

I nodded.

'She's such a nice woman, when Seb went missing she was over here making sure I was eating and she still phones me every day you know.'

I smiled, Maureen was one of the kindest, most selfless people I'd ever known, and I loved her for it. 'She's very good like that.'

'That's why when she said, did I mind having a chat with you this morning I was quite happy to. She speaks very highly of you, you know, she's ever so proud.'

I blushed.

'Maureen tells me that if anyone can find out what happened to Seb it's you.'

'I will do my best and DCI Johnston who's in charge of the case is a very good detective, I'm sure that between us we'll find who killed him.'

A tear splashed down her face, 'I can't believe he's gone. I don't understand what possible reason there could be for someone to want him dead. None of it makes sense.'

I moved to sit beside her, putting my arm around her shoulder. She rested her head against me as silent tears soaked through my top.

'Goodness,' Donna said sitting up. 'I'll get hold of myself. Sorry about that.'

'Nothing to be sorry for, I understand what it feels like to lose someone you love like this.'

'Maureen is right, you are lovely. Thank you for taking an interest in Seb, I'm glad you met him, it makes a difference I think.'

'Are you going to be by yourself for the rest of the day?' I asked.

'Sasha is coming for lunch, she still lives in Cuddieford, it's been a godsend having her so close. Luca is in Edinburgh so he doesn't get over as easily, but he's coming this weekend which will be nice, a full house will keep my mind occupied.'

'That's good.' I was relieved that I wasn't going to be leaving her alone for the rest of the day.

'Do you know when they'll be releasing his body? I want to plan the funeral and people keep asking me and I don't know what to tell them.'

'I'll speak to George, DCI Johnston, this afternoon to see if someone can get in touch with you and let you know a timescale.'

Chapter Thirty-Five

I'd left Donna's house even more convinced that Moran and Sebastian Wojcik were the same person and that he was the brother of Iris and Pamela. Had he known that his friend Iain was marrying his sister, had he been in contact with Iris? Had that been how she'd met Iain? How much did Iain know about his wife's family, did he realise that his best mate was also his brother-in-law? I had so many questions, and no one to give me answers.

George phoned and disrupted my thoughts.

'I was planning on phoning you this afternoon,' I said.

'What's up?' He asked. 'How did your visit with Mrs Wojcik go?'

'She was lovely, that's one of the reasons I was wanting to speak to you. She really wants to know when you're going to release Seb's body so she can start planning the funeral. Is there any chance someone can check in with her and give her a timescale sometime soon?'

'Of course, anything else interesting come out of your conversation?'

'Bits and pieces and now I'm convinced that he's the brother. Anyway, what were you calling for?'

'I wanted to tell you that I'm planning on going to see Elspeth tomorrow morning and tell her we've found her husband's remains and I was wondering if you would like to come?'

'Definitely. It will be interesting to see how she reacts.'

'That's what I thought. I'm going to get Natasha to come along, the old woman seems to like her and just because we think she's a bit suspicious doesn't mean I want to lose sight of the fact we're about to tell her for sure her husband is dead.'

He was right, Elspeth might be a liar and a pain in my arse but all the same this news was potentially devastating to her.

'I'll pick you up at 9am tomorrow.'

I decided to call Michael Swanage. It had been a little while since our meeting and perhaps he might be more willing to talk about whatever it was he was holding back on then.

'Hello,' he said. 'I wasn't expecting to hear from you again so soon, have you had any joy tracing Iain and Iris?'

'Not yet, I know this is a bit out of the blue but are you alright to chat for a bit?'

'Yeah, yeah, I've got a bit of free time just now.'

'Thanks. I was just visiting with Donna Wojcik this morning, Sebastian's widow, do you remember her?'

'Vaguely. I know he was besotted with her, he was a real family before everything else kind of man, suppose that makes sense given his childhood.'

'What happened in his childhood?' I asked.

'Oh, um, I don't know the specifics he always said that he'd been let down by those people who were meant to look out for him. I figured he meant his parents that's all.'

'Did he have any siblings? Donna thought there was a sister.'

'Not sure, might've done.'

'You ever meet her?'

'Don't think so.'

'Wouldn't you remember meeting your best mate's sister.'

'Guess I never met her then.'

'What did you know about Iain's relationship with his siblings?

'It was alright I think, he wasn't close with either of them, his mum had tried to keep him under her control for as long as possible, her blue-eyed boy. He hated it and I think it drove a wedge between him and his brother and sister.'

'What about his brothers in law?'

'He wasn't keen on Stewart, thought that he was domineering, said that he was concerned for Rodger.'

'In what way?'

'He thought that Rodger wasn't happy with Stewart but that he was putting up with it because he was afraid to leave.'

'Was Stewart violent towards Rodger?'

'I don't know, but I got the impression that he was controlling. He had a temper on him though. He came down to site one time and had a huge barny with Iain over something, I've no idea what. Wullie and a couple of the lads had to physically remove him.'

'And Iain never mentioned what it was about?'

'I didn't really know him as well then, he'd only been on the job a little while. Seb would've been the one who might've known, not that that's any good to you now.'

'Did Seb and Iain meet at work?'

'As far as I know, I'm not sure where else they would've met.'

And what about Max, Elspeth's husband, how did he get on with Iain?'

'He said he wouldn't spit on him if he was on fire.'

'Do you know why there was so much animosity between them?'

'All he would say is you can only fake being a good person for so long, eventually something comes along and shows you for who you really are.'

'And he didn't ever elaborate on what he meant by that?'

'Not to me.'

'Do you know someone called Jim Moriarty?'

'From Sherlock? Are you taking the piss?' Michael half laughed.

'No, I'm not. I think he's someone from Seb's past.'

'And that's his real name, is it?' I could her the condescension in his voice.

'I've no idea, he contacted Donna to give his condolences and I'm trying to track him down. You've never heard of him?'

'Sorry, no.'

'Did you ever hear Seb go by the nickname 'Moran'?'

'That's weird, why would anyone call him that?'

'No reason. Have you thought of anything else that might be relevant since we last spoke?'

'I've racked my brains, but like you said it's been a long time, a lot of water's gone under the bridge since.'

'Alright, thanks for having a chat with me today and you know, if anything springs to mind give me a shout straight away.'

'Okay will do.'

'One last thing before I go, has anyone else been in contact with you asking you about Iain and Seb, besides the police I mean.'

'No, why?'

'Curious that's all.'

I ended the call even more sure that Michael knew a lot more than he'd shared with me. I thought about heading back to Nairn and running some surveillance on Michael, but I doubted his day-to-day activities were likely to give away forty year old secrets.

Chapter Thirty-Six

The next morning George arrived outside my house at 8.50am.

'Before we set off let's set some ground rules,' he said. 'You're coming along as a courtesy and as an observer, that means keep your mouth zipped and let me do the talking, unless she asks you a question. Natasha, I need you on the tea and sympathy. From what I've seen she's already warmed to you; she doesn't see you as a threat or someone of authority so she's more likely to open up to you.'

'Gee thanks,' Natasha said.

'It's a good thing,' I said. 'It means you've won her trust, that's important, especially when neither George nor I are particularly in her good books lately. She'll feel like you're on her side and it's essential that she has someone in her corner.'

'Rowan is right, keep playing to that, even if it means shooting us dirty looks. I give you my permission. If it helps build the bond between you and Elspeth, lean into it.'

George pulled up in the gravel drive outside Elspeth's house, she was at the door before we had got a chance to knock. She scowled in my direction, 'you've brought an entourage this morning, I see.'

'Actually Mrs Thorogood, Rowan is accompanying me this morning and I think you know my colleague Natasha Findlay?'

She smiled towards Natasha, 'I suppose you'd better all come in. I'll put the kettle on.'

'I can do that for you,' Natasha said.

'That's very kind. Do you remember where everything is from last time?'

Natasha nodded and Elspeth led us through into the living room. 'I have to say I'm fascinated to discover what's brought all of you to visit me today, but I suspect I can guess.'

'You can?' George asked.

'It's obvious isn't it. You two here together,' she pointed at where George and I were sitting, 'and then Natasha on tea duty, you've come to tell me you've found my brother's remains and I wouldn't be shocked if they, as I've suspected since they were discovered, are the ones in the wood and somehow your pathologist made a mistake.' She looked smug standing by the fireplace looking down on us on the sofa.

Natasha came through and put the mugs on the wooden coffee table before taking a seat in one of the armchairs.

'I'm afraid we're not here about your brother Mrs Thorogood,' George said.

'Oh for goodness sake, call me Elspeth.'

'I think it would be best if you were to sit down, Elspeth,' George continued.

Elspeth let out an overly dramatic sigh but did as requested.

'We've come this morning about your husband, Max Thorogood.'

'What about him?' Elspeth asked.

'I regret to inform you that the remains recently uncovered in the woods off the A921 have been confirmed to be that of you husband.'

Elspeth's jaw dropped, the colour draining out of her cheeks. 'that's…that's not possible. Max died in Bulgaria.'

'I understand that is what you've always believed however we are satisfied that these are your husband's remains.'

'But how, I don't understand. Max dead and in the UK, it can't be, it just can't be.'

George said nothing, I had questions, lots of them, but for once I kept my mouth shut and my promise to George.

'I know this must have come as quite a shock, and I do have questions that I need to ask, we can come back if you don't feel up to it.'

Elspeth was quiet for a few moments, she gathered herself, 'you're here now so we might as well get on with it,' she said, returning to her usual terse tone.

'Thank you. You previously told Rowan that your husband went missing in Bulgaria where he was part of a dig, is that right?'

'He *did* go missing in Bulgaria, I didn't make it up, you can check with the other people on the dig.'

'I wasn't suggesting that you made it up,' George said. 'I'm merely trying to gather all the details for myself as the investigation into his death is now being actively carried out by my team.'

'And your team includes a private detective, does it?'

'Whilst it is unusual, I'm happy to say that on this occasion it does, Rowan has worked with me on a consultancy basis several times before and I have always found that when she does, it helps to achieve a satisfactory outcome, which I am sure you would be delighted to have in this case.'

I inwardly smiled; it was rare to hear George talk about my contribution to any investigation outside of our own conversations.

'Well, it's not like I'm keeping secrets from her,' Elspeth said before turning to address me, 'I did hire you after all to find my brother, not that you seem to be getting very far on that account.'

'I am making progress,' I said. 'But as we discussed in the beginning, finding someone who went missing four decades ago was always going to be a long and challenging process.'

'When were you informed that Max was missing?' George said.

'I can't remember the exact date, I just remember being really cross because it was some time afterwards and I thought that was utterly shocking.'

'I spoke to Christopher Phillips yesterday, you may not know the name, but he was the archaeologist in charge of the dig, and he suggested that he informed you when your husband had been missing only a day or so.'

'I don't want to call the man a liar, but I will say he must be misremembering.'

'I'm a little confused about something then, that hopefully you'll be able to clear up for me.'

'I'll do my best.'

George opened the leather document holder that he'd been carrying and took out an A4 poly pocket with a photocopy of a document inside. I tried to lean back to get a look at it without seeming too obvious, it appeared to be a list, typed on an old typewriter, but at this angle it was difficult to read.

'As I mentioned, I spoke to Mr Phillips yesterday and he was kind enough to send me over some documentation relating to your husband's disappearance. You'll see here that this is an itemised list of your husband's possessions left at the dig site,' George leaned forward handing the page to Elspeth.

'So,' she said handing it back to him.

'Well on the next page is a photocopy of a plane ticket for a student from the dig who was returning to the UK not long after Max's disappearance and Mr Phillips made me aware that you had requested you husband's possessions be returned to the UK.'

'What are you getting at?'

'If you didn't know that Max was missing then how did anyone know where to return his things to?'

'Had it occurred to you that perhaps this man, Mr Phillips, might've got his wires crossed and that he did not speak to me as I have said from the beginning and in the absence of me, he contacted my brother Rodger and arranged everything with him?'

'Are you saying that's what happened?'

'I'm saying that would seem infinitely more plausible than suggesting that *I* am lying about discovering that the man I loved was missing.'

'I'll be sure to pay a visit to your brother-in-law shortly and look into that. Can you think of any reason your husband would have to want to return to the UK without telling you?'

'Absolutely not.'

George sat back slightly, 'why don't you have a little think.'

A look of anger flashed across her face, 'I don't know how old you are detective, but communication in the 1980s was not as simple as sending someone a text and when you're out on a dig there's usually no way of getting in contact with someone without travelling to the next town and even then, depending on where you are it can be very difficult. It's also possible that he did try to contact me but for the same sort of reason I was uncontactable.'

'I understand that, but surely your husband would've found some way of getting in contact with you between leaving Bulgaria and being in Scotland?'

'If he did try, I didn't know about it.'

'Okay, why would Max leave a dig he was working on without telling any of his colleagues?'

'Max could be hot headed, he excelled in his own field, and he didn't much like being told what to do, I can imagine that working for other people rather than running the dig himself would have got his goat.'

'Then why agree to be part of it?'

'Because of the chance to uncover another temple, you can hardly imagine the excitement of being involved in such an epic find.'

'But you think that wouldn't have been enough to keep him there if he'd had a falling out with someone.'

'I can't tell you what was going on in Max's head, all I know is he must've had a good reason to leave like that.'

'Max didn't accompany you to your brother Iain's wedding, is that right?'

Elspeth frowned, 'yes, he was too busy, and the tickets were too expensive.'

'But you would've shown him pictures when you went home?'

'I imagine so.'

'And when he looked at them, did he mention that he knew Iris, your new sister-in-law?'

'What do you mean?'

'As you might remember, Iris spent much of her childhood in care and one of her placements was in Max's family home. Did you know his parents did fostering?'

'I did, but I think you might be jumping to conclusions if you're suggesting they knew each other. It's very possible that Max didn't even live there at the same time as her.'

'We checked and he did, are you saying that he didn't tell you?'

'What has this got to do with finding out who killed Max? Unless you're saying that you suspect it was Iris in which case I would agree and think that's very likely.'

'That's interesting, what was it about Iris that would make you think she would kill your husband, despite him never telling you he knew her?'

'All I'm saying is that she was the sort of person I could see killing someone, I always thought she had cold, dead eyes,' she paused for a moment. 'Could we continue this another time, I think it's only now sinking in that Max is dead, I've known for a long time, but now that he's been found I realise that there was always a part of me that hoped I was wrong.'

'Of course. Natasha can stay with you for a little while, but is there anyone else you'd like us to call, your brother-in-law maybe?'

'No, I'll be fine, I think I need a lie down that's all.'

'We'll get out of your hair then, I can come back later with any follow up questions if necessary.'

Chapter Thirty-Seven

'She was lying,' I said as George and I drove away from Elspeth's house.

'I agree, I think she had a good idea that Max had come to the UK.'

'Don't you think she looked genuinely shocked when you said he was dead?'

'I did. But where did she think he was all this time?'

I didn't say anything for a few moments, whilst I tried to organise the thoughts in my head.

'You have a theory, don't you?'

'I think Elspeth did know that Max knew Iris, what if the reason Iris was moved from the Thorogood household wasn't at her request but because someone discovered that she and Max were having a relationship, which would explain why she was removed so quickly.'

'And you think that he would ditch his marriage and his career to come back to the UK to try and rekindle a brief teenage romance?'

'I'm sketchy on the details, but I think seeing Iris again, for whatever reason, is what triggered Max to return to the UK and I think Elspeth either knew or suspected that. What if when Elspeth saw Pamela and mistook her for Iris, she wasn't trying to find out about her brother...'

'She was trying to find out about Max, because for whatever reason she thought they were together?

'Where does Seb fit into all of this, as far as we know he didn't know Max or Elspeth and we're not even a hundred percent certain that Seb, assuming that he is their brother, knew he was watching his sister getting married.'

I rubbed my eyes, 'when will Pamela wake up?'

'Should be in the next day or two, you think she might be able to give us some answers?'

'Hopefully, although if she did know Seb, it's terrible that she's going to wake up to the news that he's been murdered. I'd like to know what Elspeth had said to her though, that should at least tell us if she was looking for Max or Iain.'

I looked out of the window, 'how far is it from Elspeth's to the beach at Aberdour?'

'Ten to fifteen minutes drive, why?'

'I don't know, I was thinking about the day Pamela was attacked that's all. Elspeth said that she went to speak to Pamela, thinking she was Iris because she thought if she got her alone and off guard she would admit the truth, but Pamela always walked her dogs with Yvonne in the morning.'

'Yvonne?'

'Her friend from the bowling club, remember I told you she got a call to say her son had been in an accident.'

'Oh yeah, are you thinking that Elspeth sent her on that fool's errand?'

'If she did, she had help, Yvonne said it was a man that called her.'

'You don't think she was working with Seb?'

'No, not at all.'

'Who then?'

I shook my head, 'I don't know.'

'I need to get back to the station, where do you want dropping off?'

'I'll walk into town from the station car park.'

DC Liz Collins was peering out of the upstairs office window as we pulled into the car park and before we had got out of our seats she was striding across the tarmac towards us. She made a show of saying hello to me and smiling, I knew she was only attempting to be nice because George was here. I smiled back.

'I've discovered something I think you'll find quite interesting,' she said, her back towards me creating a human barrier between George and me. And as much as I wanted to know the interesting thing she had found out I was sure that there was no way she'd reveal it with me around and besides George would let me know later on if it was really that important.

'Thanks for the lift,' I said.

'You not staying?' He asked.

'No, I'm sure DC Collins wants to fill you in without me hanging around.'

She scowled.

'We can talk later,' I continued, knowing that the knowledge that whatever she had uncovered was going to be shared with me no matter how much she'd like to exclude me would bug her.

It was a decent day for the time of year, cold, but not windy or rainy, I slowed my usual quick pace and made the walk to the Sunshine Café leisurely, thinking over the case as I went. I could come up with several theories which would explain Elspeth wanting to hurt Iris, she probably thought that somehow Iris ran off with her husband and betrayed her brother, but what I couldn't get to add up was why that would lead to Seb being murdered. It was like buying a jigsaw puzzle second hand only to discover you don't have all the pieces and can't properly see the picture.

By the time I jingled the windchime on the door of the café I was glad to be back indoors and looking forward to a cup of camomile tea. Mohammed waved to me from the kitchen and one of their regular waitresses greeted me.

A few moments later Mohammed was walking towards me with a small tray. 'Hi Rowan, I guessed you wanted your usual, but I can change it if I'm wrong.'

'That's perfect,' I replied.

'And a slice of the traditional raw carrot cake with a cardamom and mango biscuit on the side for you to try out.'

'Thank you. You do realise that Star is never going to let you go if you keep doing as good a job as this, don't you?'

He leaned in as if he was pretending to whisper, 'don't tell anyone, but that's the plan,' he laughed. 'I'm loving it here, I don't want to step on Star's toes, this is her business, but we've been talking and she'd like to be with the baby as much as she can so this works out for us both and Chantelle has set herself up with her own wee business doing other people's ironing, I never knew there were so many people who didn't like doing it and she loves it.'

'I'll know where to send mine then, I'm so pleased the two of you are settled.'

'Me too, anyway, better get back to it.'

I took a bite of the biscuit, it melted in my mouth and the infusion of flavours was fabulous. I checked my phone to see if there was any update from George on Liz's interesting discovery, there was nothing from him, but I had missed a call from a number I didn't recognise. I checked my voicemail, nothing. I returned the call.

'Hello?' The voice that answered said.

'Hi, this is Rowan McFarlane, I missed a call from this number.'

'I dunnae ken if you'll remember me, it's Yvonne...'

'From the lawn bowling club,' I said.

'Aye, that's right.'

'Have you thought of something else that might help find out who hurt Pamela?'

'I'm no sure, but something happened this mornin and I thought it might be important, or at least the kind o' thing you'd like to know aboot.'

'What happened?'

'I think it would be easier to show you rather than just tell you, is there any chance you could come round to mine?'

I inwardly groaned, one of the rare occasions I didn't have my own car, I would need to take a taxi and hope that it was worth it. 'Of course, I've got a couple of things to finish up first,' I looked at my almost full mug and uneaten cake, 'and then I'll come over, can you text me the address.'

I finished my food quicker than I would've preferred and headed towards the door.

'Just a flying visit today?' Mohammed asked.

'Someone wants to talk to me about the case I'm working on, and I need to go hunt down a taxi.'

'You can take my car if you like.'

'Are you sure?'

'Yeah, I'll be here all day so as long as you're back before about 6.30pm it'll be fine.'

'You're a life saver,' I kissed him on the cheek.

'Come round the back and I'll meet you in the car park.'

Mohammed's car was an old Volvo estate, ideal for picking up supplies from the cash and carry. 'Thank you for this,' I said climbing into the driver's seat.

When Yvonne had told me she lived close to Pamela I hadn't realised she meant three doors down. She was stood at her front door waiting for me as I pulled into her driveway.

'I appreciate you coming oot like this,'

'No trouble at all, thanks for calling,' I said as I joined her on the front doorstep.

'Now this might be nothing,' Yvonne said, 'but I thought it was better to tell you aboot it and you decide it doesnae matter than me.'

'What happened?'

'It was about 10am and I was having a wee cup o' tea, and the dogs started yapping, like they are the noo. They do that when the delivery folk come, so I looked oot the window, because I'm no expecting anyone.'

'Was it not likely to be for one of your neighbours?'

'Unlikely, Ralph next door he died six months ago, he was 94, so nothing for you to worry about. Then the one next door to Pamela, it's one of these bloody air bnbs – hate it, anyway that's empty. And then of course there's Pamela and, well she can't have been ordering anything.'

'And what was it?'

'A blue car, and it's stopped ootside Pamela's, at first I thought maybe it was yoursel' or the polis, but I come oot to the front garden just to hae a wee check, pretend like I'm watering the roses. And it's a man, white hair, tallish, red raincoat, anyway it triggers something in ma brain and I realise I've heard that description before, the polis said they were looking for someone with that description in connection with killing Pam's brother.'

It was all I could do not to interrupt Yvonne at this point, Seb was Pamela's brother and if Yvonne knew then that meant Pamela knew. I would come back to it, but only when she'd finished telling me all the events of the morning.

'He's peering through the living room window, then he walks over tae the front door and tries the handle, starts thumping his shoulder into it like he's trying to break it doon. I wasnae concerned though, these doors are solid like.'

'Did he see you?'

'Oh no, I was very careful, come o'er.' She led me to the rose bushes that separated her front garden from the next. They were tall and made for good camouflage. 'Why don't you go up tae Pam's and take a casual glance o'er here and you'd no notice me.'

I did as she suggested and from the front of Pamela's house you wouldn't see Yvonne through the roses, which was just as well, if it had been Seb's murderer then Yvonne might've put herself in danger. I came back along the path.

'You're right,' I said.

'I heard him go roond the side tae the garage, so I nipped oot intae the road and took doon the make, model and registration o' the car, then I went back indoors. A few minutes later I see the car drive back doon. What do you think?'

'I think you did the right thing giving me a call and that this might be very important.'

'Hmm, that's what I thought. You want tae come in for a cuppa?' She asked.

'That would be great.'

'You know before Pamela, that hoose had been rented oot for the last five years. When it went up for sale I worried what type o' neighbour I might be getting – you never know these days do you. But then Pam moved in, I saw the photos in the ad online and the place was an absolute state inside. She did it up real nice, of course her brother did a lot of the work.'

'Seb?'

'That's the one, only I didn't realise he was her brother at first because he had a bit o' an accent and I thought, to my shame, that he was hired help. But then Pam explained, same mum, different dad.' Yvonne put a mug of tea in front of me and sat down in the brown leather armchair.

'You and Pamela were really close?'

'I'd say she was ma best friend, but that makes us sound like school bairns.'

It's strange how as we get older that some things start to sound wrong, I thought, like best friend and boyfriend.

'I didnae marry and some folk think that's odd. But I went into the army, not as infantry, you couldn't do that as a woman when I was younger, I went in as a post person,' she paused. 'People laugh when I say that, because they think o' me wondering aroond barracks posting letters, but that's not what it is. I was oot in the first Iran-Iraq war, sometimes documents need delivering in person and by then I had the sort o' clearance that allowed that, so I would hae to have an armed escort from one place to another.'

Having spent a little bit of time with Yvonne it didn't surprise me at all that she'd had an interesting life.

'Had Pamela and Seb been raised apart?' I asked not wanting to seem impolite but desperately wanting to get the conversation back on topic.

'Aye. They were all with their mother in the beginning, but then she got sick, reading between the lines I always thought it was drugs, but I could be wrong.'

I said nothing, not wanting to betray either the investigation or Pamela's privacy, if she'd chosen to keep it from her closest friend then it wasn't my secret to tell.

'After their mum died, Seb's father took him in, he'd married or remarried, again I dunnae know the details and for a while they went back to Poland to live, that's where his father was fae and I understand they lost contact for quite a while when they were younger. Pamela lived for a long time in France, not sure if you knew that.'

'Do you know what brought her back to Scotland?' I asked.

'Finding her brother. Not sure how they managed it, but I know she was keen to rebuild that relationship and that was happening, she'll be heart broken when she wakes and finds oot he's deed. I'm guessing you think the two things are connected,' she looked at me, her eyes narrowing in thought for a brief moment. 'Not that you'd be able to tell me.'

'What about their other sister, had they managed to track her down?' I asked thinking it was worth taking a punt and asking the question.

'Irene…no, Iris, I think. Pam couldnae believe it that Seb had been in contact wi' her for years, she couldnae wait to be reunited.'

I tried not to let the gravity of what she had just said show on my face, hoping that my poker face was still strong after months of Zoom and telephone only communications.

'I never met her though,' Yvonne frowned.

'What is it?'

'I'm no sure, but I got the impression that there was something…going on there. She asked me not to talk aboot her family with anyone else, particularly at the bowls, that was just after her and Elspeth had that falling oot. To be honest I'm only telling you now because I think it's the right thing to do and that it might help catch whoever did this.'

'I'm sure Pamela would agree,' I said. 'What did you mean when you said you thought there was something going on there?'

'I can't quite put my finger on it, but I wondered if this Iris might've been in prison or maybe a nursing home, that there was some reason that she couldnae come tae Pamela.'

'Have you mentioned any of this to anyone else?' I asked.

'Oh no, I wouldnae.'

'That's good,' I said, not sure if she realised how much risk her knowledge put her in. 'I hope you don't mind but I'm going to need to share this with DCI Johnston and he might want you to make an official statement about what happened this morning.'

'That's fine.'

'If you see this man again, you should phone the police,' I added.

'Will do.'

'I'd better be off, I borrowed my friend's car to come here and he'll want it back.'

'Do you no hae your own car?'

'I do, just not with me when you called.'

I said goodbye to Yvonne and headed back into town, the Volvo was a bit older than my car with no hands-free capability so the news that Iris was very much still alive and that Pamela had known this would have to wait until I got to the police station for me to share it with George.

Chapter Thirty-Eight

Mohammed was busy serving when I parked the car, so I gave the keys to one of the waitresses and started to walk towards the station. Checking my phone, I saw that I had a missed call from George.

I dialled his number.

'I wondered when you'd come back to me,' he said when he answered. 'That information Liz found out, I think you'll find it very interesting.'

'We can do an exchange then,' I said telling him that I'd been out to see Yvonne. 'I'm on my way over to you now.'

'I'll ask Natasha to come down to meet you and bring you up to my office.'

We hung up, no point trying to have a conversation over the phone when we would be face to face in a few moments. It was getting colder, my breath billowed out clouds of steam as I quickened my step, intrigued by what Liz had discovered.

Natasha was stood behind the front desk when I went in, she buzzed me through and we walked up the stairs together.

'Being summoned into the inner sanctum again, you must've done something right,' she laughed.

'Either that or I've done something wrong, it's one of the two. How do you get on with Liz Collins?'

'She's alright, she's had to take a lot of stick from some of the others since she transferred here.'

We were almost at the top of the stairs but I stood still eager to finish this conversation first. 'Why?'

Natasha frowned, 'I thought it was common knowledge.'

'Maybe in here, but all I know is that she doesn't like me because of what happened after Jack died.' I knew that Natasha knew who I was, she'd said as much when we first met so there was no need to go over old ground.

'Not sure why she would care, she wasn't even here then. I'm guessing she was trying to fit in, if she was agreeing with some of the more vocal people against you then they weren't focussing on her.'

'What happened, why did she need to transfer?'

'She told her boss that she believed a local politician was soliciting underage girls, she didn't have solid proof, her information had come from one of the women that she had used as an informant in the past. The woman was a prostitute, so it was brushed off as being not credible.'

'What did she do about it?'

'She started investigating and was told to stand down, she went out on a date and didn't realise the guy was a journalist, had one too many drinks and gave him the story. Do you really not remember it being in the papers?'

I shook my head.

'To be honest, it might have been at the same time as...' she paused for a moment. 'Your dad was killed.' She finished.

'Can't say I was giving much time to the headlines then. That was a while before she came here though, wasn't it?'

'She was suspended, previously she'd been a DS and part of her punishment was a downgrade and a transfer.'

'That must've stung.'

'Especially as before that she was the golden girl, on the fast track for DI.'

It didn't make me like her any more, the way she'd behaved towards me last year had been unacceptable, but I did understand that she was trying to keep her head above water and make working here tolerable, although I'd like to think that if George had any idea that she was being bullied he wouldn't have stood for it.

'Right, we'd better get on before George sends a search party for us,' I said.

We walked across the room, Liz was stood beside George's desk as we entered, I sat down in the seat opposite George, Liz frowned at me, I smiled back.

'Thanks Natasha,' George said.

She went to leave and then when she got to the door she turned to face the room, 'before I go, I found out that information about the car you asked me to get, Liz, you know the one that belonged to Iain Blair.'

Liz blushed and I remembered that George had asked her to look into that, I wondered how much of that Natasha was aware of.

'We kept it for a while, but when we changed our storage provider in 1997 it was sent for crushing, there was a note made in the file that the car was no longer in a fit state to be used as evidence. There was a photo included and it was mostly rust, you could barely tell what colour it used to be. It also said the upholstery had been destroyed by an infestation of rodents. Which means that if it's not in the original file then we aren't going to get any more evidence from it.'

'Thank you for checking that,' Liz said.

Natasha closed the door behind her, I had hoped that this meeting would be just George and I, but if Liz had found something useful I could see why George would let her have the spotlight.

'George says you've uncovered some information that could really help the case,' I said to Liz.

'I think so, it certainly turns things in a new direction,' she replied.

I prickled slightly at the implied suggestion that the direction I'd been going in was the wrong one. 'Great,' I said not letting my emotions play out on my face.

'I asked Liz to delve into the foster records of Max's parents, see if there had been any problems in the past and to look for any of the other children that might've been fostered at the same time and in the process of doing that she found something unexpected,' George said.

'For the four years prior to Iris Hatfield being placed with the Thorogoods they had one foster child that was with them that whole period and then some shorter placements of other children, who on the most part seemed to later return to live with their parents, but it's the long-term placement that caught my eye.'

'What was interesting about it?' I asked.

'The boy was called Adam Forrester, he had been in foster care since the age of six, had one failed adoption where the parents had returned him to the system after almost two years with them, saying he hadn't been able to integrate into their family, he bounced around between group homes and foster families until he was twelve when he went to the Thorogoods. He seemed to find his feet there.' Liz paused

'What happened when Iris went to live with them?' I asked.

'Well, this is where it gets interesting. When Iris was removed from their care, he was also removed and because of the length of the investigation into the family, Adam had to complete his time in foster care in a group home where it would seem that he didn't have a very good time of it, with three hospital admissions for broken bones in a short space of time. Eventually he voluntarily left care just before his seventeenth birthday where he spent seven months or so being homeless. The Thorogoods invited him to stay with them for a little while to let him get back on his feet.'

'And where is he now?' I asked.

'You'll like this bit,' George said.

'He's been under our noses this whole time, 'Adam Stewart Forrester was his name before marriage. He goes by his middle name now, we know him as Stewart Blair.'

'Then it stands to reason that he would have recognised Iris when Iain introduced her to his family,' I said.

'I'd say so,' George said.

'And if Elspeth saw Pamela and thought that she was Iris she might also have told her brother-in-law that she'd found her,' I said.

'Do you think Stewart would hold a grudge after all this time?' George asked.

I shrugged, 'if he thought she was to blame for screwing up his happy life, probably.' I looked at Liz, 'you said there was an investigation when Iris was taken out of their care, do we know what happened?'

'The family were cleared of any wrongdoing, and it was chalked up to a misunderstanding.'

'What was?' I asked.

'Didn't I say? Iris accused Max's father of trying to sexually assault her.'

'How could that be a misunderstanding?' I asked.

'You mean other than it was the 1970s and a lot of things were swept under the carpet if they weren't considered important, and let's face it, a teenage foster girl accusing someone of sexual assault wasn't going to be taken seriously then,' Liz said.

She was right, now there would be an actual investigation, then though they seemed more interested in hushing things up, there must've been good people involved in foster care, but the only cases you tend to hear about are the awful ones.'

'The question is, did Iris recognise Stewart?' George said.

'I guess we'll have to ask him,' I replied.

'Thanks for sharing that Liz, can you find out where we might find Stewart, I'd like to pay him a visit later,' George said.

Liz smiled and left the room, I wondered if she felt put out that she had to share with me but in return wasn't going to get to hear what I had uncovered.

'What about you, this woman you went to see, what information did she have for you?' George asked.

I told him about the man Yvonne had seen and gave him the car details, 'from what we now know I'm going to guess that it's Stewart's car. There was one other thing, Seb was a regular visitor at Pamela's house, and she described him as her brother. I know we don't have the DNA results back yet, but I think it's safe to say that Sebastian Wojcik was Iris and Pamela's brother and the reason he was killed is related to Pamela's attack. And that was the other thing – the description you gave out for your potential witness, red jacket etc – Yvonne said that the man she saw matched it.'

Chapter Thirty-Nine

I'd offered to go with George when he went to question Stewart, but he said he wanted to take Amadeus with him instead and that he would update me later if there was anything to share.

I'd considered going back to the Sunshine Café, but instead I got the bus home for a late lunch, it was a little after 3pm when I finally sat down at my desk. I opened my laptop and tried FaceTiming Alana, I'd checked her class schedule and this was free time, not that it meant she'd be able to pick up. I was glad when I saw her face appear on my screen.

'Are you okay?' She said.

'Yeah, I'm fine, just seeing if you're free for a chat.'

'You had me worried for a moment there,' she smiled. 'I'm free, I was just watching a bit of tv, nothing important. How's the case going?'

I filled her in on all the details.

'Interesting, do you think Elspeth and Stewart are in it together?' She asked.

'Possibly, could also be that Stewart is in it alone and it's coincidental that Elspeth is connected.'

'You don't believe in coincidences, remember.'

'I know, it is a bit far fetched to think they're unconnected.'

'When did this Elspeth woman hire you to find her brother, was it before or after Pamela was attacked?'

'After, why?'

'Is it possible that when she attacked Pamela she found out that she wasn't Iris and Elspeth thought by hiring you to look for her brother you would by default find Iris?'

'I guess, but she seemed genuinely shocked when I told her that Pamela wasn't Iris, I don't think she could've faked that reaction.'

'You said yourself she's been lying to you throughout, which means she's probably a practiced liar, she could've been rehearsing that reaction for weeks in case you ever found out.'

'Thing is,' I said. 'I can understand to some degree why Stewart felt aggrieved by Iris, his whole world was turned upside down by her allegations, and even assuming she was telling the truth, it would still be easier to blame her over the people he considered family. But why would Elspeth get involved?'

'Are you sure it was the father that she said assaulted her?' Alana asked. 'What if it was Max.'

'Even if it was, there were no consequences for him, why would that bother Elspeth?'

'There were no legal consequences, but what if he was obsessed with Iris and never really got past that, and then he discovers that she's become his sister-in-law. Maybe Elspeth thought that her husband was in love with her, so in love that she believed it was possible for him to abandon her and everything else he'd worked for to go looking for Iris.'

'And when he didn't come back, she thought they'd run off together?'

'Why not, that could be why she wasn't bothered when Iain went missing, she thought that he'd gone off somewhere to lick his wounds, she expected him to come back home in time and say that his marriage failed.'

'Why look for him now though?'

'Seeing Pamela might have triggered old feelings, it's possible that when she told you she needed closure before she died, she really meant it, she wanted to know if her suspicions were true. It would also explain why she was so convinced that the skeletal remains were her brother, she'd have known Max well enough to believe that he would have shot Iain if he had to in order to get Iris.'

'When she was told the remains were Max, she said she thought Iris killed him, which I thought was a bit odd.'

'Not if in her head the scenario was Max trying to take Iris away from Iain, she clearly doesn't think Iain was capable of killing someone, but was happy to believe Iris was, after all in her mind Iris is the villain in this story, not Max.'

'The question is where are Iris and Iain now? If only Seb had told me who he was…' I trailed off.

'He might've done, but he wouldn't have trusted you right away, think about how you'd behave in that situation,' Alana said.

'I'm thinking of heading back up to Nairn to speak to Michael Swanage again, do you fancy coming with me for a little road trip?'

'When were you thinking of going?'

'Tomorrow morning,' I said, I'd checked her calendar, she didn't have any lectures, but I wasn't sure if she had any lab time booked.

'As long as we're not away for more than one night.'

'Brilliant, I'll pick you up tomorrow.'

The prospect of spending some quality time with Alana over the next two days distracted me from the fact that George hadn't called to let me know the outcome of his conversation with

Stewart. I suppose that either it hadn't yielded any new information or that he hadn't been able to pin him down to have it yet.

A text pinged onto my phone, it was Sonya letting me know that DNA results indicated as expected that Pamela and Seb were siblings and that George had said he was happy for Seb's body to be released to his wife and family. I was pleased for Donna, I would check with Maureen to find out where and when the funeral was going to be.

Chapter Forty

The next morning I set off at 8.45am, I told Alana I'd pick her up outside her halls at 10am and the traffic was always heavy at this time of day. Still, once I was past Glenrothes the traffic quietened down, and I arrived five minutes early. Alana was already outside and waiting.

'I know that technically this is a business trip for you, but I was thinking before we go hunting down suspects, we should get some fish and chips for lunch, because everyone knows you can't do this kind of work on an empty stomach,' Alana said as she climbed into the passenger seat, chucking her bag onto the back seat.

'Might've known you would want feeding before we got started,' I laughed.

For the rest of the journey to Nairn we talked about how her course was going and how she was finding living in halls.

'It's just so busy all the time,' Alana said, 'I guess I'm still not used to it, not sure if I ever will be.'

The intention had always been to look at private housing for her second year, but then the pandemic came and her whole first year was online learning from home and so halls this year had felt like a good idea.

'When I've wrapped up this case how about we look at getting something different sorted out for next term?'

'I dunno, I've been looking at privately renting and it's so expensive.'

'What about if we bought a little flat for you?'

'Can we afford that?'

'It might need to be a bit of a project in the beginning, but I'm sure we could and if not I could always sell the house and move somewhere a bit smaller.'

'You can't sell the house,' Alana said, all of a sudden her voice much softer than before.

'It's just a house, Jack's with us wherever we go,' I replied.

'No, I'd rather stay in halls the whole time I was at uni than you sell the house,' Alana replied. 'It's not just that it was Jack's house, it's our house too, it's where I grew up, there's lots of memories tied up in those walls.' She paused. 'It's not that I'm saying you should never sell it, it's that I don't want the reason to be because I don't want to live in halls.'

'It was only a suggestion, I've got some savings, so we'll figure something out. I just want you to be happy whilst you're staying in Dundee.'

'I'm sure I can manage until the end of second year and then if I can get together with enough other people there are some decent student flats, at least then I'd only be living with 3 or 4 other people.'

'Leave it with me, we can discuss it more when you're home at Christmas,' I said. I pulled the car into a little car park near the waterfront, 'if you want fish and chips we can walk from here.'

We sat on a park bench not far from the chippy to eat.

'What's the plan?' Alana asked.

'I'm going to call Michael and say that I'm in the area, see if he's free to catch up.'

'You think he'll admit to knowing that Seb and Iris were related?'

'Maybe, I think it depends on what he's got to lose.' I wiped my fingers on the paper napkin before scrolling through my phone to find his details.

'Michael hi, it's Rowan McFarlane, I'm in Nairn and I was hoping that we could meet up, there's a couple of things I'd really like to run by you.'

'I wasn't expecting this,' he said.

'I know, sorry to spring it on you out of the blue but I didn't know I was coming up until last night and I thought I'd give you a call and hope for the best.'

'Umm, yeah alright. I'm busy just now but I can meet you in the Fisherman's Catch pub in a couple of hours. It's right down by the water, you should be able to find it easy enough.'

'No problem, see you then.'

He hung up.

'How did he sound?' Alana asked.

'A bit shocked, but he agreed to meet so that's something.'

It was nearly three o'clock, we walked back to the car and drove round to the small hotel I'd booked us into. 'I got us a twin room, so don't be expecting to hog the bathroom,' I smiled as we walked up to the receptionist.

The hotel had nine rooms, all with a theme, the one we were in was called 'Traditionally Scottish' which in reality meant tartan bedcovers, curtains and a large tartan armchair.

'We've got shortbread,' Alana said opening one of the individually wrapped lengths of biscuit.

'I'm going to grab a shower before we go back out,' I said. 'Try to save at least one biscuit for me.'

'I can't make any promises,' Alana replied.

By the time I had finished in the bathroom Alana had eaten three biscuits, which had left one for me, and she had found the way to the pub on Google Maps.

'Have you got your ID with you?' I asked.

'I'm only going to have a coke,' she replied.

'I know, but sometimes places can be a bit weird about things and it's better to be safe than sorry.'

'I've got my driver's licence,' she said tapping the top pocket of her jacket.

It was dusk when we left the hotel, so far it had been a mild October, even so we could see our breath it the air as we made our way to the pub.

'Let me do the talking,' I said. 'You observe him, see how he behaves.'

'Okay. Does George know we're here?'

I hadn't heard from him since our conversation yesterday morning and if I was being honest, I'd been a bit irritated that he hadn't been keeping me fully in the loop with what had happened with Stewart. Once that would've meant that I wouldn't have told him what I was doing either, but this time I had sent him a text letting him know that I was picking Alana up and then heading here to see Michael. His reply had been 'ok, stay safe, G'. Which I'd taken to mean that he must be busy.

'Yes.'

'Good.'

I knew that her desire to have him know what was going on had nothing to do with her having no faith in me and my ability to do my job, rather the desire to keep us safe.

Inside the pub it was warm, we found a table near one of the windows and I went to the bar to get our drinks. It was another twenty minutes before Michael arrived. I waved so he could find us amongst the other patrons. He went to the bar and came back with a pint and a packet of salt and vinegar crisps.

'Thanks for seeing me at such short notice,' I said. 'This is my daughter, Alana.'

'Hi,' Alana said.

'You don't look old enough,' Michael said to me. It was a phrase I had heard more times than I could remember. I smiled and said nothing. 'I thought you were sisters,' he continued and when we gave no response, 'how are you getting on with your investigation?'

'It's going well, actually I recently discovered something interesting and I'm hoping you can help me with what people knew at the time.'

Michael frowned, 'what's that then,' he took a sip of his pint and opened his crisps, tearing the packet along its length after opening the top so it lay flat like a plate on the table. 'Help yourself,' he said as he took one.

'Did Iain get the job working on the roads because he was Seb's brother-in-law?' I asked.

Michael looked at me for a few moments, 'who told you that?'

'His other sister's neighbour and a DNA test.'

'Other sister?'

'Pamela, she was attacked a couple of weeks ago, she's in hospital unconscious at the moment. Someone bludgeoned her across the head with a rock because they thought she was Iris.'

Before Michael had a chance to reply a woman from the table next to us burled round, 'Oh my God, is Pammy going to be okay, I didn't know. Michael why didn't you mention this last time.'

I recognised her immediately, even after all this time the resemblance to her sister was uncanny. 'Hello Iris, I thought you might be here,' I said. I leant out of my chair slightly so I could see past her to the man she was sitting with, 'and you must be Iain, I think it might be a good idea if you joined us.'

Chapter Forty-One

With five chairs around it the little table felt cramped and with the pub getting busy with evening trade I was half wondering if this was the best place to be having this conversation, but we were all here and I wasn't going to let the opportunity go.

'Does someone want to explain what's going on?' I asked.

'First I need to know what happened to Pammy,' Iris said.

'Seb didn't tell you?' I asked, surprised that her brother wouldn't have let her know about the attack.

'No, he messaged Michael telling him something had happened, that everything was going to be okay, but we needed a break in contact to keep everyone safe,' she paused. 'Not that it worked, Seb wasn't safe, someone murdered him.'

'Is Michael the go between?' I asked.

'What happened to Pam?'

'Alright, a couple of weeks ago she was out walking her dogs in the morning, on the beach…'

'By herself? She never went by herself,' Iris interrupted.

'She should've been with her friend Yvonne, but she was called away last minute,' I left out the fact that it was a hoax and clearly part of the plan to get Pamela alone. 'And whilst she was out someone attacked her, hitting her over the head with a rock. She was taken to hospital and because of some swelling on the brain they put her in a medically induced coma, she should be awake in the next few days, the doctors have said she'll make a full recovery.'

'Have they got the person that did it?'

'Not yet.'

'I can't believe it, who would want to hurt Pammy?'

Iain had been watching the conversation unfold then spoke for the first time since joining our table. 'Do they think it's the same person that killed Seb?'

I thought for a moment, cautious of not giving too much away, it was likely that Iris and Iain were as much victims in this as Pamela and Seb, but I didn't have enough information to know that. 'It's possible, but the police are looking into all angles. I've told you what I know about Pamela, now it's time for you to tell me what happened in 1983 and why you've been hiding from your family ever since.'

Iris and Iain looked at each other for a moment before Iris began to talk, 'it started when I was in foster care.'

'At Max Thorogood's house or before that?' I asked.

'Both I guess, it was the 70s, they didn't try so hard to keep families together then, and Seb he was lucky, his dad had always been in the picture, he did try to take us all but because we weren't his kids he wasn't allowed, which if you ask me was a bloody joke, it wasn't like they really cared what happened to us or checked up on the god awful places they sent us to live.'

'It must've been really difficult,' Alana said, reaching across the table to touch the woman's hand.

Iris smiled at her, 'you've no idea, thank goodness. In the first group home we went to Pamela and I were together, which was something because it meant I could look out for her, I was the oldest, and I'd been looking out for her and Seb since mum got addicted. It wasn't just the wardens that were dangerous, the other kids were too, I didn't properly understand at first why they hated us, but it was hard for them too. Your things would get stolen and Pamela, she was a gentle soul and an easy target for bullies, until I stepped in and beat seven bells out of them.'

'You were brave,' Alana said, 'you must've been scared as well.'

'It was a long time ago, and I'd I got used to being a bit scared, some of the men our mother brought around were frightening, I had to hit one of them in the face with a rolling pin once,' Iris smiled at the memory. 'Anyway, I realised early on that the only way to protect Pamela was to get her into a long-term family. She was younger than me which made it easier, I made sure she was never in trouble, if she did something wrong, I took the blame, it didn't take long before she was out of there.'

'Did you keep in touch?'

'As much as possible, her foster family were lovely, but they only wanted one child and I don't hold it against them, they took good care of Pammy, even adopted her in the end, she had a wonderful life living in Paris, becoming a pastry chef. I was proud.'

'Not such an easy life for you though?' I asked.

She tilted her head to the side, 'not so much. I had a few good foster families, but if a younger child came along, I would be off back to the group home with the other leftovers. People don't want teenagers, they come with too much baggage, and I was already seen as a problem child.'

'And then you were placed at the Thorogood's?'

'That's right, I didn't expect much of them, I was told they had another two foster children, a boy a bit older than me who'd been there for years and a girl a bit younger and a son of their own, Max.'

'What happened when you got there?'

'It was fine, nice house, plenty of room, the other girl was sweet, we all had our own rooms, which felt like luxury, the other boy was quiet but no problem, but Max, he creeped me out.'

'In what way?'

'It was little things at first, I'd catch him staring at me over breakfast and he'd lick his lips when I looked at him, then it was more explicit, he'd sit next to me when we had family movie time and whisper in my ear that I made him hard and ask me if I wanted to see.'

'Did you tell anyone?'

'Not at first, I hoped that if I ignored him, he'd get bored and stop. I did complain to the foster boy once...'

'You mean Stewart?' I asked.

'Oh, I wasn't sure if you knew that, I was trying to find a way to work it into the conversation. Yes, Stewart or Adam as he was then.'

'And what was his reaction?'

'He called me a liar, he got defensive about it. I should've known he'd be like that, he'd been with them three or four years and he was nearly finished his time, even if he did believe me, he wouldn't have wanted the boat rocked.'

'Did you try talking to Max's parents?'

'I told them Max was making me feel a bit uncomfortable and asked if they could tell him to leave me alone, but they said we were "family" and that I just didn't know what that felt like.'

'What about a social worker?' I asked.

'They would've just told me I was being ridiculous and making something out of nothing, so I put up with it for a while, I would come in from school and he'd be on my bed naked, or

I'd be in the shower and when I pulled the curtain back to get my towel he'd be there. He told me he was in love with me, that I should be flattered that someone like him wanted someone like me, as if he was doing me a favour. He came into my bedroom one Saturday morning, pushed me up against the wall and kissed me and groped me, told me I had two choices, be his girlfriend or get out of his house, he said he'd make up a story to his parents that he'd caught me stealing and that Stewart would back him up. I agreed to be his girlfriend just to give me time to think.'

'Did he believe you?' I asked.

'Oh yeah, I'm not sure I ever met anyone so full of themselves as him, he really thought he was god's gift to the world, and his parents treated him like he could do no wrong, Stewart followed him around like a pathetic little lap dog, asking how high when Max said jump.'

'How did Stewart react when he found out that Max had made you his girlfriend?'

'I'm not sure he knew. I was trying to think of a way out, but Max wanted to be with me every moment, it was suffocating, even if I had liked him like that, which I absolutely didn't, I would've hated it. He said that now I was his girlfriend that meant we had to be together properly. I knew what he meant of course, but I tried to pretend like I didn't.'

'You've got to understand that this was a lifetime ago and things were very different, Iris wasn't left with many options, if she complained she would be seen as the troublemaker, not Max,' Iain said.

'I understand,' I replied, then looking at Iris I said, 'the information I have is that you said that Max's father came on to you.'

'I don't know why that would be. After a few days of trying to avoid Max, he came into my room, told me it was time and tried to force himself on me. I knee'd him in the balls, hard and he went off, tail between his legs but not before he hit me across the face and gave me a split lip. I phoned the social worker and they had to come out, told me to pack my things and they took me to a group home.'

'What happened?'

'They said they did an investigation, but it was clear from the start it was only a form filling exercise, they were pissed off that they'd had to pull three kids out of a home. It all came to nothing, Max said that I was lying, that he'd caught me stealing and that I had made up the other story to cover my back, Stewart backed him of course, said he'd seen the whole thing. In the end it was marked up as a "misunderstanding" and I spent the rest of my foster care time in a group home.'

'When did you get back in touch with Seb?'

'By the time I left foster care I'd lost contact with both him and Pammy, it had become harder to write to her and pretend everything was alright, I never wanted her to feel guilty for being adopted and leaving me behind. I knew Seb was travelling about, I got myself a job as a secretary in a law firm, and a wee flat and then one day Seb turned up at my door.'

'That must've been nice.'

'It was amazing, he was married and settled and really happy.'

'When did you meet Iain?' I asked.

'By the time we met, I'd been on my own for a while, I'm not going to say my foster experience was well behind me, but I was moving forward with my life, I'd got Seb back, we tried to find Pammy, but it was difficult, not like now with the internet.'

'Where did you two meet?' Alana asked.

'The pub, I wasn't a drinker, but I'd gone with some work colleagues, I think we were celebrating something.'

'Wasn't it your boss's 60th?' Iain said.

'I think you might be right. Anyway, I was in the pub and so was Iain…'

'Drowning my sorrows.'

'In a shandy as I recall,' Iris laughed.

'Why were you drowning your sorrows?' I asked.

'I was miserable, doing a PhD that I didn't care about, and never really had, I only did it because it was what was expected of me. Then suddenly, I look up and this beautiful woman was stood next to me waiting to be served. I smiled at her, but I honestly didn't think she'd give me a second glance.'

'You looked so bloody miserable, I felt sorry for you.'

'She asked me what was wrong, and I blurted it all out and she just said, well leave and do something else then. Like it was that easy.'

'Because it was,' Iris said. 'My lot were finishing up at the pub and heading off somewhere else and I was done for the evening, Iain was still there, still looking for answers at the bottom of the same glass. I sat down beside him, and we got to talking.'

'Turned out to be the best night of my life,' Iain said.

'Oh aye,' Michael laughed.

'Not like that,' Iris said gently punching Michael on the arm. 'We started dating – I introduced him to Seb, and he said, and I think he was joking at the start, that he could get Iain a job on the roads if he wanted.

'When did you meet Iain's family and realise who they were?'

'I met Rodger and Stewart first, I think we thought they'd be the most accepting of our relationship. I didn't recognise Stewart right away and originally, I didn't think he'd recognised me. Then when Iain and I got engaged he told me he knew who I was and he wouldn't let me destroy another family, that he would do everything he could to ruin our relationship and me.'

'But she didn't tell me that in the beginning.' Iain said.

'I didn't want to cause waves, and there was a part of me that was scared that Iain might believe whatever Stewart told him, I knew he was close with his brother, and I didn't want to risk losing him.'

'On the run up to the wedding I started receiving anonymous letters, telling me that Iris was a stripper, that she was a prostitute, that she was cheating on me, really horrible graphic language,' Iain said, 'I didn't believe it, but I was concerned and that's when she told me how she knew Stewart, he'd already threatened her that he would split us up so it was logical that it was him behind the letters.'

'Did you confront him?' I asked.

'Not straight away, I'd written to Elspeth telling her I was going to get married and when she wrote back telling me how she thought Iris was a gold digger just looking for a way out of a horrible lifestyle I knew I had to say something.'

'How did Stewart react when you spoke to him?'

'He didn't deny any of it, he said that he was doing it for my own good and that Iris would hurt me, and I would realise he was right eventually, and he was just trying to save me time. I was so angry with him.'

'Why did you invite him to the wedding then?'

'We didn't,' Iris said, we told Rodger he was welcome, explained what Stewart had done and said he would need to come alone, he wasn't happy, but he agreed to it and then on the day Rodger arrived by himself and five minutes later Stewart walked in as if nothing had happened.'

'I was going to kick him out, but Iris told me not to.'

'He was hoping that him turning up would create a scene, spoil our special day and I wasn't about to give him the satisfaction. I said, ignore him, smile and be polite, give him no reason to behave like a dickhead and if he kicks off let Seb and Michael deal with him,' Iris said.

'Did you invite your parents to the wedding?' I asked.

'We did,' Iain said, 'but they refused to come. Stewart had done a good job on his smear campaign, and they'd already made up their minds on Iris before they met her and they weren't shy about telling her all the ways that she wasn't good enough for me and that she'd destroyed my chance of happiness and a good career by forcing me to leave my PhD. I'd explained over and over that I left because I wasn't happy, but they preferred Stewart's explanation that Iris hadn't wanted me to complete it. I told them that they could sit at home all they liked, it wasn't going to change a thing.'

'What had your relationship with Stewart been like before that Iain?' I asked.

'Honestly, and I'm not saying this because of what he tried to do to Iris, I never liked him, well perhaps that's not completely true. He could be charming and when Rodger first introduced him to me I was glad that he'd found someone, being gay was still illegal then, which sounds crazy now, but I knew that Rodger had to be careful and of course he couldn't be honest with our parents about who Stewart was.'

'What changed?'

'Rodger changed, he used to be really outgoing but he'd started changing the way he dressed, the hobbies he liked to do, he gave away his dog, because apparently Stewart was allergic, which I never believed. He couldn't make decisions for himself, it was always that he'd have to check with Stewart first.'

'Domestic abuse,' Alana said.

'I never saw him hit Rodger or any sign that he'd been physically abused, but emotionally, definitely.'

'What made him stay with Stewart do you think?' I asked and then because I was concerned it sounded like I was blaming Rodger I added, 'of course I know that leaving is much, much harder than it sounds, especially when you've had all your self-confidence eroded.'

'It was simpler than that, Rodger told me once that Stewart said if he ever left him he'd go to the police and say that Rodger tried to convert him to homosexuality and like I said it was a crime to be gay at the start of the 80s, and by the time it wasn't Stewart had control of him.'

'I'm really sorry to hear that,' I replied.

'It was awful for sure, but I had no idea that my family was harbouring so many psychopaths.'

'When did you realise who Elspeth's husband was?' I asked thinking that Iain was alluding to Max.

'Stewart told me,' Iris said, 'he delighted in revealing that knowledge, I told Iain about it at the same time as I explained how Stewart knew me. I was never sure if Elspeth was aware though.'

I thought about all my interactions with Elspeth, it would be hard for me to say for certain what she thought back then, her memory had become so twisted against Iris that she'd probably have skewed it anyway.

'When we invited her to the wedding, I didn't imagine that she would come all the way from Singapore, but she did, and we were just grateful that she came alone.'

'You must've thought that with Max and Elspeth in Singapore you wouldn't need to see much, if anything of them.'

'We hoped that it would only be occasionally at best and I thought that I could handle that,' Iris said.

'Why don't you tell me what happened, how that all changed and how Max ended up dead,' I said.

Iain looked around the now very busy pub, 'not here,' he said. 'We'll tell you, but come to ours tomorrow morning and we'll explain everything and then you can do whatever you need to do.

Chapter Forty-Two

'I'd say that was a shock, but I'm not sure you were that surprised,' Alana said as we walked back to the hotel.

'I had an inkling they were still alive, even more so when Sonya confirmed that it was Max's remains, and then I thought where would I go if I were trying to start a new life, and somewhere that I'd have at least one friend made sense to me.'

'What happens now, are you going to tell George you've found them?'

'Not yet, I'll see what they have to say tomorrow.'

'Will they get in trouble, even if they killed Max by accident?'

'Technically concealing a body is a crime, but that will be up to George and the Procurator Fiscal to decide, I hope they don't take it any further though, not sure what good it would do anyone.'

Back at the hotel it was too late for dinner and our fish and chips felt like they'd been a long time ago, I was glad that we'd had the sense to stop off at a supermarket on the way here and had bought plenty of snacks and a couple of Pot Noodles to keep us going. We sat back on the bed together watching the tv.

'I've missed this,' Alana said quietly.

'Me too, but it's not like you're never going to be home.'

'I know, but sometimes I think I should've gone to Edinburgh University and then I could have stayed home like Becky does.'

'Dundee had the best course for you,' I reminded her. Her grades had been so good that she'd had the pick of all the universities that she'd applied to.

'I know.'

'It's okay to get a little home sick though, I get a little Alana sick sometimes as well and then I remind myself how brilliant you are and that you're doing something that you love and that usually sorts me out and if that doesn't work, I eat chocolate.'

'Some people run when they get stressed you know, it's generally better for you,' Alana laughed.

'I beg to differ, people who go out running have a greater risk of finding dead bodies and I see enough of those in my day job, I don't want to be stumbling over them in my relaxation time as well.'

Alana shook her head and laughed. 'You used to like running.'

'I know I still do it, usually on the treadmill these days though, especially this time of year, it's too cold to go out in the morning.'

We had breakfast in bed before checking out the next morning, they didn't do a cooked breakfast, but the croissants were nice and would keep us going for a while. Michael had text the address to us this morning, the drive saw us leaving the touristy part of the town behind and entering the more built up section of housing. After a couple of minutes we came to a stop at the end of a row of terrace houses. Iris and Iain were stood in the open doorway waiting for us.

'Glad you found us okay,' Iris said.

In the living room a pot of tea, cups and a plate of biscuits were already laid out on the coffee table.

'I thought it would be easier if we were ready to kick off without fussing with all the pleasantries first, help yourself.'

I poured Alana and I a cup of tea and took a biscuit each, another one of Jack's rules was never turn down the opportunity to eat a biscuit, especially the good ones covered in chocolate, because you don't know what the rest of your day might bring.

Iris was sat perched on the edge of the brown suede sofa, she looked apprehensive. Iain was sat next to her, equally on the edge of the seat. The room was simply decorated, on the mantel piece I saw the same black and white photograph of three children, two sisters and a brother, that I had seen in Pamela's house.

'How are we going to do this?' Iain asked.

'That's up to you, I'm interested in what happened that day and how it got to this stage, it's your story though, you tell it as you see best.'

'Not long after we sent the wedding invitation to Elspeth I got a letter from Max,' Iris said. 'He was declaring his undying love to me, said he didn't understand why we'd been separated all those years ago, it was like he was remembering a whole different thing to what happened. He said he would leave Elspeth and we could be together. I showed it to Iain, but we decided it was best to ignore it.'

'But they didn't stop,' Iain said. 'In fact, it felt like he must've been writing to her every day, sometimes we'd even receive two in the same post. I wrote back to him and told him to stop, not that it did any good.'

'Did you consider telling Elspeth about the letters?'

'No, we weren't sure how much she knew and anyway she'd only stick her head in the sand and more than likely think we were making it up, she worshipped Max, I'm sure she probably gave you the full independent woman routine, but she would've walked over hot coals for that man.'

'Did you know he had come back to the UK?'

'No, first I knew of it was when I got home from work and found Max and Stewart in our flat, Iris was terrified, she'd told them to leave, but Max had said he wasn't going anywhere without her. There was a bit of a scuffle,' Iain said, 'but I made them leave.'

'Why didn't you go to the police?'

'And say my brothers in law came to visit and wouldn't go home, I'm sure things are very much better now, but in 1983 that would've been a domestic and not one the police would've had any interest in getting involved in.' Iris said.

It was a fair statement and probably true, 'what happened on the day you disappeared?' I asked.

'It was a Saturday, Iain had popped to the shop round the corner to grab a couple of things and I was in the flat getting ready for the day, I heard the door go and I thought it was Iain, so I shouted that I was in the kitchen, I turn around and there's Max. He tells me this is our moment, we can get away from everyone, start a new life. I tell him that's not what I want, and that Iain will be home soon, but he wasn't listening. He took hold of my wrist and started pulling me to the door. I tried to resist and in the end, he picked me up, sort of put me over his shoulder, I didn't weigh very much then and it wasn't hard for him. I screamed and screamed but no one heard me.'

'How did you know what had happened?' I asked Iain.

'I came back to see Max in my car, Iris in the passenger seat, he practically ran me over to get out of there. I ran into the house and phoned Seb, he came round and we went out looking for them, I called Michael as well and he said he would get out in his car and let us know if he saw anything.'

'How did you keep in touch without a mobile phone?' Alana asked.

'Seb and Michael had CB radios in their cars, I used to tease them about the enormous aerials, said that they'd catch low flying aircraft, but it turns out they were useful after all,' Iris said.

'They only worked if you were within a couple of miles of one another,' Iain said 'but we got a message from Michael that he'd seen my car pulled off the side of the old A92, so we headed that way. Seb let me out and said he and Michael would meet me at the other side of the woods as there was a car park there.'

Debbie had seen two people arguing and I'd always assumed it was Iris and Iain, but it had been Iris and Max that she'd seen that day.'

'Max's behaviour was all over the place, he was driving really erratically, then at one point he slowed down enough that I thought if I open the door now, I can jump out and probably make it. I tried, but instead of me jumping out, he crashed the car into the ditch. I opened the door and started running up the hill, I could see a little house and I just kept thinking if I got to it then maybe I could get help, but Max was quick, and he caught up to me.'

'You must've been so scared,' Alana said.

'I was, but I was also determined that I wouldn't get back in another vehicle with him, I kept walking, hoping that in the woods we'd bump into a dog walker or someone I could get help from. Unfortunately there was no one about, then I heard Iain shouting my name and I knew it would all be okay,' she smiled at Iain, he reached over and took her hand.

'I caught up with them, Max was yelling about how I didn't deserve Iris, that they were meant to be together, that he'd known it from the moment he laid eyes on her all those years ago. I told him that was all in his head and that she never even liked him,' Iain said. 'That was when things changed, he let go of Iris and pulled a gun out of his jacket.'

'You didn't know he had a gun?' I asked.

'No,' Iris said. 'I would've warned Iain if I knew.'

'What happened?'

'I told her to run, to get to the car park on the other side, that Michael and her brother were waiting for her. She started to go, but then for some reason she came back.' Iain said.

'Because I couldn't leave you alone with that maniac and I'd rather have died with you in those woods than run away and left you to die there by yourself, the last face you ever saw being his,' Iris said.

'She had a lot of faith in me,' Iain chuckled. 'Honestly, I didn't want anyone to get hurt that day, let alone die. Max was waving the gun around, shouting that this wasn't supposed to be the way it was, that he didn't understand what went wrong. We tried to make a run for it whilst he was so engrossed in his morose monologue. We got a few steps and one of us stood on a branch, it cracked and he realised what was going on. He ran towards us, I pushed Iris out the way and he battered into me, I'm not sure exactly what happened in the next few moments, but during the struggle the gun fired and for a second, I didn't know if I'd been shot, then Max collapsed to the ground.'

'Why didn't you call for help?'

'We thought about it, but it would've been hard to explain.'

'You explained it well enough to me just now.'

'I know, you're right, we should've gone to the house down the path and got the occupant to call the police, but we were scared. Michael and Seb had arrived a couple of moments after the shot,' Iain said.

'Seb took control of everything,' Iris said. 'He pushed Max's body into a little dip in the ground and covered it with moss and leaves, it wasn't completely covered and for ages afterwards we expected to hear on the news that his body had been discovered and then years went by and nothing, until you turned up.'

'The blood soaked handkerchief you threw away that day on the way to the woods, whose blood was that?' I asked.

'It was Max's, he hit his face into the steering wheel when he crashed the car, it gave him a nosebleed.'

'How did you know about that?' Iain asked.

'The woman who lived in the cottage told me, she also said there was a glove and a wedding ring.'

'When I saw my car in the ditch the first thing I thought was that Iris might be hurt so I went to check. I saw the bloody cloth and a wedding ring on the seat and one of Iris' favourite gloves in the footwell. I threw them away because I didn't want anything leading back to Iris.'

'When you saw on the news that human remains had been discovered in those woods you must've known it was Max, why not come forward then?' I asked.

'We thought about it and then before we'd decided what to do you contacted Michael so we thought we'd wait and see what you said, but when you told Michael about Seb, I was afraid and now I know about Pammy, I'm glad we didn't,' Iris said. 'But now I suppose there's no choice.'

'I will have to tell my colleague DCI George Johnston what you've told me, I can assure you he's a very fair man, he'll hear you out just like I have.'

'I don't mean to be nosey,' Alana said. 'But how did you get away that day?'

Iris smiled, 'there's no secrets left to tell so you might as well know the whole thing. Michael and Seb were amazing, Michael was already planning on moving up here and he'd got a house sorted out, so that day we drove there and Seb went to our flat and packed up some things – we thought it would be enough to make it look like we went on holiday or something, it wasn't like we had much stuff, the flat was rented and all the furniture belonged to the landlords. We went to an ATM and took out as much as we could but accepted that the rest of it was lost. Then we changed our names, which was much easier then – as everything was paper based. Then we started a new life and hoped that when we were reported missing that no one looked too hard.'

'Actually, you were never reported missing,' I said to Iris. 'Iain's family only ever reported him missing and I always thought that was strange, even if they really hated you, I couldn't understand why they didn't tell the police and try to suggest that you were in some way responsible, now I understand though, they thought that you and Max had run off together.' I said. 'Stewart must've told Elspeth that Max was back in the UK, when none of you returned they jumped to the wrong conclusion.'

'Do you think they're responsible for attacking Pammy and killing Seb?' Iris asked.

'I don't know,' I replied, although it was looking very likely that it was true. I excused myself from the room to call George.

Chapter Forty-Three

'Okay tell all three of them to sit tight, I'll send a car up to collect them and bring them here,' George said.

'Do you need me to stay with them?'

'Are they likely to do a runner?'

'I doubt it.'

'They did once before,' George replied.

'I know, and I think if it weren't for Pamela then I might feel differently, but Iris wants to see her sister.'

'Stay if you can, but if you need to get Alana back to Dundee then I'll understand, still not sure why you thought it was a good idea to have her tag along.'

'She has a good way with people, especially older people and I thought her observations might be useful. You never told me how you got on with Stewart,' I said.

'We haven't been able to speak to him, he's gone to ground.'

'Have you checked that he's not taken his boat out?'

'What boat, you didn't mention he had a bloody boat.'

'Because I assumed you knew, I told you I spoke to him at the sailing club, so I figured it was obvious.'

George sighed, 'Right, I'll get Liz on to it now.'

'Okay, speak later,' I said before hanging up.

Back in the room Alana appeared deep in conversation with Iris. Iain and Michael sat quietly either side of her. I cleared my throat. 'DCI Johnston is going to send a car for you all to bring you back to Fife.'

Michael looked at his watch, 'we've got about three hours I reckon, should I make a few calls, arrange lawyers, that sort of thing?'

'If you'd like to, the police want to take a statement from you in the beginning though as far as I know you're not going to be arrested.'

Michael turned away from me to look at his friends and smiled, 'I'd do it again in a heartbeat. I just wish Seb and Donna had come with us.'

'I can't believe he's gone,' Iris said, tears trickling down her cheeks for the first time since we met.

The wait was awkward, silence interrupted with sporadic conversations about not very much, should we eat lunch before the police come, who could they get to feed the cat, should they take a change of clothes.

Alana made us all sandwiches, because she didn't think sitting in a police car hungry was sensible, Michael phoned one of his children who agreed to feed the cat, and despite being asked several times Michael gave nothing away to his family and Iris popped upstairs and came back with a small black holdall, just enough to keep them going, she said and some of Iain's clothes to tide Michael over.

By the time the police cars drew up outside the house there felt like there was nothing left to say. I saw Natasha and Amadeus get out of the first car and two uniformed officers I didn't recognise get out the second.

I went to the front door to let them in. 'Everyone's waiting in the living room,' I said. A few moments later we were all outside, Iris locked her front door and placed the palm of her hand against it as though she was saying goodbye; goodbye to the house or goodbye to the life she'd been living for the last forty years I wondered.

'It's been nice having you with me the last couple of days,' I said to Alana as we drove towards Dundee.

'I've enjoyed it, but don't be getting any ideas about me joining the family business,' she smiled.

'I know, you plan to be a world class forensic anthropologist.'

'I do. In some ways what I want to do and what you do aren't so different, I want to investigate the dead and that's what you do,' she replied.

'I'm so incredibly proud of you, you know that don't you?'

'Obviously, you tell me at least once every time I see you these days.'

Pulling up outside her halls I felt a fleeting pang of sadness, 'come home for a visit soon,' I said.

'I will. Let me know what happens with Iris.'

After I waved goodbye, I drove straight to the police station. Natasha buzzed me through. 'DCI Johnston says to take you to his office, he'll meet you there,' she said as we walked up the stairs.

'Did he find Stewart?'

'Yes, you were right, he'd taken his boat out, had the thing fully stocked so we think he was planning on making his escape, he's in one of the interview rooms waiting on DCI Johnston.'

I didn't have long to wait before George appeared. 'You been taking their statements?' I asked.

He nodded.

'What are you thinking, will there be charges?'

'It'll be down to the Procurator Fiscal, but my recommendation will be not to charge them, I believe their version of events and Sonya says that damage caused to the bones by the bullet is consistent with Max accidentally shooting himself, although she does say with the absence of soft tissue a case could be argued the other way. Even so, it was forty years ago and from what I can tell the three of them have been model citizens for the rest of their lives, and even if Iain did shoot Max it was clearly in self-defence. I had Liz run some checks and we know that Max's dad owned a handgun in 1983, one which he later reported as being stolen.'

'Can I sit in on your interview with Stewart?'

'No. Can you imagine what that would look like in court, you can sit in the other room though and watch it on the screens. We've brought in Elspeth as well and hopefully they'll be in a talkative mood.'

'Who are you going to interview first?'

'Stewart, he matches the description of the man seen in the vicinity of the hills where Sebastian Wojcik's body was found, so that's grounds enough to bring him in for questioning.'

Natasha walked me round to the back room where we would watch the interview on the television screens. 'I bet you'd like to be the one asking the questions,' she said.

'I would, but this is a decent second option.'

> **DCI Johnston:** Mr Blair can you tell me where you were going on your boat?
> **Stewart:** I decided to take a trip across to France.
> **DCI Johnston:** October isn't exactly a great time of year for sailing, is it?
> **Stewart:** Isn't it, anyway even if it wasn't perfect that's hardly a crime.

DCI Johnston: No, it's not. Can you tell me how you know Sebastian Wojcik.
Stewart: I don't, never heard of the bloke.
DCI Johnston: For the tape I'm showing Mr Blair a photograph of the victim
Stewart: Never seen him before.

Stewart pushed the photograph back towards George without giving it so much as a second glance, then sat back in the chair folding his arms.

DCI Johnston: Okay, tell me about your relationship with your brother-in-law, Max Thorogood.
Stewart: There's nothing to tell, he was my brother-in-law, he sadly died in Bulgaria, or there abouts, but that was almost forty years ago.
DCI Johnston: But you knew him before then though didn't you, he was your foster brother for a long time.

Stewart shifted in the seat, frowning at George

Stewart: Yes, he was my foster brother, we were very close.
DCI Johnston: You must've been very angry when you were taken from the Thorogood's home, from what I've read that derailed your life for a bit.
Stewart: I was angry, that's true. Max was a gentle kind soul, he would never have done what that little bitch accused him of.
DCI Johnston: You hated Iris Hatfield
Stewart: I did

DCI Johnston: It must've come as quite a shock when Iain introduced you to his fiancé and you realised who she was

Stewart: It was unbelievable, I told him not to marry her, that he'd only end up getting hurt, but he wouldn't listen, he was like that you see, so used to being mummy's favourite child, the special one, so clever, so brilliant, it was all his bloody mother could chatter on about. But even then he was so selfish that he didn't care that leaving university and marrying that tart would hurt his mother after everything she'd done for him, all her sacrifices.

DCI Johnston: He didn't know how lucky he was to have parents like that did he. Is that why you made up lies about Iris being a stripper and a prostitute?

Stewart: Who says I was lying?

DCI Johnston: You *were* lying, there is nothing to substantiate your allegations.

Stewart: It's not like she's around to say otherwise though is it.

DCI Johnston: How do you get on with your other sister-in-law, Elspeth?

Stewart: We get on fine, I think she's a bit full of her own sense of importance and I was surprised she didn't take her husband's disappearance more seriously.

DCI Johnston: Okay I think we'll take a break for now, I'll have an officer bring you something to eat and drink shortly. Oh, and for the record, I can ask Iris what she was doing for work in the 1980s, because she's just a few doors down from you, helping us with our enquiries.

George stood up. The colour drained slightly from Stewart's cheeks as the door was closed leaving him sat in the room with a PC for company. The door to the back room opened a few moments later.

'What do you think?' He asked.

'He's not too pleased about how much you know about him, and he was genuinely shocked that Iris is here. Oh, and he was lying when he said he didn't recognise Seb.' I replied.

'Well let's see what Elspeth has to say for herself.' George glugged down a mug of what must've been barely lukewarm coffee and went back out.

On another monitor a door opened and George entered introducing himself to Elspeth

>**Elspeth:** I know who you are, we've met before.
>**DCI Johnston:** Indeed we have, but I'm not sure you've ever been entirely honest with me though, have you.
>**Elspeth:** I'm not sure I know what you mean.
>**DCI Johnston:** Let me lay it out for you, when you employed my colleague private detective Rowan McFarlane to find your brother, I think you were really hoping to find your missing husband, Max. Because I think you believed that he'd run off with your sister-in-law Iris Hatfield and that she or they had killed your brother to facilitate this. I think you'd become obsessed with the idea of finding Max the moment you laid eyes on Pamela after mistaking her for Iris. Why don't you tell me how it went from desire for knowledge to murder?
>**Elspeth:** I saw it as soon as I showed him the wedding photographs, although he knew by then of course, his bum chum Stewart hadn't wasted any time in sharing the news, no one thought to keep me in the loop though.
>**DCI Johnston:** What did you see when Max looked at Iris?

Elspeth: Lust, he wanted her. I've seen him have that look before – not when he was looking at me, no he never looked at me that way and I suppose I always knew that he didn't love me the way I loved him, he was always putting me down, laughing when someone wanted my expert opinion. He didn't even try to hide it, he told me he'd taken her virginity and they were destined to be together, that he couldn't believe that she would be interested in a limp wristed academic like Iain, he was utterly convinced that the only reason Iris married Iain was to get to him. After a while I actually believed him.

DCI Johnston: When your husband took the job in Bulgaria did you know what his plans were?'

Elspeth: No, I was glad to not have him around. I hated him and I despised her, he hadn't even seen her in real life in years and here she was destroying what I told myself was a happy successful marriage.

DCI Johnston: When did you suspect that he might've returned to the UK?

Elspeth: As soon as Christopher Phillips contacted me, I knew what he was up to, so I contacted Stewart and he confirmed it.

DCI Johnston: What was the relationship like between Stewart and Max?

Elspeth: Stewart would've done anything for him, and I mean anything. I think he was in love with Max, I'm not sure if Rodger realised it, but he would've forgiven Stewart anything. I mean he *did* forgive Stewart anything, all the time. But Max wasn't interested in Stewart that way, he just liked having an obedient loyal lap dog.

DCI Johnston: When your parents wrote to you asking you to come home because Iain was missing what did you think?

Elspeth: Stewart had told me that he'd helped Iris and Max get away, not that he ever went into very much detail, I figured that Iain was heartbroken and had taken himself off somewhere to lick his wounds. Stewart and I agreed we wouldn't mention Iris or the marriage to the police, him because he was helping Max and me because I was so completely humiliated. I suppose I hoped it would burn itself out and he'd come back to me.

DCI Johnston: It must have come as quite a shock then when you were told that Max's body had been lying in the woods for four decades.

Elspeth: I didn't know what to think. I didn't understand.

DCI Johnston: Whose idea was it to attack Pamela Blackstock?

Elspeth: No one was meant to attack her, Stewart and I planned to confront her, and we thought if we could get her by herself, make her admit to who she was, then we could find out what happen to Max.

DCI Johnston: And Iain?

Elspeth: Of course.

DCI Johnston: But she didn't know what you were talking about did she?

Elspeth: No, Stewart was enraged, I didn't realise what he'd done until it was too late. I swear I didn't know he'd hit her, I didn't know he had that fishing priest with him. I said we should phone for help, but he checked her pulse and said it was too late and we needed to get out of there before someone saw us.

DCI Johnston: What do you mean – fishing priest?

Elspeth: Rodger gave it to him as a gift, it was made of antler or bone or something, you use it to kill the fish once you've caught them. I swear I had no idea he was planning on hurting her.
DCI Johnston: And what about Sebastian Wojcik?
Elspeth: I didn't know Iris *had* a brother, not till after he was dead, you'll need to ask Stewart about that.

Chapter Forty-Four

George stopped the interview for a break and a few moments later he was stood beside me. 'What are your thoughts?'

'I don't know, it was very premeditated to get Pamela alone that morning, all of that would've had to have been Elspeth's idea, she was the one that knew Pamela and Yvonne's morning routine. With them both going to confront Pamela they certainly meant to intimidate her if nothing else. I suppose it's possible that Stewart didn't share with her that he'd discovered that Seb was Pamela's brother. And I think it's worth remembering that when Seb was killed they were both still under the impression that Pamela was Iris and she was lying to them about her identity.'

'Trouble is we have no physical evidence to link Stewart to either the attack on Pamela or the murder of Sebastian,' George said. 'And it could easily turn into a situation where they point the finger at the other one and say 'they did it' and without anything to corroborate either version of events it's difficult.'

'What about the fishing priest, I don't believe he's clever enough to be forensically aware and I doubt he would have disposed of it afterwards seeing as it was a gift from his husband. If we believe Elspeth then Stewart attacked Pamela in a fit of anger, the same might be true of Seb, and people like that tend to be sloppy, they leave traces behind.'

'I've got some officers over at his house just now looking to see if we can find anything and on his boat, as well. I'll get them to be on the lookout for the fishing priest. I'm going to go back in and have another chat with him.'

DCI Johnston: You said that you were surprised Elspeth didn't take her husband's disappearance more seriously.

Stewart: Yes, you'd think that if she loved him as much as she said she did she would be out of her mind with worry.

DCI Johnston: But she knew where he was because you told her. You contacted her to say that her husband, your best friend, had come back to Scotland to try to persuade Iris to leave with him.

Stewart: I forgot.

DCI Johnston: Which bit?

Stewart: That I'd told Elspeth.

DCI Johnston: What did you think had happened when none of the three of them came back that day?

Stewart: I didn't know, I hoped that Iris had seen sense and gone with Max.

DCI Johnston: And Iain?

Stewart: I thought he was dead. I didn't tell Elspeth, it would've made her angry.

DCI Johnston: Why would you assume he was dead?

Stewart: Because Max had a gun.

DCI Johnston: He told you about the gun?

Stewart: He asked me to get it for him and I did.

DCI Johnston: So you weren't bothered if he killed Iain or Iris?

Stewart: As long as he didn't kill himself, I couldn't give a damn about the other two.

DCI Johnston: How would Rodger have felt about that?

Stewart: He was very fond of his brother, ridiculously so in my opinion, he always took his side. Even when I told him that his new sister-in-law was a whore, he told me it was none of my business what Iain did and if he was happy then that's all that mattered.

DCI Johnston: Did Rodger know that you were in love with Max?

Stewart: What...I wasn't...it wasn't like that...Max wasn't...he wasn't gay, I loved him as a brother.

DCI Johnston: It's funny though isn't it that you say you only loved Max as a brother and yet you were willing to help him kill the brother of the man you claim to love and yet when Rodger stated all he wanted was for Iain to be happy that irritated you. No what I think is that you were in love with Max, you had been since your teens, infatuated with him and I don't know if he led you on at all, gave you moments of hope to make sure he secured your loyalty, but whatever he did, you loved him. You loved him so much you were prepared to destroy the family that had accepted you as one of their own.

Stewart: Do you have any idea what it was like for me after I had to leave Max's house, what I went through? Maybe you're right and I did love Max but I also loved the life I had there and that little tart destroyed it so believe me I hated her more than I ever loved anyone.

DCI Johnston: She didn't destroy your life, Max did. He tried to force himself on her, all she did was stand up for herself. Max didn't care about you, or what happened to you afterwards he was just angry that he lost control over Iris. How often did he reach out to you afterwards, was he there to support you like a real brother would?

Stewart: He wanted to be, but it's not that easy.

DCI Johnston: Are you sure about that, it seems like it would've been much simpler to keep in touch with you and help you than it was for him to get Iris to accept him. But he was prepared to abandon a job that by all accounts he loved, his wife, his whole life to be with her, but I doubt he even gave you a second's thought, that was until you were useful to him again.

Stewart: You're wrong, Max cared about me, you didn't know him.

DCI Johnston: I think I can see what Max saw in you, he saw that you were kindred spirits, he was prepared to kill to have Iris and you were prepared to kill to find Max. He knew it, he could see that you had that dark side in you, that's what he liked about you.

Stewart: He understood me, in his own way he loved me.

DCI Johnston: I bet it made you so angry when Pamela said she wasn't Iris.

Stewart: I had no idea there was a sister, Iris hadn't ever mentioned her.

DCI Johnston: Probably because you didn't spend any time getting to know Iris. What I'd like to know is how you discovered that Sebastian Wojcik was Iris' brother, that was clever.

Stewart: It happened by accident, I like to go hill walking, I'd said hello to Sebastian before, I knew his name. I didn't go there to hurt him, I'm not a murderer. I saw him sat on a rock having a drink from his water bottle, I went over to be nice, that was all and then he started talking to me and he said he was worried about his sister, that she'd been attacked whilst walking her dogs. He didn't know who I was, and he looked so confused when I asked him where Max was and why Iris was lying about her name. He tried to fight back but I was so angry I smashed his head in and threw him over the edge, I really thought he had fallen further, I didn't realise his body had become caught in the gorse.

DCI Johnston: And all the time Max was already dead.

Stewart: It was Iris wasn't it, that murdered him, I mean.

DCI Johnston: No, he shot himself.

Stewart: That's not possible, he can't have, she's lying to you.

Chapter Forty-Five

'What happens to them now?' I asked George once we were back in his office.

'Stewart will be formally charged with murder and attempted murder and Elspeth as an accessory to murder.'

'Do you think they'll plead guilty?'

'I hope so, but once they get chatting with a lawyer it can all change.'

'What about Iris and Iain?'

'The Procurator Fiscal isn't going to press charges, in the circumstances they've accepted their version of events, they'll be able to head home.'

'That's good.'

Natasha knocked on the office door, 'sorry to interrupt but Elspeth Thorogood is asking if she can speak to Rowan.'

'What about?' George asked.

'Wouldn't say, just that she wanted to speak to Rowan.'

'Okay, but please remember that in an interview room everything is recorded and she could be trying to be clever and make you say or do something that will help her case if she pleads not guilty,' George said.

'I promise to be on my best behaviour.'

'Okay,' George sighed.

Natasha walked me to the interview rooms, 'you know I'm obviously glad that we've caught them, but I'm going to miss being part of the team, back to routine uniform work for me.'

'You've impressed George though, keep your eye out for an opportunity and I think that he'd happily have you there permanently.'

She smiled, 'fingers crossed. Okay here you are, I'm going to go into the recording room so if anything weird happens I'll be here and there will be an officer in the room with you at all times for everyone's safety.'

I opened the door, Elspeth was sitting in one of the chairs, she looked considerably older than when we'd met a few weeks ago.

'You asked to talk to me,' I said sitting down opposite her.

'Yes, thank you for coming.'

'What was it you wanted to say?'

'Firstly, I want to apologise to you, I tried to manipulate and use you to find Max under the guise of concern for my brother.'

'Why not ask me to look for Max in the first place?'

'He was legally dead; you'd have had questions that I didn't want to answer.'

'For what it's worth I think Max treated you very poorly.'

'I loved him though, and I couldn't see past that.'

'Seb's wife loved him too, as did his children and grandchildren and now he's dead because of this obsession to find Max.'

'I'm sorry,' Elspeth said. 'You don't have to believe me, but I'm truly sorry for them, I had no idea what Stewart was capable of. I think I must've been a very bad sister, Rodger loved Stewart and I thought that meant he was a good kind man, looking back though there were signs that my brother wasn't happy, I chose to ignore them, instead I spent most of my life hiding in other countries pretending it was for the love of my work when in reality, I just didn't want to come home and face what I thought the truth was.'

'You should've stayed away,' I said. It sounded cruel but if she'd chosen to live out her life somewhere else Donna wouldn't be planning her husband's funeral.

'I'm sorry.'

'So you keep saying, but it doesn't undo what's happened.'

'I know.'

'The break in at the university in 1996, that was you, wasn't it?'

'Yes.'

'You wanted Max's notebooks?'

'Yes, initially I hadn't given it any thought that the university had held on to them, it wasn't like I was interested in his notes, then one day I decided to have a look at them, that's when I realised that in the back of one of them was the plan he'd made for leaving the dig and coming back to the UK. He stole some artifacts from site and sold them to pay for his travel. I could tell looking through them what he'd stolen, he had a very particular shorthand style and because we'd worked together for so long I understood it. I panicked and thought if these were ever properly examined then someone might figure it out.'

'Where are they now?'

'I burnt them, I didn't want a memory of his unfaithfulness, so I destroyed them as soon as I took them home.'

'And what about the other things?'

'I didn't want to just take the notebooks, I thought that would look suspicious, I felt bad about that though. You'll find them in my house in a box under the bed, I'd appreciate it if you could arrange for them to be returned.'

'I'll get the keys from DCI Johnston once they've finished with them.'

'Thank you.' She bowed her head for a moment, 'I wish I'd known all those years ago that he was dead, it would've been a relief. I've been so consumed with bitterness that it spoiled my life. I could've moved on, been happy even.'

Did I feel sorry for her? Perhaps a little, she'd spent the last forty years thinking her husband abandoned her completely. Then again, she let an innocent woman be attacked and did nothing to help her. Even if she'd known that he was dead it wouldn't have changed the fact that he did leave her to pursue Iris. She lost her brother and her husband at the same time, but it was pity I felt for her more than anything else. What a wasted opportunity for living.

'Was it you that wrote me that letter about Iain?' I asked. It had been in the back of my mind since I'd received it, not because of the contents, more because it seemed wrong somehow.

'That was Stewart's idea, he said it would intrigue you and make you more determined to look for him and therefore more likely to find Max. Did it work at all?'

'No, you had employed me to look for your brother, I didn't need jockeying along, it was foolish.'

'You're quite right of course,' she said quietly.

'Was there anything else?' I asked.

'I also want you to know that I intend to instruct my solicitor to settle your bill in full, please send an itemised bill to me and I'll make sure you're compensated for all of your hard work.' She half laughed, 'ironically you did the one thing I thought was going to be impossible, you found Iain. You know I asked if I could see him, I wanted to have the chance to explain face to face but he told the officers he didn't want to see me, to tell me I was dead to him.'

'I appreciate you paying my bill, I'll make sure it's sent out in the next couple of days.' I stood up, 'Goodbye Elspeth.'

I stood in the hallway waiting for Natasha to walk me back to George's office only to find him striding out of it pulling his jacket on as he went.

'Sorry Rowan, the boss has called a press conference already,' George said. 'Natasha can you take Rowan out through the back door please, no offence.'

'Good luck with the press,' I replied as he sped by me. 'God I'd hate that part of the job,' I said to Natasha as we walked down the back staircase. 'A journalist wanted to interview me a couple of years ago after I found Sally Mitchell, I turned them down.'

'Wouldn't it have been great publicity for your business though?'

'Maybe, but I'm pretty busy anyway, and it felt wrong to exploit her story like that and in my experience, journalists always like to put their own twists on things.'

I waved to Natasha as I walked across the car park, once back in my car I closed my eyes for a couple of moments, realising for the first time how exhausting the last couple of days had been. I couldn't wait to drive home and get in the shower.

I wasn't even halfway home when my phone rang, it was Iris.

'Sorry to bother you,' she said. 'I thought you'd like to know that Pamela has woken up, the doctor says she's not up to visitors today, but I can go tomorrow.'

'That's great news I'm really pleased.'

'I know this might be taking liberties, but I wondered if you could help me with something?'

'It depends what it is,' I'd learnt to be cautious before agreeing to things.

'It's actually a couple of things and I'll understand if you say you don't feel comfortable…'

'I'll tell you if I won't or can't do it, what is it?'

'I don't know how much Pamela knew about why we had gone to Nairn and were in hiding so to speak, I'm terrified that she'll blame me for Seb's death and not understand, I was hoping you would agree to explain everything to her.'

'I think the police will want to interview her first about her attack, to corroborate the information they took from Elspeth and Stewart.'

'Yes, DCI Johnston said they would talk to her about that, but that it was up to us what we said about everything else.'

'I'm happy to talk to her, although I would suggest you visit at the same time or just after, she'll be looking to you for a deeper understanding, but I can go through the facts with her. I'll liaise with the police to get a suitable time. What was the second thing?'

'I know Seb had a wife, Donna, we met many years ago and she was lovely, I don't know how he explained me disappearing out of their lives, he always told me not to worry about it. I would've loved the chance to be a proper aunty to his children, of course I completely understood that we couldn't take that risk. Now that he's gone it feels even more important to get to know them and his grandchildren, I'd love to be a proper part of her life.'

'I'll speak to Donna and let you know what she says.'

'Thank you.'

I hung up then called Donna to ask if I could visit, my shower would have to wait. Twenty minutes later I pulled up outside her house. The door opened revealing Maureen, not Donna.

'Hello petal,' she said. 'I was already here when you called so I thought I'd hang on to see you and be around in case Donna needed me. I've put the kettle on, come on in,' Maureen said

Donna smiled as I entered the living room, 'hello Rowan, the police have released Seb's body, Maureen is helping me plan his funeral, you will come, won't you?'

'If you'd like me to.'

'I would.'

Maureen arrived with mugs of tea and slices of Victoria sponge cake. 'Now don't either of you tell me you're not hungry, you both could do with a slice of cake. I expect clean plates,' she said as she handed them out.

I was grateful for the fork on the side of the plate which allowed me to eat the cake without having to lift the wedge to my mouth and risk spreading cream and jam on my face.

'You said there was something you wanted to tell me about Seb's death,' Donna said.

'Yes, I think you know that Seb had two sisters and they were separated when they went into foster care?'

Donna nodded.

'And you met Iris, his older sister, when Seb introduced you to her as Iain's wife, did you know she was his sister then?'

'Seb treated them like family. I thought it was because finally he found someone on the job that really understood him, that he could have long talks with and discuss books, that kind of thing. I wish he'd told me.'

'He was also in touch with his other sister Pamela, she's the woman that was attacked on the beach a couple of weeks ago,' I said.

'I don't understand,' Donna said, 'he was all about family, why didn't he tell me?'

'This is where it gets more complicated, but I think it's important to remember that everything Seb did was done with keeping you and his children away from trouble.'

'Safe from what?' Donna asked.

Maureen, who was sitting next to Donna, put her hand on her friend's arm, 'give Rowan a chance to explain, sometimes things aren't what we thought or even hoped, but that doesn't mean to say they don't come with blessings.' She smiled at me.

I took my time trying to explain her husband's actions the best I could, knowing that it would be hard for her to reconcile the man she loved with one who helped conceal Max's death, but I hoped that, ultimately, she would accept that he was doing what he thought was the right thing to keep Iris safe.

'He did what was best for his sister and he would've hated lying to you about it, I'm sure,' Maureen said sympathetically. 'Just because our loved ones keep things from us it doesn't mean they don't love us. Seb would have wanted to find a way to protect you all.'

'You know when Sasha was a teenager he would say to her, you're absolutely amazing and brilliant, you don't need no boy to complete you, what you need in life is a partner who respects you and loves you and lifts you up, someone who'll help you through the hard times and celebrate your achievements. And to Luca he would say, never disrespect a woman, you don't put a hand on her unless you've been given permission and then you make sure that the hand is kind and gentle, if they're not interested in you then you walk away, no girl owes you anything.'

'From all accounts he was a fantastic dad,' I said.

'He was. I wish he'd told me about helping Iris, there's nothing that he wouldn't do to protect family…' she took a sharp intake of breath before her body began to shake with emotion, tears streaming down her face. 'He died doing it.'

Maureen put her arm around Donna, 'that's it, you let it out my love.'

'I'm sorry,' Donna said moments later when she was drying her eyes on a tissue.

'You've nothing to be sorry for, Rowan understands grief, don't you worry,' Maureen said.

'I know that Iris would like to meet you again, and the rest of your family and I'm sure Pamela will feel the same. But Iris is worried that you'll feel she's to blame for what happened to Seb.'

'You tell her she's family, that she's welcome here and I know my children will feel the same way, family first and there's only one person to blame for Seb's death, and that's the man that took his life.'

I stayed for a little while listening to Donna talk about Seb and their life together, eating a second piece of cake supplied by Maureen and then when Donna seemed like she talked all she wanted or needed to I finally headed home for my much overdue shower and a long sleep.

Chapter Forty-Six

Explaining the past to Pamela had been considerably easier than I expected, George had already broken the news of Seb's death and when Iris came into the room after our conversation the two sisters held each other as though they never wanted to let go.

I'd arranged to meet George in the Sunshine Café for a debrief, as usual I was there before him.

'You're looking tired,' Billy said as he put a cup of camomile tea and a slice of carrot cake on the table in front of me.

'Always the charmer,' I laughed.

'Is that the case solved now then?'

'It is.'

'Good, another success story I hear as well.'

'I did alright,' I replied, it would have been more of a success if Seb hadn't died.

'At least now you should be able to get some rest for a bit.'

'Till the next case comes along. How's Star doing, can't be long until her due date now.'

'Four weeks tomorrow, she says she feels the size of a whale, I tell her she still looks beautiful but she's frustrated she can't do all the things she used to do. Mohammed has been an absolute saviour though, he's done great here, and Star is even letting him tinker with the menu so she must be relaxed about it.'

'It must be nice having them around to help.'

'Don't know how we'd have managed without them,' Billy looked up as the door chimes jangled. 'Here's your partner in crime, I'd better get his coffee.'

'Sorry I'm late.'

'Aren't you always?' I laughed.

'You'll be pleased to know that both Stewart and Elspeth have decided to plead guilty.'

'What do you think sentencing will be?'

'Hard to say, Elspeth might get very little, or even a suspended sentence, she wasn't involved in Sebastian Wojcik's death at all, and she had no intention of causing physical harm to Pamela Blackstock, her main charge is Defeating the Ends of Justice, perverting the course of justice as it's more commonly known, but that's out of my hands. Stewart Blair should spend the rest of his life in prison in my opinion.'

'Does this mean you're ready to propose to Mel then?'

'I've booked some time off for the end of this month, I thought about what you said about not doing it publicly and Becky screwed her nose up at that idea as well, so instead I thought I'd take her away for a few days, maybe Belgium or something, what do you think?'

'That sounds nice.'

'Although I keep having the fear that I've misread the signs and she's going to say no.'

I stifled a laugh, I wasn't mocking George, it was just amusing that he was panicking so much, I didn't think I'd ever seen him panic. 'You'll be fine, Becky would've told you if you were barking up the wrong tree. Talking of barking what's happening with Jock and Wallace?'

'Safely returned to their rightful owner, I was sorry to see them go, they were great little guys, but I'm not missing the early all weathers morning walks or picking up dog turd. They were pleased to see Pamela and she them, Iris and Iain are staying with her for a bit until she's feeling fully recovered…'

Billy clattered through the chairs towards us taking his apron off as he moved, 'it's Star, he said breathlessly, Chantelle called, she's gone into labour, they're on the way to the hospital just now. I don't have the car with me today, any chance of a lift.'

George stood, 'I'll take you; we can put the blue lights on and should get you there not long after they've arrived.'

'Thank you,'

'Let me know when the baby's here,' I called after them as they scuttled out the door.

Chapter Forty-Seven

Fourteen hours later Star and Billy welcomed a little girl into the world, Willow Alana Slater weighing 6lb 4oz. Alana had cried when I'd called to tell her that they'd given the middle name after her and I had cried when I'd visited laden down with gifts when they'd asked me if I would be one of Willow's Guide Parents, with neither Star or Billy being religious they'd chosen to have a naming ceremony for their daughter and picked the winter solstice for the event.

A few weeks later and despite it being a cold December day, all our friends had made the effort to dress up and it was lovely to be back in the same village hall where Star and Billy had their wedding reception. The couple had chosen six Guide Parents, Chantelle and Mohammed, Me, George, Maureen and Eddie. Maureen had cried more than me when they'd asked her.

Willow was dressed in a green velvet dress and matching booties and looked every bit a winter princess. We'd been asked to write our own commitment statement to Willow, when Alana found out she joked that I had to say more than 'if anyone hurts you Willow, I'll hunt them down and kill them.' In truth I'd agonised over what to say. Mohammed read a poem that he'd written about what it meant to him to guide Willow in the world, Chantelle sung a song, revealing a beautiful voice that no one realised she possessed. Maureen and Eddie gave a joint statement about always having a slice of cake at the ready and their door always being open. George, who'd worried that he would be too formal, spoke of how proud he was of Billy, and to call Willow's parents his friends, and a vow to remind Willow that it wasn't about the mistakes you made in your life, it mattered what you did when the chips were down, and then it was my turn.

'Dear sweet Willow, a few years ago your daddy saved my life and put his own at risk to protect my daughter. Before that time, I thought that all the family I needed was contained in three people, but I was wrong. I've been blessed to build a new family in my collection of friends that are so wonderful they enrich my life in ways I never knew were possible. As I look at you today, I know that we would all go to any lengths to keep you safe, but just as importantly we'd go to any lengths to help you have a happy and fulfilled life. One day I hope you look at your parents and know how lucky you are to have been born to two of the most special people I've ever met. My promise to you Willow Alana Slater is to protect you fiercely against anyone who wishes you harm, love you completely, especially when you make daft decisions and be there for you unconditionally.'

The humanist leading the ceremony looked on the verge of tears herself, 'A naming ceremony is always a wonderful thing,' she said, 'but still it's a rare thing to conduct one with a group of people so committed to the love, protection, and wellbeing of little Willow, every one of you spoke of family in the non-traditional sense and the importance of love and self-acceptance. Billy and Star, you find yourselves in the very privileged situation that so many people are invested in the unconditional love of your daughter, and it is my absolute pleasure to introduce Willow Alana Slater'

'I liked your speech,' Sonya said afterwards.

'Thanks, I found it quite hard to come up with the right thing.'

'You did good,' Mel said.

I glanced at the beautiful engagement ring on Mel's finger, she had of course accepted George's proposal which he'd made over a croissant and a mug of hot chocolate sitting on their hotel room balcony. Mel had described the moment as perfect, very relieved that he'd not made a public display and later, privately George had told me that he had been so nervous that he'd messed up the three other opportunities he'd tried to orchestrate earlier in their trip.

I'd suggested that Alana invite Xavier as her plus one, but she said they'd decided to just be friends, she liked him, but he was too intense, and she liked being able to do as she pleased without thinking about anyone else. I'd told her that she shouldn't be closed off to a relationship, worried that she was going to miss out and she'd laughed at me, reminding me that she was still young and there would be plenty of time for that later.

Willow's party ran on until 5pm when the little girl was showing signs of being tired and completely fed up of wearing unusually fussy clothes. Maureen insisted they went home and left the tidying up to everyone else, although when it came to it she did everything herself with the exception of permitting Mohammed to box up any leftover food.

Back home Alana and I opted to change from our glad rags to our pyjamas, make hot chocolate and find a cheesy Christmas film to watch on tv. It had been brilliant having her at home for the holidays, the house had felt like it had come out of hibernation, and I knew it would miss her presence when she headed back to Uni next year.

We'd looked at flats to buy and hadn't found anything within my price range that didn't also mean selling our home as well, which I'd been told by Alana in no uncertain terms wasn't happening. She had however found an ad from some fourth year students who'd lost their fourth flat mate for the next term as she was going to study abroad. They'd advertised for a fourth year only, but Alana had chanced her arm anyway and applied and once they'd met her they'd agreed the room could be hers for the term, which at least pushed back our housing issues till after the Easter break.

Later that evening as Alana lay slumped on the sofa sleeping, I looked at my emails for the first time in days. There was one from Ellie, I opened it.

> Hi Rowan
> Hope you're doing okay and not working too hard,
> I'm sorry I've not been in touch for a little while. Lots of things have changed for me, after what happened with Harmony I decided to take a break from chasing stardom and took a job with the Highlands Art Committee, now I travel round schools in the remote parts of Scotland teaching drama, or helping villages to put on their own plays. I'm absolutely loving the change.
> Anyway, the job comes with a beautiful cottage, and I was wondering if you and Alana fancied coming up to stay with me for a few days over Hogmanay and New Year?
> No problem if you already have plans, but there is a smashing wee pub here that's putting on a Hogmanay event, with food and a couple of bands (traditional music). Let me know what you think.
> Love
> Ellie xxx

Lies She Didn't Tell

I looked down at Alana, perhaps a few days up in the Highlands would be fun.

Acknowledgements

Writing is a solitary activity, but getting a book ready for publication is a team effort and I know I couldn't do it without my team.

As always, my husband Gavin, whose belief in my stories makes more difference than he'll ever know. To my editor for correcting my grammar, spelling and much, much more.

To my friends, Rachel Chapman, Debbie Fleming, Marion Todd and Laura Shepherd.

My readers – I'm forever grateful that you're always there waiting for the next Rowan McFarlane adventure.

Sonya Drysdale and Alana McGrath, I hope your namesakes continue to do you proud, thank you for your belief and support. The Best Seller Experiment, the two Marks and all the other writers so willing to help and uplift one another.

To F,J & P for being by my side throughout it all.

About The Author

Born in the Kingdom of Fife, Angela spent her teenage years in Penzance before returning to Scotland. She had a varied career from Nursery Nurse to Bank Manager before becoming a full-time writer. Her Rowan McFarlane Detective Mysteries are set in the fictional town of Cuddieford, which lies somewhere between Dunfermline & Kirkcaldy. Angela now lives with her husband in Fife looking out on the River Forth where she can easily see her favourite bridge, the Forth Rail Bridge. When she's not writing she can be found walking the coast or touring the countryside in her campervan.

For more information and to sign up to my newsletter you can visit Angela's website:

www.angelacnurse.com

Printed in Great Britain
by Amazon